Thy Neighbor's Wife

Georgia Beers

Yellow Rose Books

Nederland, Texas

ISBN 1-932300-15-5

First Printing 2003

9 8 7 6 5 4 3 2 1

Cover design by Donna Pawlowski

Published by:

Yellow Rose Books
PMB 210, 8691 9th Avenue
Port Arthur, Texas 77642-8025

Find us on the World Wide Web at
http://www.regalcrest.biz

Printed in the United States of America

Acknowledgments:

There are a handful of folks who have made this book better because of their hard work and support...

Thank you to Stacy Harp for the sharp eyes, the patience, and the ability to boost my ego right when it needs it the most.

Thank you to the staff of Yellow Rose and Regal Crest for making both the editing process and the business end of my writing run smoothly and painlessly. I'm a very lucky author to be associated with such professionals.

Thank you to the small city of Canandaigua, New York, for being such a beautiful and inspirational place. I did take a few liberties—natives will recognize them—but all in all, I tried to keep it as true to life on paper as I could. I hope I succeeded.

Lastly, thank you to Tonya Muir—wherever you are...

For Bonnie.
Always.

Chapter
One

"What do you think, honey?"

The excitement in Eric Wainwright's voice was unmistakable to his wife, Jennifer. She smiled at the little-boy expression on his face, the twinkling in his brown eyes. It wasn't terribly often that he asked for her opinion on something he was looking to purchase, but for some reason, he really wanted her to be as enamored with the lake house as he was. It was important to him. He waited, studying her.

Jennifer was completely taken with the house, but she didn't want to let him off the hook too soon, so she pretended to ponder, wandering slowly around. She turned in a casual circle in the expansive great room and then stopped to look out the floor-to-ceiling windows that offered a stunning view of Canandaigua Lake. The waves lapped gently at the shores of the yard, which was impeccably landscaped, the grass, a lush green nearly impossible to find this early in the season.

Above her head were wood beams, accentuating the high ceiling and drawing the eyes to the railing of the loft that overlooked the great room. She'd been up there already and had been equally impressed with the open design of the master and guest bedrooms, accented in the same wood as the ceiling beams. Ideas for painting and decorating were already bombarding her, colors and patterns spinning in her mind.

She knew that, whether or not she liked the place, Eric did and that they'd probably end up buying it anyway, but she was pleased he seemed so anxious for her opinion. She smiled at him again.

"I think it's beautiful," she pronounced.

Eric let out an audible sigh of relief and hugged her, catching her off guard. He turned to Jake, his cousin and their real estate agent, and grinned. "She thinks it's beautiful."

"Of course she does," Jake replied easily. "Let's take care of the paperwork, shall we?"

As the two men headed for the kitchen where they could use

the counter space to write on, Jennifer slid open the sliding glass doors and stepped out onto the massive back deck. It was empty, so she was sure that was why it seemed so huge. The house had been empty for over a week, following the death of the elderly previous owner. She rested her palms on the railing, closing her eyes and taking a lung full of fresh lake air, so different from that of the city.

So this is going to be our summer home. Not bad. Not bad at all.

Eric had wanted a house on the water for ages and grudgingly admitted to knowing that it was more a status symbol than anything else for him. It would be added to the list of material things he'd acquired, all before the age of thirty: the Mercedes, the boat, the membership at Oak Hill, the most exclusive golf club in the area, a huge house in the heart of Pittsford, one of the wealthiest suburbs of Rochester, New York.

She despised the whole money game. She'd spent all twenty-nine of her years right in the middle of it, but she hated being wealthy. She also knew how snobbish that sounded and she didn't run around telling people how much she abhorred being rich, but it was the truth. The role of high society wife was not one that she treasured, nor was she good at it. She was the first to say so. Her mother, as well as Eric's mother, would be in line right behind her.

Still, the house was gorgeous and she already felt a sense of peace simply standing on the deck. She also reluctantly admitted to herself that she happily anticipated being there alone quite often. Eric's offices were in the city—about forty-five minutes from Canandaigua – and lately he'd been helping set up the new division in Buffalo—a good two hours away. It would be very inconvenient for him to make such a commute every day during the summer, given the late hours he tended to work, and he would most likely stay at the Pittsford house more often than not. The idea of spending time on the lakeshore alone was very appealing to Jennifer; she could feel the calm and solitude calling to her on the breeze coming off the shore.

She turned to look up at the house. The exterior was a faded gray, a finish that made it appear more weathered than it actually was. Looking back to the water, she sighed, let the sudden relaxation she felt seep into her very being, and admired the sunset over the water. She heard children laughing in the distance; a dog barked.

She'd never had a dog growing up, even though she'd always wanted one. Her mother had had a million reasons why she wouldn't allow it. Dogs were messy. Dogs were smelly. Dogs were silly, shedding creatures that didn't belong in a house full of nice things like theirs. Something was bound to get broken or stained or...she'd go on and on and on until her daughter would stop her begging simply to get the woman to shut up. Jennifer could hear her mother's voice ringing clearly in her head as if it had happened yesterday. She still got a headache any time she thought about Dina Remington's No Pets and Here's Why speech.

Despite the shrillness and insistence of her mother, Jennifer's desire for a dog had never gone away. She supposed that childhood want was what made her smile at the little white pooch that she noticed running through her new back yard. He was adorable, all furry with pointy ears, short, stubby legs, and big expressive brown eyes. He was clearly in his glory, running free in the spring grass. Part of an unraveled rope flew unconstrained behind him, clasped to his plaid collar but nothing else. He stopped to pee every few feet, lifting a short back leg with relish, as if his mission in life was to mark everything in sight. Jennifer chuckled at his antics.

The chuckling died swiftly as she had a sickening vision of a car screeching to a halt to avoid him. She couldn't bear the thought of his broken little body, should he find his way up to the main road, so she headed down into the large yard, squatted, and called to him, clapping her hands and using a playful voice.

"Come here, buddy. Come on. Come here."

He stopped his romping when he heard her and cocked his head as if listening intently. His little black lips were visible on his white-furred face and Jennifer was sure he was grinning at her.

"Yeah, you." She giggled. "Come here."

Much to her surprise, he trotted right over to her, his tail pointing straight up and wagging slightly as he sniffed the hand she held out to him. After a minute or two, he decided she was safe and allowed her to scratch his head. Soon, she was able to grasp his collar, tug him a little closer, and picked him up in her arms to get a closer look at him.

He immediately set to bathing her face with his pink tongue. He was surprisingly gentle, like a mother with a pup, and it made her smile.

"Oh, I'm dirty, am I? Well, thanks so much for taking care of that."

She was relieved to see that he had an ID tag hanging from his collar. She had picked up enough strays in her life and she was always happy when she had a number to call to return the animal to its owner. A pet without an ID tag was a sign of a glaringly irresponsible owner in her book.

This tag said simply *Kinsey* and had a local phone number.

"Is Kinsey your name or is that your mommy? Hmm?" He cocked his head as if seriously contemplating the question, but offered her no answer. "Well, what do you say we find out?"

She carried him into the house. She could hear Eric and Jake discussing the details of the purchase of the house, so she decided not to interrupt. Instead, she fished her cell phone out of her shoulder bag and dialed the number on the tag. It was picked up after three rings.

"Hello?" The voice was female, deep and smooth.

"Um, hi. My name is Jennifer Wainwright and I was just wondering if you or somebody there had, by any chance, lost a dog."

"Lost a—hang on a sec..." Jennifer heard a door slide open, then a muffled curse. The woman came back on the line. "A little white one?" she asked anxiously.

"Yep. His tag says Kinsey. Is that you or him?"

"That's him, the little stinker. I can't believe he broke that rope. I swear he's an escape artist!"

"He's a sweetie." She giggled as Kinsey licked her ear.

"Oh, he's very smooth with the ladies, that's for sure." The woman chuckled warmly. "Listen, I can't thank you enough for grabbing him. Where are you? I'll come right over and get him out of your hair."

"Well, let's see." Jennifer stepped back out onto the deck to scrutinize her surroundings, which were completely new to her. "I'm on the lake. My house is new...I mean, I don't even live here yet, so I'm not exactly sure how to tell you where I am. Um, I know we're on East Lake Road. I think it might be number seventeen." She felt like a complete dolt, unable to give the voice on the phone a solid address, and she rolled her eyes at herself.

"Number seventeen?" the voice said with surprise. Jennifer could hear the door slide open again.

"I think so. Do you know where that is?"

The woman laughed. "I believe I do. Take a look to your right."

Jennifer furrowed her brows in confusion, then looked to her right. Not fifty yards away, a dark-haired woman stood on the deck next door, a cordless phone pressed to her ear. She waved.

"Found you."

Jennifer laughed as she snapped the cell phone shut, set it on the railing of the deck, and walked toward her new neighbor, Kinsey still in her arms.

It was impossible not to notice how attractive the woman was. *God, I hope Eric can keep himself from drooling on her,* she thought with a smile. Her dark hair was pulled back into a loose ponytail, her bangs ruffling in the lake breeze. She had soft, dark eyes framed by almost-black lashes and brows, and an easy smile played at the corners of her mouth. She was dressed casually in jeans and a black, v-neck t-shirt.

How come my *jeans don't fit me that well?* Jennifer's brain whined enviously. *It's so unfair.*

The woman was tall, several inches above Jennifer's five foot four inch frame. Her facial structure was near perfect, as though she'd been carved out of marble, then painstakingly buffed until her skin glowed. She looked visibly relieved to see her dog and smiled an impeccable white smile as she reached out for him.

"Didn't get so far after all, did you, rat boy? I oughta skin you and have you for dinner."

Kinsey set to work bathing his owner's face this time, his tail wagging rapidly. She accepted the treatment for another minute, then set him down inside her sliding glass door and snapped it shut. The dog stood pathetically, looking out through the glass like a doomed prisoner.

The woman turned and held out her hand to Jennifer. "Alex Foster."

Jennifer placed her hand in Alex's, feeling both warmth and strength radiating from her. "Jennifer Wainwright. Nice to meet you."

"Thank you so much for grabbing him, Jennifer. He can't be trusted. He's got a one-track mind and when he puts that nose to the ground, he's off like a shot. He would have just kept going and probably would have ended up a doggie pancake on the main road." She kept her tone light, but the worry in her eyes betrayed her voice. She was obviously attached to the little guy and the prospect of such an accident made her queasy.

"No problem," Jennifer replied. "I'm glad I saw him. Has he gotten out before?"

"Once or twice, yeah. It's really in his blood, just a characteristic of the breed."

"He's a terrier, right?"

"Yup. He's a Westie—a West Highland White Terrier. He's bred to be a rodent hunter, so like I said, he puts that nose to the ground, trying to sniff up the mice or the chipmunks and nothing else in the world exists for him. Especially now, in the spring, when everything's coming out of hibernation."

Jennifer smiled at the image of the adorable little pooch pretending not to hear his mommy calling him. "So, I take it walking him without a leash is out of the question?"

"Absolutely. I've tried that." Alex then added sheepishly, "Three times."

"*Three* times?"

"What? I thought maybe he was just a slow learner."

"Sounds like the slow learner was you," Jennifer commented with a smirk.

"Hey! You just met me. You can't insult me for at least twenty-four hours." She laughed, taking Jennifer's ribbing as the fun for which it was meant. "So, you said you just bought the place?" She gestured behind Jennifer to the house.

"Yeah. My husband, Eric, is inside taking care of the details right now. I'm not sure exactly when we'll move in, but it's ours. I'm pretty excited, so I hope I don't sound like a total goof. Have you been here long?"

Alex smiled at the enthusiasm in her new neighbor's voice. "This used to be my aunt's place. I spent a lot of time here as a kid and now I'm living here."

"Well, this is my first time on the lake, so maybe you can show me around sometime?"

"You've got yourself a deal, young lady." She smiled a dazzling white smile and Jennifer wondered how many men had simply fallen at Alex's feet.

They stood quietly, but not awkwardly, in easy familiarity for a couple minutes just looking out at the water. Jennifer was surprised to feel a tiny pang of disappointment when she heard Eric's voice calling for her. She was baffled by the little part of her that didn't really want to introduce Eric to Alex. It had been so long since she'd had something that was hers and only hers and she was feeling a bit possessive; she wanted to keep Alex all to herself. Strange, since she'd only known the woman for ten minutes.

* * *

Alexandra Foster was so pleasantly surprised by her new neighbor that she could hardly keep the smile from plastering itself on her face. She had begun to feel a little lonely in her new home and was excited by the prospect of a new friendship...and one with such an attractive woman.

Jennifer's strawberry blonde hair was pulled back into a French braid, a look Alex found incredibly sexy. Her green blouse accented her eyes nicely. The beige designer jeans perfectly hugged her lower body and Alex had trouble keeping her eyes from sliding over the smaller woman's backside, not wanting to frighten off her new neighbor before their friendship had time to begin. She chuckled to herself as she had a vision of Jennifer catching her ogling her, then sprinting back to her house in horror, hoping to prevent the final signatures from making their way onto the contract. Instead, they made small talk and enjoyed one another's company.

Because she found Jennifer so appealing, Alex's inner child really wanted to hate Eric Wainwright. She was determined to dislike him. He was obviously rich, judging from the house they just bought and the Mercedes in the driveway. He was devastatingly handsome, she could see as he approached, and he was married to Jennifer. What reason was there not to hate him?

"Making friends already, honey?" he asked with a smile as he reached a hand out to Alex. "Eric Wainwright."

"This is Alex Foster. We were just talking about living on the lake." Jennifer's green eyes sparkled as she introduced Alex to her husband.

They shook hands. "You lived here long?" he asked, as Jennifer noticed his subtle appraisal of Alex and gave herself a point for predicting his impression of her.

"I spent most of my summers here as a kid."

"This used to be her aunt's house," Jennifer filled in.

"Were you friends with the previous owners of our place?"

Alex was barely able to keep from rolling her eyes. "Um, no. Mrs. Cavanaugh wasn't exactly...approachable." She managed to keep herself from going on too long about her ex-neighbor, not wanting to speak ill of the dead. Ethel Cavanaugh had been a rich old biddy who considered herself higher up on the food chain than most of the rest of mankind. She could barely be bothered to give Alex the time of day, but did favor her with disapproving looks any chance she could. Alex had not been disappointed when the woman's homophobic heart had given out and the idea of having young neighbors was almost too appealing for words. "You're going to love it here. There's nothing like living on the water."

"I hope I get time to enjoy it," Eric muttered.

"You will," Jennifer scolded gently as he put his arm around her.

"We should go finish up with Jake," he said. "It was nice to meet you, Alex. I'm sure we'll be seeing each other often."

"Same here," she replied. "And if you need any help with moving or anything, just holler."

Jennifer seemed to want to linger, but Eric took her hand and tugged her along behind him. Alex was surprised to feel disappointment at her departure.

"I'll be back in twenty-four hours to deliver a proper insult, okay?" Jennifer called over her shoulder.

"Don't be late." Alex laughed. Jennifer waved goodbye. "Back to high society wife," Alex said softly.

It was going to be an interesting summer.

She headed back into the house and Kinsey looked up at her expectantly. "What? You think you get some kind of reward for that little escapade of yours?" He cocked his head to one side, the way he always did when his owner scolded him, his ears pointed straight up, his brown eyes wide with the attention he was certainly paying her. He looked so damn cute like that and he knew it. Alex couldn't resist him and he knew that, too. She swooped him up in her arms, let him rain kisses all over her face, and told herself they were surely kisses of apology.

Chapter
Two

"Eric, honey, they do this for a living. Would you please just relax and let them work?" Jennifer spoke through clenched teeth, trying not to explode on her husband. She was getting fed up with him constantly trying to tell the furniture deliverymen how to do their job. He'd been directing them all morning and she'd had just about enough of it. Judging from the disgusted scowls on their worn faces, so had they.

"Well, he's right, dear. That will never fit through the doorway." Claire Wainwright had decided to "help" with the move, much to Jennifer's dismay. Her mother-in-law never failed to take the opposite side as Jennifer and she had been antagonizing the poor deliverymen nearly as often as Eric had. Between the two of them, Jennifer was ready to scream.

"How 'bout we let them try?" she growled. She caught the grateful glance tossed her way by the largest of the three hulky men and she tried to smile her reassurance that she was doing the best she could for them.

They stood in silence as the men from Stickley spun the new sofa into several various positions until they did indeed find the one that would allow them to bring it through the front door. Jennifer bit her tongue to keep from sneering, "neener, neener, neener" at her husband and his mother. Claire shot her a look, one that clearly said how much she hated when Jennifer was right.

Claire Wainwright was a beautiful woman. Even if she hadn't had enough money to buy herself the perfect hairstyle in the perfect color, the most expensive manicures, and the best in designer clothes, she still would have been beautiful. At age fifty-eight, she looked like she was in her mid-forties. Her bottle-blonde hair was impeccable, not a strand out of place, and it gently brushed the back of her neck. Her eyes were the same chocolate brown as Eric's, made up with subtle perfection. Jennifer had managed to keep from rolling her eyes when Claire had arrived in her typical moving attire: a beautifully tailored black pantsuit and pumps of Italian leather.

Jennifer had known Claire for as long as she could remember. She was five and Eric was six when Jennifer's father had made partner at Eric's father's law firm. Michael Remington and Daniel Wainwright had become fast friends, as had their wives, Kathleen and Claire. They did the same things, moved in the same circles, and became members of the same country club. Both their families were small—Jennifer had a brother and Eric had an older sister—and it wasn't long before they became a nearly inseparable group. Because Eric and Jennifer seemed to get along so well from the beginning, it became a sort of predetermined destiny that they would end up together.

Claire was a typical mother in the sense that nothing—and no woman—would ever be good enough for her baby boy. She and Daniel had never had what could be called a happy marriage, so it often seemed like she'd decided to try her best to control her son's. Jennifer understood this behavior and had spent much of her life trying to accept it, but Claire was interminably hard on her and every once in a while, it really got on her nerves.

Like that moving day. Claire continued to supervise the movers, despite Jennifer's kind attempts to get her to stop. She took issue with the way Jennifer sought to arrange her kitchen cupboards and directed her to stock them the way Claire saw fit. She had several opinions on the window dressings that were needed, none of which agreed with Jennifer's. She even pointed out streaks on the glass that Jennifer had missed in her cleaning. Jennifer's irritation bubbled slowly in the pit of her stomach all day long until she started to worry that she might say something nasty. She knew she had to get away before her mouth went on a rampage without her permission, one she would truly live to regret for Claire Wainwright could hold a grudge longer than anybody had a right.

"I need some air," was all she could manage to grind out before stomping out the back door sliding it shut with such force that she was sure Claire had a comment. She walked through the thick green grass of the backyard straight down to the dock. Much to her surprise, the gentle lapping of the water against the wood immediately calmed her racing heart and boiling blood. She took a deep, cleansing breath, walked all the way to the end, and just looked out onto the peaceful surface of the lake.

The air was still fairly cool so early in the season. Jennifer had grown up in a suburb much closer to the city and had yet to get used to the temperature difference near the water. She felt goose bumps break out on her arms and rubbed them vigorously, choosing to be chilly rather than return to the hostile environment of the house behind her. She tried not to think about the fact that Eric never sided with her and against his mother and she was annoyed at herself for not being used to such behavior by that point. Eric was simply accustomed to Claire's antics and had no trouble just tuning her out. Jennifer was exceedingly envious, wishing she could do the same, but knowing it was impossible for her.

Apparently, I prefer to take all remarks as personally as I possibly can, she thought, then smiled at the sarcastic tone in her head, suddenly feeling a little better. She decided she'd just wait out the movers, give Claire time to go home, and then she'd have the whole week to arrange the place the way *she* wanted it.

The simple plan clear in her mind, she let her head drop back so she could absorb the sunshine beaming down on her. The combination of the cool, soft breeze, the fresh smell of the lake, and the warm sun acted like a drug and her anxiety slipped away.

The silence of the moment was broken by a sharp series of barks. She smiled, realizing they must be coming from her furry little friend who lived next door. She turned her gaze and squinted against the sun just as she heard a gently scolding voice.

"Kinsey. Quiet. Nobody wants your opinion."

Alex was perched on the section of her deck that faced the water, looking very comfortable in the lounge chair she occupied. She seemed to be reading, but she looked out onto the water more than at what she held in her lap. Jennifer debated whether or not to disturb her, but she knew she wasn't ready to go back into the house just yet.

"Howdy, neighbor," she called out.

Alex looked up and met Jennifer's gaze with a wide smile and a friendly wave. "Hi there, Jennifer. How goes the move?"

"Ugh. Don't ask," Jennifer said with a groan.

"Need a break?" Alex held up the glass she'd been drinking from as incentive.

Jennifer was moving before she even had time to think about it, retracing her steps off the dock, across the lawn, and up the stairs of Alex's deck.

Kinsey was excited to see her, his ears flat against his head, his tail wagging furiously. He was clipped to a chain that attached him to one of the posts on the deck and Jennifer smiled at the fact that Alex wasn't taking any chances on his escape that day. As she bent to scratch the dog, he curled his lips in a goofy manner, showing his teeth in a gesture so comical Jennifer laughed out loud.

"Is he smiling at you?" Alex asked from her chair.

"Yes!" Jennifer giggled at the description, for that was exactly what he was doing. "God, he's cute."

"And he knows it, too," Alex said. "He uses it to his advantage every chance he gets. Have a seat."

Jennifer took a quick look around the deck. It was spacious, the wood natural in color, but well taken care of with no cracks or chips, no rotting to be seen. A large glass table, the legs and framework a deep forest green, occupied one corner. Four matching chairs surrounded it, their cushions a floral print of greens and burgundies. A bit to the right was a pair of lounge chairs, with thick, comfortable looking cushions that matched those of the other chairs. Several pots and flower boxes lined the railing and sat in corners, but all were still empty given that it was only mid-May. Jennifer thought how great the whole area must look when the flowers were in bloom and she made a mental note to start thinking about what types of greenery she thought might look best on her own property.

She chose the matching lounge and sat down next to her smiling neighbor who had a legal pad propped on her lap and a simple Bic pen in her hand. A groan of pleasure escaped Jennifer's lips as she got off her feet for the first time in several hours and sank comfortably into the surprisingly deep cushion.

"Oh my God, that's nice."

Alex smiled knowingly. "Wait until you get the chance to nap in one."

"Don't tempt me."

"You'll never leave my deck."

"I said don't tempt me." Jennifer smiled, closed her eyes, and reveled in the warm spring sun, her chill gone.

"You look stressed."

"Do I?" Jennifer opened her eyes, shielding the sun with a hand, and mildly flattered at the look of concern on Alex's face. "I always was a bit transparent. I've been meaning to work on that little character flaw."

Alex jumped up. "Stay right there." She set her pad and paper down and ran into the house. Jennifer noticed how incredibly warm and approachable she looked in her navy blue sweatpants and candy apple red Henley—the sleeves pulled up to reveal her forearms. She had nothing on her feet but white athletic socks and another peek of white was visible in the form of a t-shirt that Jennifer could see inside the buttons of the Henley. It was about as comfortable as one could dress without actually wearing pajamas, yet Alex didn't look even a little rumpled.

Again, Jennifer felt the excitement of having a new friend, somebody totally removed from her usual circle. Most of the women she was used to associating with were very much like Claire...wives of wealthy businessmen who spent more time shopping and gossiping about one another than anything else and Jennifer didn't really like the person she became when she was with them. She was glad to be in a completely different environment, away from all that. She didn't feel the least bit awkward relaxing on Alex's deck; she felt *relieved*.

As she snuggled into the soft-cushioned chair, Kinsey took it upon himself to jump into her lap and perch his little butt on her thighs. His chain was plenty long enough to allow him access to most of the deck, just not most of the neighborhood. She chuckled at his assertiveness and scratched his side. As she did so, he lifted his right front paw, as if directing her to scratch under his little arm. She, of course, did as she was requested and that's the position they were in when Alex returned with a tall glass in her hand.

"Kinsey! Get down!" she scolded, slightly embarrassed. He blinked up at her in wide-eyed innocence, but made no move.

"Oh, no. He's okay, Alex. Really. I don't mind." The truth was, Jennifer was flattered by the way he had taken to her and was not quite ready to give him up.

Alex looked uncertain, but relented. "If he bugs you, just tell him to get down. He's very bossy. Aren't you, bad boy?" She affectionately scratched the top of his head and handed Jennifer the glass. "Here you go. Guaranteed to allay any type of stress."

It looked like a glass of cola, but Jennifer had the sneaking suspicion there was more to it than that. She took a sip, immediately loving the creamy, spiced taste as it slid down her throat and she hummed her approval, raising an eyebrow in question.

"Captain Morgan's and Coke," Alex announced with a smile. "There's no pressure the Captain can't relieve."

Jennifer smiled back at her. It had been a long time since somebody had done something to brighten her day and she was flattered. She took another sip, relishing the feel of the rum as it settled into her stomach and spread throughout her body. Her goose bumps had disappeared.

"So, the move's not going so well?" Alex ventured. A couple strands of her dark hair had escaped her ponytail and skimmed along the side of her face in the soft breeze as she met Jennifer's gaze.

"Oh, it's going all right," Jennifer said. "It would be a lot less stressful, though, if I could figure out a way to tactfully get rid of my mother-in-law."

"Ah. Too much help is she?"

Jennifer laughed. "Yeah, that's about it. Plus, everything she says is right and everything I say is wrong."

"And this surprises you? Isn't that the first thing they teach you in Being the Model Daughter-In-Law 101?"

"I think I was sick that day."

"And didn't study for the final, apparently."

"Jesus, I guess not." They both chuckled. "First, she was absolutely certain the sofa was not going to fit through the doorway, despite the fact that the delivery guys didn't see it as a problem."

"And then?"

"Then, she swears that the oversized chair doesn't match it."

"The sofa?"

"Right."

"Does it?"

"The *matching* oversized chair?" Jennifer smirked. "Yeah, it does. I picked it out myself. Thus the term 'matched set.'"

"I see. Any other furniture give her a hard time?"

"No, but she hates my dishes."

"Your dishes."

"Yes. She can't put her finger on it, but they're 'just not right.'" Jennifer launched into her best imitation of Claire, one she had damn near perfected over the years, mixing the perfect combination of haughtiness and egotism. She sat up straight as a rod, her voice taking on the mysterious almost-English accent that Claire had affected over the years for no apparent reason. "These...these dishes, Jennifah, where on earth did you get them? The pattern is so...so..." She waved her hand in the air as if she couldn't be bothered with finding the right word. "They're just not right."

"Wow." Alex laughed. "She sounds...um...difficult."

Jennifer was amused by Alex's obvious attempt to tread carefully when speaking about a woman she'd never met who was related to Jennifer. "Oh, it's okay. Don't be polite on my account. She's a bitch."

"We should introduce her to *my* mother."

"Yeah? She the same way?"

"Without the polish or the money, yes. I never do anything right."

"Are you married?"

"Nope."

"Well, hopefully when you are, you won't get a mother-in-law who's as bad. If you do, come and see me and I'll give you my best advice on how to deal with two of them at once."

"You're mom's just as bad?"

"She's close."

"My God, Jennifer. How do you stay sane?"

"Who says I am?"

They laughed over that. Jennifer sighed and took another swig from her glass. "I didn't think it was going to be this hard."

"What? Moving?"

"Yeah," Jennifer replied, almost honestly.

Alex looked at her, waiting for her to elaborate.

Jennifer wasn't sure where it came from and was very surprised to feel it, but she had the sudden, almost irresistible urge to spill her guts, to pour out her heart to this complete stranger. She was able to control herself and to keep from doing just that, but it was such a weird feeling. She knew that if things had been the other way around, if Alex had come to her home and began to tell her woes after they'd only met once, Jennifer probably would have figured out how to shoo her away and would have rolled her eyes about Alex later. As it was, she just felt so comfortable sitting there that she couldn't bring herself to leave. Alex gazed openly at her, expectantly, like she really *cared* what her new friend was about to say, like she really *intended* to listen. For the first time in years, Jennifer felt like she could be herself and she wouldn't be judged.

"How long have you and Eric been married?" Alex asked.

"Almost eight years. I'm twenty-nine."

"You're a baby."

"Wipe that smirk off your face. What are you, thirty?"

"Many moons ago. I'm looking at the big three-five next January." She grimaced at the thought, only half-jokingly.

"Ouch. You'll have to let me know how that goes. I'm already dreading it and I've got five more years."

"Eric the same age as you?"

"A year older."

"You guys married young, huh?"

"Yeah, I suppose we did."

"I bet you had a beautiful wedding." She had an image of a huge extravaganza, probably at Oak Hill Country Club or someplace equally gorgeous. Expensive food, tons of guests, Jennifer looking beautiful in a flowing, white gown, Eric all handsome in his tailored tux.

"It was." Jennifer nodded. "Though I think our parents were more excited about it than we were." *I wasn't ready to get married and neither was Eric*, she wanted to add.

"He seems like a nice guy," Alex commented sincerely.

"He is. He's been a little stressed lately with his job, but I suppose that's to be expected in his line of work."

"What does he do?"

"He's a lawyer in his dad's firm. He's being groomed to take over as partner when his father retires next year. Daniel's been handing his clients over to Eric little by little and with the addition of the Buffalo office, I think Eric's a bit overwhelmed. He's really a great guy, though. I could do a lot worse, that's for sure. Feels like I've known him forever."

"Are you high school sweethearts?"

"Yup. Actually, we grew up together. We've known each other

for..." She did a quick calculation in her head. "Jesus, twenty years."

"Wow."

"His family and my family are very tight. When Eric and I started dating in high school, our parents sort of latched onto the pairing and the rest is history."

"That's really very sweet."

"Yeah, I suppose it is." She drained the rest of her glass.

They gazed steadily out at the water, watching the seagulls dive and swoop. They were quiet and the silence was comfortable and warm. Kinsey had curled up in Jennifer's lap and twitched restlessly every now and then as he chased something in his sleep, small snoring sounds emanating from his little black nose.

Finally, Jennifer broke the silence. "What are you working on?" She gestured at the pad Alex held. "A letter?"

"An outline, actually." She glanced at it and said, somewhat self-consciously, "I'm writing a novel."

"Really?" Jennifer couldn't hide her excitement. "You're a writer?"

"I hope so." Alex chuckled, flattered by Jennifer's glee. "One day. We'll have to see what happens."

Jennifer was confused and her expression said so.

"It's sort of a long story—no pun intended—but the short and sweet version is this: I used to teach and now I'm trying my hand at being a novelist. I've written short stories before, even sold a few, but I've never written anything longer than fifty pages."

"So you're giving it a shot."

"Right. It's quite a challenge for me, given my tiny little attention span, and I want to see if I'm up to it."

Jennifer was dying to ask what it was about, what was in the outline, but Alex's failure to offer it up herself told her that maybe she was still too much of a stranger to trust with such personal information. She chose another topic instead. "What did you teach?"

"Freshman English." A flicker of emotion zipped across Alex's face, but she offered no more than those two words.

It would seem the mysterious Ms. Foster has a few secrets, Jennifer thought, vowing to get to know this woman better and maybe uncover a few of them.

"So, are you and Eric officially moved in today?" Alex asked. "Are you staying over tonight?"

"I know I am. I'm not sure about Eric yet. Remember I said his firm has a new branch opening up in Buffalo that he's been helping to set up? I know he has an early meeting tomorrow, so he'll probably go back to Pittsford and stay there tonight. That'll cut half an hour off his morning commute."

"Wait. You've got *another* house in Pittsford?" Alex asked, her eyes twinkling.

"Yes," Jennifer drawled back, loving the playful tone of Alex's voice.

"Jennifer?"

"Yes?"

"Are you loaded?"

"Loaded as in drunk or loaded as in rich?"

"Either."

"Yes."

They burst into laughter. Kinsey lifted his head and gave them an annoyed glare. They laughed at him, too.

"Can I get you another drink, lightweight?" Alex asked with a smirk.

"Only if you want to carry me back to my place." Jennifer chuckled, holding up a hand. "No, I'm good. Thanks."

"You have tomorrow off?"

Jennifer cringed inwardly at the question. The fact that she didn't work wasn't something that normally concerned her, but in the presence of her new friend, it bothered her a great deal. "Yeah. Yeah, I do."

"Well, I'm here most of the time, so if you need anything...help with moving stuff around or whatever...just come on over."

"I may take you up on that. Thank you."

"Are you a morning person?"

"Sleeping until eight is considered sleeping in for me. Eric whines that I run from the bed too early on the weekends."

"Kinsey is an early riser, so we're usually up by six or seven. I highly recommend having your morning coffee or tea on the deck, although it's still a bit chilly yet. It's quiet and peaceful. The water's like glass. Nobody's in sight but a few fishermen. It's heaven. There's nothing like morning on the lake."

The look on her face was so full of passion, causing Jennifer to vow then and there that she'd follow Alex's directions the next morning, no matter what. "Sounds wonderful. I'll have to give it a try."

They sat in companionable silence for several minutes, looking out onto the sun as it reflected on the water. Jennifer felt the burning need to find out more about this new person in her life.

"So, you're not married?"

"No." Alex looked fondly at her sleeping dog. "Kinsey's the only man in my life."

"Ever been married?"

"Nope."

Alex offered no more detail, always a little uncomfortable with that particular line of questioning. Fortunately, she was saved any further interrogation by the sound of Eric's voice.

"Jen!" he hollered. "I have to get going soon. Can you make me something to eat?"

"Be right there," Jennifer hollered back.

"Hi, Alex!"

"Hey, Eric." Alex waved. "Welcome to the neighborhood!"

Jennifer sighed, her respite over. "Why can't men cook for themselves?"

Alex smiled. "It's an age-old question passed down from generation to generation."

"I suppose I should go." She made no move to leave.

"I suppose."

"Am I up yet?" she asked after a few minutes.

Alex chuckled. "Not quite."

"Damn." A few more minutes passed. "How 'bout now?"

This time Alex laughed out loud. "Um, no."

"It's this friggin' chair of yours, you know."

"Don't say I didn't warn you."

"Jen!" came Eric's voice again.

This time, Jennifer smiled and gently moved Kinsey. "God has spoken. I've got to go."

Alex stood and picked the dog up off Jennifer's lap, sorry to see her leave.

"Thank you so much. For the drink as well as the company. It's just what I needed."

"Any time. You know where I live. You're always welcome. And I mean it about tomorrow. If you need anything, just come on over, okay?"

"I will." She gave Kinsey a final scratch on his head as he yawned, then hurried down the stairs. "I'll see you again soon."

"Definitely," Alex replied, watching her walk quickly away and unable to keep from enjoying the gentle sway of her hips as she moved. She turned to the dog in her arms. "Well, you certainly had the best seat in the house, didn't you? Little stinker."

She thought about her new neighbors and wondered what their life was like. Were they happy? They seemed to be, though she hadn't seen them together more than a couple minutes. An idea sparked in her brain. She set Kinsey down, picked up her pad and pen, and jotted notes as they came to her.

She focused on Eric and Jennifer, trying to picture what their life must be like. They were young, rich, and good-looking. Was Eric the sweet guy Jennifer insisted he was? Maybe he was possessive and bossy. Did he love her? She seemed so sweet and charming.

Did he love her like a sweet and charming woman deserved to be loved? Was he good to her? Did he buy her presents and bring her flowers? Did he tell her how beautiful she was on a regular basis? Did he hug her often?

What about her? Did she love him? Was she happy? Was she bored? Much to her surprise, Alex made a list of all the questions bombarding her mind, and crumpled and tossed aside the sparse notes she'd jotted down before Jennifer had visited. The creative juices that had merely trickled earlier suddenly flowed abundantly and she kept them going as best she could. An idea took form in her head. She'd been having trouble smoothing out the details for the story she'd planned to write, but the whole thing took a back seat to the new piece now taking shape.

Was Eric romantic? Was he gentle and sweet when he made love to Jennifer? Or did he simply take what he wanted and leave her unsatisfied? Alex laughed quietly to herself when she realized her brain was quickly thinking up several different methods of keeping Jennifer *very* satisfied. *A good fantasy never hurt anybody*, she rationalized.

She kept working on her lists and before she knew it, she had created two fictional characters based not-so-loosely on Jennifer and Eric. A teacher friend of Alex's had once told her that a writer should always know everything there was to know about a character…what she would do in any given situation, how she would answer any given question. Alex's outlines grew lengthy as she created backgrounds and families and idiosyncrasies for two of her main characters. She gave them good jobs, bad habits, an unfulfilling sex life…

…and a neighbor.

Alex laughed aloud.

This could be good. This could be very, very good.

Chapter
Three

Alex blinked in surprise when she opened her eyes the Saturday morning of the annual First Picnic of the Summer party. The weather in Upstate New York was fickle, to say the least, and the chances of having good weather in the summer, on a weekend, when something's been planned are slim to none. When she realized the sun was shining and the sky was blue, she actually wondered if she might be dreaming.

Even Kinsey did a double take out the window. Then he yawned, his pink tongue impossibly long, and did his morning stretch—first his front legs, then his back legs. Next, he padded onto Alex's chest where he stood on her like he was king of the mountain—or mountains in that case—and proceeded to give her a wake-up bath. It had become a morning ritual that Alex adored, though she didn't tell many people about it for fear of embarrassment; not everybody understood the value of doggie kisses. Kinsey had been with her for five years and there had been more than one time in her life when she'd felt like he was her only friend.

"Hey, leave my eyeballs in the sockets, pal," she scolded with a chuckle as he became a tad overzealous in his washing. "We've got company coming today. Gotta get moving." She stretched her way out of the queen-size bed, made a quick detour to the bathroom, and then tossed on some cleaning sweats. Although they'd most likely spend the better part of the day on the deck, it would be the first time her friends would see the lake house since it had officially become *hers* and she wanted it spotless.

It was a small house by lake standards—less than half the size of Jennifer and Eric's—but it was valuable by sheer location alone. It had started out as a cottage decades before, but was gradually refurbished and solidified so that it became suitable for year-round living. It was only one level. The L-shaped deck supported two entrances—a sliding glass door from the back, facing the water, and a regular door from the side. Both entered into the kitchen. The front door led to a good-sized living room with a small fireplace. A hallway off the living room led to the master bedroom, bathroom, and guest room. Alex was still trying to get used to sleeping in the master. Whenever she'd stayed with Aunt Margie growing up, she'd slept in the guest bedroom, so the adjustment was strange, even after several months.

Exactly one hour before the party was to officially start, Kinsey began to bark. Alex, smiling, came out of the bedroom in fresh jeans and a white t-shirt. She knew it would be Jackie and Rita. They always arrived early so Alex could have extra time with their daughter. Kinsey continued to bark excitedly as Alex opened the side door and clipped his chain onto his collar, as she watched her friends clamor out of their minivan.

"Awek!" The beautiful baby girl voice of her goddaughter never failed to melt Alex's heart.

"Hannah Banana? Is that you?"

No sooner had Jackie set the toddler on the ground, than her little feet carried her as quickly as they could to her godmother's outstretched arms. Alex swooped her up, smothered her giggling face with kisses, and inhaled the incomparable toddler smell of baby powder and sweetness.

"Nothing warms the heart like a three-year-old who thinks you're the Queen of All Things, does it?" Jackie asked with a wry grin.

"Not a thing."

"How's it going, Stretch?" Jackie kissed Alex's cheek.

"Not bad. Not bad at all. You?"

"It's all good."

The resemblance between Jackie and Hannah was remarkable, given that they did not share the same blood. Rita had been inseminated with sperm from a donor she and Jackie had picked together. Rita had wanted the father to be as similar physically to Jackie as possible. As a result, both mother and child had fine, blonde hair, big, blue eyes, and long, thin frames. Rita, with her mostly Hispanic background, had given Hannah her fiery temper and her passion for the things she loved. The child was the perfect mix of Alex's two dearest friends and it couldn't have worked any better if they'd been heterosexual and conceived her the old fashioned way.

Jackie glanced up at the house, hefting a diaper bag over her shoulder as Rita approached from the vehicle with a large bowl in her arms. "It's really yours, huh?"

Alex sighed and set Hannah on her feet so she could go pay attention to Kinsey, who was still barking. "Yup. All mine. I still can't believe it."

"So tell me how this came about," Rita ordered. "Jackie didn't give me any details."

"I did, too," Jackie whined.

"'Alex's aunt gave her the lake house' doesn't constitute details, my love," she said sweetly, an unruly dark curl hanging over one eye.

"I was quick and to the point," Jackie said.

"Hope you're not like that in bed," Alex teased.

"Funny."

Alex took the bowl from Rita's arms and led them into the house. "As you know, I was staying here on and off, keeping an eye on the place for Aunt Margie while she was away with Rafael. The lease on my apartment was up at the end of February and Aunt Margie suggested I just move my stuff in and live here indefinitely. I didn't want to, really, but after the fiasco at school, things were getting tight money-wise so I took her up on it. Earlier this month, I got a call from her. She said she was going to stay in Cancun with Rafael." She could still remember the giddiness in her aunt's voice.

"Permanently?" Rita asked incredulously. "Aunt Margie's become a one-man woman?"

"Apparently." Alex nodded with a smile. "She sounded so happy about it. Anyway, she said that since I was in need of a place and she didn't really want to go through the hassle of getting a realtor and trying to sell, that I should just have it."

"No way!" Rita shrieked.

"I know! I couldn't believe it, either. I told her I'd be glad to take care of selling it for her, but she said she knew how much I loved it when I was growing up and if I wanted it, she wanted me to have it."

"Oh my God," Rita said.

"I tried to argue with her," she turned to Jackie, "but you know what it's like to take on Aunt Margie when she's got an idea in her head."

"Yeah. Impossible. I spent enough time here as a kid to know that."

"Her lawyer contacted me with all the paperwork the next day, the deed was transferred into my name, and that was that."

"Free and clear?" Rita asked in disbelief as she unloaded some of Hannah's toys and got her settled on the floor with her crayons.

"Well, I have taxes and utilities, but nothing I can't handle." The tone in Alex's voice made it clear that she too was still in awe.

Jackie helped herself to a beer from the fridge. "What does Leona think of all this?"

At the mention of her mother's name, Alex rolled her eyes—her usual reaction. "What do you think?"

Jackie smirked and swigged from her bottle.

"What?" Rita asked. Not hooking up with Jackie until after

college, she had missed the pleasure of growing up around Alex's mother.

"She's pissed off and upset that Margie gave the house to Alex and not her," Jackie predicted.

Alex tapped her forefinger to the tip of her nose. "Bingo. That phone call was fun. Not."

"Awek, will you cuwwer wiff me?" Hannah's sweet little voice drifted up from the floor where she was spread out with her coloring books and crayons.

"I would love to color with you, baby." Alex stretched out on her stomach and picked up a burnt sienna crayon.

"You cuwwer dis one," the toddler directed, pointing to the opposite page.

"Yes, ma'am."

Alex looked up and smiled at her friends. The house was set up so that the kitchen looked across the small dining area and into the living room. Rita had made herself at home near the sink, as she always did, taking it upon herself to cut up different cheeses and veggies and laying out several varieties of crackers. Jackie fondly watched her daughter and best friend, sipped her beer as she leaned against the counter that separated the kitchen from the dining area, and propped her foot on one of the chairs.

"So, this writing thing." She always referred to Alex's writing as such. "How's that going?"

"Very well. I came up with what I think might really be a good tale. Something new. Not the one I told you about before." She stopped and continued working on her picture.

"Yeah—?" Jackie prompted, making continuation motions with her arm.

"A little mystery, a little romance..."

"And—?"

Alex took a big breath, trying to decide on how much to reveal. "It's about a guy who falls desperately in love with the new girl next door. Problem is, she's married."

Jackie blinked at her for several seconds, waiting. Finally, when it was clear Alex would say no more, she whined, "That's it? That's all I get?"

"For now." Alex smiled and went back to her picture as Jackie grumbled on and on about how she was the best friend and she of all people should get a full synopsis of the story and so on and so forth. Alex kept coloring and smiling, noting Kinsey with amusement. He had settled next to Hannah, his snout resting possessively on her butt as she colored. Her swinging feet occasionally bonked him in the head, but he didn't seem to mind. He was as enamored of her as Alex was.

It wasn't long before slamming car doors could be heard and Kinsey jumped up to bark at the sound.

"More guests," Jackie commented. "Whoa! What have we here?"

Alex looked up and tried to follow Jackie's gaze out the window, but couldn't from her spot on the floor. She stood up, much to Hannah's annoyance.

Across the way, Jennifer was out on her deck working on some flowerpots. She wore a tight, red, scoop-neck t-shirt and snug, ripped jeans. Her blonde hair was pulled back into a loose, casual ponytail and she looked good enough to eat. Alex swallowed hard, wondering why she couldn't quite catch her breath.

"That's Jennifer. My new neighbor."

"New neighbor?" Jackie smiled at her knowingly. Alex grimaced, hating the feeling that Jackie could see exactly what was in her head. "Well, at least you'll have some inspiration for the story, hmm?"

Alex felt herself flush a deep, deep red.

* * *

The day had somehow managed to stay gorgeous, which was a miracle in itself. Alex and her guests sat on the deck eating, drinking, and shooting the breeze, soaking up the rays of sunshine and planning the upcoming summer. In addition to Jackie and Rita, there was Alex's good friend Steve and his girlfriend, Shelley. At the end of the deck on one of the lounges was Alex's ex, Nikki, and her girlfriend Diane. The atmosphere was one of fun and anticipation and laughter surrounded them.

Throughout the afternoon, out of the corner of her eye, Alex kept unintentional track of Jennifer as she practically landscaped her entire yard. She was sure Jackie caught her once or twice, but wisely said nothing. She was also sure Jackie would use it against her later.

"Hey, volleyball starts in a couple weeks, you know." Steve was one of Alex's most cherished friends. The two of them had worked together while in college making pizza for Vito's in an attempt to cover the unexpected costs of college life—like food and beer. They had a lot in common and became instant buddies. It was during college that Alex had struggled with her sexuality, and when poor Steve had pursued her romantically, she ran away screaming like the last female left in a horror movie, leaving him dazed and confused. Fortunately, she'd accepted things readily and Steve was the first close friend to whom she had ever come out. He had always remained sweet and supportive and she couldn't imagine her life without him. "We should get in a couple practices. Work out the kinks." His dark, unruly hair always looked like it needed to be cut and he regularly tossed his head to the side, temporarily flinging his bangs out of his eyes.

"Kinks?" Jackie teased. "Getting old, Stevie my boy?"

"I'm afraid so," he responded with an easy smile. "I spend a lot more time stretching these days."

"Those early thirties are a killer," Rita commented. At thirty-nine she was the eldest of the group.

Alex smirked. "Apparently, Shelley's not giving you enough of a workout."

"Hey!" Shelley protested from her spot at the table. She was a petite blonde who had been with Steve for three years and simply adored him. "I give him plenty of workouts. It's not my fault he can't keep up any more."

That earned Steve a couple of sympathetic pats on the shoulder and many pitiful looks. He blushed, even though he knew Shelley was just teasing him. He was so easy to embarrass.

"We still need a setter," Alex said as she flipped a burger on the grill. "I don't think three days after giving birth is enough time for Tina to come back, do you?"

Jackie chuckled at the mention of her work friend who had served as their setter last year. "Are you kidding me? I talked to her on the phone yesterday. She's so in love with her son, we may never see her again. You sure you don't want to play, Di? We could use you."

Alex cringed, but hid it well by pretending to fuss with a burger.

Diane turned her sunglassed face toward Jackie as she sat on the lounge, her feet in Nikki's lap. "Nah. I don't think so."

Kinsey wandered over to them, sniffing. Diane blatantly pushed him away and he moved on to Nikki, who scratched his head sweetly. "You'd be a great setter, honey," she said to Diane, smiling gently.

"Yeah, I know I would. Volleyball's just not my thing; it never has been. They wanted me to play in school, too, but I turned them down. It's kind of boring."

Alex rolled her eyes. *Yes, I can see how a game where you don't physically knock down your opponent would be boring for you*, she thought—and actually managed to keep herself from muttering it out loud. She shot Jackie a look. Jackie's return expression told her to keep quiet, for Nikki's sake.

She flipped another burger and tightly clenched her teeth.

* * *

Jennifer was having a hard time explaining to herself why she felt such a pang in her stomach when she realized Alex was having some sort of party. After all, she'd only known the woman for a very short time, so it wasn't like she expected to be invited. After a long while of listening to the laughing and joking coming from the deck as she worked on her plants, she decided she was simply envious of the good time they were having.

She thought about the get-togethers that she and Eric had thrown in the past; there weren't very many, aside from the housewarming party they'd thrown when they'd moved into their house in Pittsford. It had included some of their school friends and had been a good time, but they had drifted from that group since. Eric's job required long hours and constant contact with the same group of people in his office, so Jennifer thought it might be good to get to know some of them on a more personal level. She decided to have a sort of happy hour at their house, telling Eric to invite his colleagues from the office and their spouses to drop by after work one Friday night. It had turned out to be one of the most boring affairs she'd ever been a part of. The people were wooden to say the least, talking only of money and their clients. The group was almost unbelievably stereotypical. If she did her best to picture a room full of snooty, rich people, she invariably came up with the exact group that had occupied her home that night. It was a chillingly sterile party. When the last guest had departed, she and Eric had stood in the foyer, looking at each other in disbelief.

"Wow," he'd said, eyes wide. "That was...frightening."

"I'm glad I'm not the only one who thought so," she'd responded. "You work all day long with them?"

He nodded. "Thus, the term 'frightening.' Let's not do that again, okay?"

"You've got yourself a deal, babe."

There were still occasions where they had to socialize with Eric's colleagues, but they hadn't invited any of them over since that night.

The party going on next door was obviously not like that at all, and that's where the pang of envy came from. They were laughing. They laughed a lot. Jennifer managed to keep herself from glancing often in their direction, but she had no trouble picking Alex's rumbling chuckle out of the air; hers seemed to carry further than the rest and was contagious. More than once, she caught herself smiling at the sound of it.

Finding it difficult to look in from the outside as it were, she concentrated on her flowers. She'd filled several flowerpots and flower boxes with various annuals, adding a satisfying splash of color to the other wise monochromatic deck. That morning, she had taken Alex's advice and had stood on the deck with her coffee, surveying the entire area. Alex had been right: the air was fresh and crisp, the lake smooth and quiet. It was incredibly peaceful and she'd taken the opportunity to visualize what she wanted the deck and yard to look like, deciding what colors would go where, how she would arrange things, where she would dig. It was relaxing and invigorating at the same time. Having a plan for the day was something that always got her going and helped her look forward to the hours ahead.

She'd spent almost two hours at the garden store, picking several annuals in differing but complimentary shades and vowing to return in the fall for some perennials. She'd had the entire design all sketched out in her head; she could see exactly how she wanted it to look when she was finished.

The day was cool, but cheerfully sunny and she worked for several hours without a break, creating three flowerbeds from scratch. She had decided to stick with pastels and whites, so she planted petunias and impatiens in varying shades of pinks and purples. She lined the borders with white and lavender alyssum and she intended to use some shredded mulch as the finishing touch, saving that for the next day. She sat back on her heels after patting dirt around the very last plant and smiled with satisfaction.

"That looks fantastic!" Alex's voice surprised her in its close proximity, but it was a pleasant surprise. She looked up to see her neighbor smiling down at her, holding out a bottle of LaBatts. "You've been working nonstop for hours. I thought you could use this."

Jennifer smiled warmly, accepting the beer. "Thanks, Alex."

"Listen, we're having a little beginning-of-the-summer party over there. We've got tons of food. Why don't you join us? Eat something. You must be starving by now."

Jennifer was instantly nervous at the prospect of meeting new friends, feeling out of practice and worried about the impression she'd make. Alex's gentle, welcoming smile, however, shooed those concerns away. "You're right. I *am* starving." She stood up, peeled off her gardening gloves, and noticed with dismay her brownish knees. She tried in vain to brush them clean.

"Please." Alex chuckled, grabbing her arm and tugging her toward the gathering. "Don't worry about it. You look great."

* * *

Jennifer's fears turned out to be unfounded; Alex's friends welcomed her with open arms and she was glad she had agreed to join them. Four of the women obviously made up two couples, which made Jennifer wonder about Alex's sexuality, but she decided she'd broach that subject at another time.

"Here. Sit down." Alex ushered her to the table next to Steve. "I'll get you a plate." Jennifer was flattered by Alex's enthusiasm and smiled as she skittered off into the kitchen.

"So, Jennifer. Alex says you're new here?" Jackie sat down across from her, balancing her chin in her hand, her blue eyes friendly and curious.

"We just moved in a couple weeks ago."

"We?" This came from the corner, where Nikki and Diane sat. Nikki regarded her openly, waiting for a response, but Jennifer shifted uncomfortably as she was sure that behind her sunglasses, Diane was giving her a very lascivious appraisal.

"My husband and I, yes."

Alex returned from inside with a plate and set it in front of her. It was loaded with generous helpings of potato salad, beans, pasta salad, pickles, and pieces of fresh fruit. She smiled gratefully at her, realizing only at that moment just how hungry she really was.

"I can throw a hot dog or a burger on the grill, too, if you'd like."

"This is great, Alex. Really. I'm fine. Thank you."

Suddenly, Kinsey barked playfully from around the corner of the deck and a friendly male voice could be heard talking to him. Seconds later, an extremely handsome man appeared to the delight of the whole crowd. He was at least six foot three with hugely broad shoulders and smiling eyes. He wore wire-rimmed glasses, cargo shorts, and a navy blue long sleeve t-shirt. Jennifer couldn't take her eyes off him.

"Hey, big guy." Jackie stood up to hug him. She was quite tall, but the newcomer's height made her seem average.

Alex was next. She practically disappeared in his embrace and his face told Jennifer that he cared a great deal for her.

"Hey, where's the volleyball net?" he asked.

Alex chuckled. "It's still a little early in the season for me," she replied as he made his rounds, greeting the rest of the partygoers. "We were just talking about having a practice or two. Think you can get some guys together to scrimmage with us?"

His eyes roamed the deck and rested on Jennifer. She smiled around her fork.

"Sure. Is this our new setter?"

Alex followed his pointing finger and chuckled again. "Oh, no. This is my new neighbor, Jennifer. Jennifer, this is my dear friend David."

David held out his hand and Jennifer took it, her own engulfed within his. "Hmm. Nice, strong hands." He turned back to Alex. "Are you sure she's not a setter?"

"You don't play volleyball, do you, Jennifer?" Alex asked playfully.

"Not in quite a while, no," she answered smugly. Alex's eyebrows shot up in surprise.

"You mean you do play?" Jackie looked from Alex to Jennifer and back again, her eyes sparkling.

"Well, I did in school. It's been a long time and I'm really rusty." She saw where this was going and it made her a little nervous. She wasn't a bad player, but she wasn't an outstanding player and she didn't want to embarrass herself or Alex by claiming to be better than she was.

"Rust can be worked away." Jackie smiled. "Just needs a little elbow grease. Right, Alex?"

Alex was smiling, too, and Jennifer soon realized what she'd just gotten herself into.

Alex sensed her unease because the expression on her face softened and she sat down next to Jennifer. "Why don't you come to a practice? It's really just recreational. We like to play, but we're not out for blood. We just like to have fun. Come to practice and see what you think. Okay?" Her brown eyes were soft and gentle and Jennifer felt the complete and total inability to say no to her.

"One practice." She held up a finger to stress her point.

"Terrific." Alex looked incredibly pleased and Jennifer grinned back at her.

"What position did you play in school?" Jackie asked.

Jennifer's grin grew a little wider. "I was a setter."

Chapter
Four

The following Thursday, the weather didn't exactly look promising. It was warm enough, but the sky was overcast with a few threatening, black clouds rolling by on occasion. It looked about ready to pour any minute. The impending rain didn't stop the volleyball team from having a riot practicing, though.

They were just about the only bunch of people on the beach. Jennifer assumed the smart people of town were actually under roofs of some sort. She sat in the sand with Rita and Hannah, alternating between watching the team practice and helping the little blonde toddler build a sandcastle. She was reluctant to jump right into the game and Alex seemed to understand when Jennifer told her that she'd rather observe for a while. She wanted to know exactly where her skill level would fall.

The team was quite good. Alex and Jackie were definitely the strongest players. Jackie had a vertical leap that was shocking and her lean, lanky frame was deceiving; she could spike the ball with startling force. Jennifer would bet that she fooled many an opponent the same way. Alex wasn't quite as strong as Jackie, but she was amazingly consistent and Jennifer guessed that the team looked to her to hold them together. David was also very good and she got the impression that he hadn't been playing very long. He seemed a little unsure of his position on the court, but once he figured it out, he was rock solid. Steve was wiry and fast and all over the sand. Jennifer laughed more than once at his diving saves, realizing with great clarity just exactly why he had to stretch so much before a game; Rita referred to him as the 'floor mop.' Nikki was definitely the weak link. She did her best to set, but had a very stiff touch, often sending the ball careening away instead of up to her hitter. She got frustrated very quickly, but Jennifer was sure if she could just relax and focus, she could be quite good. Alex was constantly reassuring her, reminding her that it was just practice, the first of the season.

The interaction between the two of them was very interesting to Jennifer and she watched them carefully. Alex seemed very caring, very concerned with Nikki, but there was an obvious line she wouldn't cross. She was physical in a sisterly way, stroking an arm or patting a shoulder when Nikki seemed upset. Nikki, on the other hand, looked at Alex with complete love and devotion. It was absolutely unmistakable and Jennifer's immediate reaction was that they had been lovers, but were not any more. Either that or Nikki wanted something Alex wouldn't give her. Or both. It was at that moment that Jennifer stopped wondering and became quite certain that Alex was gay.

On the other side of the net were four men. None of them were very good, but all of them put one hundred and ten percent into their efforts. Jennifer predicted that if they continued to play together, in time they'd make a formidable opponent to Alex's team. The best part was, everybody was having fun. Lots of laughter carried through the air. Playful name calling and bending of the rules abounded.

"So, Jennifer." Rita's friendly voice pulled her from her speculations. "What do you do?"

Jennifer blinked several times, trying to figure out why she despised answering that particular question so much. "I'm...between jobs right now. How 'bout you?" *Nice, Jen,* her inner voice mocked her. *Redirect the focus. Very smooth.*

"I'm a stay at home mom." She said it proudly, which surprised Jennifer. Rita glanced lovingly at Hannah and Jennifer felt her heart warm.

"Really? Lucky Hannah," she commented, meaning it sincerely.

"Jackie and I discussed it long and hard before we even got pregnant. I was the vice president of a bank, made a pretty good living, but..." Her voice drifted off and she looked out onto the churning water of the lake. Bringing her own brown gaze back to Jennifer, she shrugged and smiled. "I remember my mom always being there when my sisters and I got home from school. The house was always bright, there were always cookies, she was always able to help us with our homework or school projects. I just wanted that for my kids, too, you know?"

Jennifer nodded, smiling back at her. "It's hard to do that now, both because of the high cost of living and the attitude that society has today about women who don't work." She knew that all too well. She was one of those women. She was also one of those people with the attitude.

"Jackie makes a decent living and I was able to do some smart investing while I was still working, so we do okay."

"Will you have more kids?"

"Oh, absolutely." She said it with such enthusiasm that it made

Jennifer laugh. "What about you? Any children in the future for you and your husband?"

The question made the laughter die in Jennifer's throat. "Oh, I don't know..." She had a quick flashback of her most recent conversation with Eric on that very subject. He thought they were ready, but for her, the thought of children caused the sound of a slamming prison door to reverberate in her head.

"Well, you're great with Hannah." Rita gestured to the fact that Jennifer sat close to the toddler, up to her elbows in sand.

"That's because she's a little doll." She grinned, winking at the child.

"Jennifer! Come on!"

Jennifer looked up at Alex as she waved her toward the court, eternally grateful for being saved from the conversation. Smiling apologetically at Rita, she jumped up, eager to leave the topic to die in the sand, and jogged onto the court.

"Six on four?" she asked as she looked around. "Hardly seems fair."

"You're right," Jackie agreed. "Nikki, why don't you help the boys out? They need a setter."

Nikki looked less than pleased to switch teams, but she went.

"Here." Alex tossed Jennifer the ball. "Thought you might like to actually touch it before you play."

Jennifer tossed it back at her, causing the brunette's eyebrows to raise. "Not necessary," she said, her voice cocky.

"Is that so?"

"Yup. Think you can hit?"

"If you think you can set me."

"Oh, I'll set you."

"Really."

"You just be ready."

"Baby, I was born ready."

They grinned playfully at each other, holding one another's gaze until it felt like the rest of the court had disappeared.

Jackie cleared her throat. "Can the rest of us play, too?" she asked teasingly.

Alex sighed. "I suppose."

"And what did I tell you about flirting with the straight girls?"

Alex pouted. "She started it."

"Did not," Jennifer whined back.

"Did, too." They grinned at one another as Alex tossed the ball to Jackie for the serve and the game began in earnest.

Jennifer was amazed by how quickly everything came back to her. She hadn't played in several years, since intramural volleyball her first semester in college and quite simply, she had forgotten how much she enjoyed the game.

She and Alex played like they'd been teammates for years. Jennifer instinctively knew just where to set the taller woman in order to get her to hit most effectively. Alex was spiking kills left and right, much to even her own surprise. The other team was left strewn in the sand on more than one occasion. They all had a fantastic time and the rain actually held off until just before they decided to call it a day.

Rita had seen it coming and had Hannah all packed up in the car when the players scrambled for their belongings. The poor toddler was completely tuckered out and had fallen asleep in her car seat in a matter of minutes after being strapped in. Rita really wanted to get her home and into her own bed.

Knowing Jackie and Rita had picked up Alex, Jennifer offered to give her a ride home.

"You're sure?" she asked. "I don't want to inconvenience you."

"Of course I'm sure. Alex, you live next door. How inconvenient can it be?"

Alex smiled a goofy grin. "Okay. I'd appreciate it." She jogged over to Rita's car and leaned in the passenger side window to talk to Jackie. Jackie punched her playfully on the arm and waggled a finger at her, like a mother scolding a child. Alex slapped her in return, then hurried back to Jennifer as her friends drove away. She just got into the car when the sky opened up and drops of rain the size of ping pong balls fell.

"Damn," Jennifer muttered. "I can't see a thing."

"It's okay. We can just sit here for a bit. This won't last long."

It only took a few minutes for the combination of the body heat inside and the falling rain outside to cause the car windows to fog over. Jennifer looked around at the sudden cocoon they'd found themselves in.

"People are going to wonder what we're doing in here," Alex said, waggling her eyebrows.

Jennifer smiled. "Or they're going to assume they *know* what we're doing in here." She swiped at the windshield and they sat in comfortable silence, watching the clouds roll over the lake. Jennifer was not usually okay with a total lack of conversation, but with Alex it was relaxing. She reveled in the simplicity of just being in the other woman's presence, of having a friend who expected nothing from her, who had no role for her to play. It was the most peace she'd felt in a long time.

"So, did you have fun?" Alex asked, breaking the silence gently.

Jennifer smiled widely. "I had a blast. Your friends are wonderful."

"Does that mean you'll at least consider becoming a regular? We sure could use you."

"I don't even have to consider it. I'd love to."

"Terrific."

They were quiet again until the rain died down to an acceptable rate of descent, and Jennifer turned the key in the ignition and pointed them home.

"Can I ask you something?" she ventured, hoping she wasn't about to step out of line.

"Sure."

"What's the deal with you and Nikki?"

Alex felt her heart skip a beat, as it usually did when that particular type of subject was broached. "Um...what do you mean?"

"She seems kind of...possessive is the wrong word..." Jennifer searched the air. "Clingy. She seems to cling to you. Are you lovers?"

Alex's face visibly blanched and Jennifer hid her smile. Amused by her shyness, she allowed Alex to stutter and stammer for a minute or two before trying to help.

"You *are* gay, right?"

"Me?"

"Yes, you."

Alex cleared her throat awkwardly. "Yes."

Jennifer furrowed her brow. "What's the matter?"

"I'm...um...just surprised. That's all."

"Surprised that I knew or surprised that I asked?"

"Yes."

"Alex." Jennifer chuckled. "It is the twenty-first century, you know. *Will & Grace. Ellen. Queer as Folk.* It's not an uncommon thing."

She smiled shyly. "No, I suppose it isn't."

"So, what about Nikki?"

"Nikki." She took a deep breath as if trying to decide how much to reveal.

"I don't mean to pry," Jennifer said, suddenly worried that maybe she had offended Alex. "It's none of my business. I was just curious."

"No, no. It's okay. Nikki is my ex. We were together for a fairly short period of time."

"Oh. And you still hang around together?"

"Yeah. The Curse of Lesbianism. You're doomed to remain friends with all your exes."

"Ick." Jennifer thought about how awkward that could be. "Why?"

"Nobody knows." Alex smiled. "Actually, Jackie and Rita are

really fond of Nikki, so she gets invited to the same gatherings as I do."

"That must be hard for you."

"I got used to it, I guess."

"How come you broke up?"

"It just didn't work, you know?"

"Yeah. Sometimes it doesn't. Is she seeing that other woman at the party?"

"Diane? Yeah, she's seeing her." Alex scowled as she answered and Jennifer laughed aloud.

"Tell me how you *really* feel about her."

Alex laughed, too. "She's a bitch and a control freak."

Jennifer kept laughing. "No, no. Don't sugar coat it for me."

Alex sighed and hastened to correct herself. "You know what? I shouldn't say that. That's not very nice of me. Nikki loves her—I think—and Nikki's my friend and I shouldn't say things like that. I don't care much for Diane. How's that?"

"Much more PC," Jennifer commended. "She's not great to Nikki, is she?"

"You noticed, huh?"

"At the party. All anybody has to do is watch them for a few minutes. Diane sat around the whole time I was there and Nikki waited on her. I don't think I heard Diane say thank you once...or anything nice that I noticed."

"Yeah, well, that pretty much sums up that relationship."

"Poor Nikki."

"It's too bad. She's a nice girl."

They pulled into Jennifer's driveway just as the sun broke through the clouds.

"What weird weather," Jennifer remarked.

"You'll get used to it."

"Hey, have you had dinner?" Jennifer asked as she reached for the door handle.

"No."

"Eric's staying in Buffalo tonight, so I'm on my own. I was just going to whip up a salad. Would you care to join me? Keep me company?"

Alex smiled widely. "Can I run home and grab a shower first? I have sand in places where sand has no business being."

"Me, too. See you back here in half an hour?"

"Sounds great."

Jennifer watched as Alex jogged across the yard to her own place. "And bring Kinsey!" she hollered after her, smiling as she waved back. She couldn't recall ever having connected with another woman so quickly. Well, at least not since...

She literally waved the thought away with her hand and she grabbed her shoes and towel from the back seat. *I will not go there,* she told herself. Several times.

Chapter
Five

As Alex approached the back deck of Jennifer's place, she stopped and ran her fingers through her hair one last time. The dinner invitation was totally unexpected, but she'd been more than happy to accept. She was finding herself more and more excited about this new friendship and she was looking forward to getting to know her neighbor better. The fact that Jennifer had pegged her on her sexuality unnerved her a bit, though she was unsure as to why. It wasn't a big secret or anything. Jennifer had seemed so straightforward and unaffected by the whole thing; Alex found it refreshing and odd at the same time. As had happened in the past, she began to suspect that maybe the hang-up about her gayness was her own and not anybody else's.

She looked down at Kinsey, who sat at her feet scowling with barely disguised impatience.

"How do I look?" she asked him quietly.

She could have sworn he rolled his brown eyes at her.

"Oh, thanks a lot. Come on." She led him up the stairs, maneuvering his leash and a bottle of wine in one hand while she rapped lightly on the sliding glass door with the other.

Jennifer appeared momentarily, bouncing to the door and smiling; she looked happy to see them as she slid the door open.

"Hi. Long time, no see." She looked fresh as a flower and smelled just as sweet. Alex squinted suspiciously at her.

"Hey. Didn't you just finish playing over an hour of intense volleyball in the sand? Weren't you as dirty and sweaty as the rest of us? How is it you look like *this* so fast?"

Jennifer blushed an attractive pink and Alex made a mental note to make her new friend blush as often as possible. It was adorable.

She held out the wine. "I come bearing gifts."

"I see that. You didn't have to do that, you know."

"You didn't have to invite me. It was very sweet of you. We were going to have cereal." Alex looked down at Kinsey as Jennifer laughed. "She thinks I'm kidding," she muttered to her dog.

"Hi there, handsome." Jennifer squatted down and gave Kinsey the attention for which he'd been waiting patiently.

Alex took the opportunity to study her new neighbor from above. Her hair was still damp. She had pulled it back into a quick braid that reached just past her shoulders and Alex noticed for the first time several streaks of red that ran through it. She wore baggy gray sweatpants emblazoned with NYU on the hip and a maroon sweatshirt with the sleeves cut off, which showed her surprisingly muscular shoulders. Alex's eyes lingered there for several delicious seconds before sliding down and taking note of the rest of her pleasing shape.

Kinsey sufficiently bathed Jennifer's face, but Jennifer apparently couldn't get enough and scooped him right up in her arms, much to his delight. It was Alex's turn to roll her eyes when the pooch shot her a look of pure glee.

"You're such a ladies' man," she accused him, laughing.

"He is just a doll." Jennifer was as much in her glory as Kinsey was, evidently.

Alex gave them a few more minutes before playfully interrupting. "I hate to bust in on your little love fest, but some of us came here to eat."

Jennifer laughed a sweet, musical sound that made Alex smile. She finally put Kinsey down, and unsnapped his leash from his collar. "The queen has spoken," she whispered to him. "Come on." She picked up the bottle of wine off the table where she had placed it and handed it to Alex. "You can open this."

Alex followed Jennifer and her dog into the kitchen, unable to keep her eyes from drifting over the blonde woman's rear end. She smiled inwardly, pretending to chide herself for her wandering eyes. *So I love to look at women. Is that so wrong?* she thought with a grin.

Jennifer opened a drawer and handed Alex a corkscrew. As she set to work on the bottle, Alex let her eyes wander around the room. She tried hard to keep her gaze neutral, though she was unsure about her success. It wasn't often that she was so obviously surrounded by money.

The kitchen was a cook's dream, which surprised Alex given how much she knew about—and disliked—Mrs. Cavanaugh. Alex wasn't much of a cook, but the modern design of the room wasn't lost on her. The appliances were all state of the art, the counter tops were Corian, the floor was ceramic tile. The color scheme was black and gray, with all the appliances stainless steel. It had a very professional, *expensive* feel to it. She wondered if Jennifer was as good a cook as her kitchen would have somebody believe, or if it was all just for show.

She popped the cork and Jennifer handed her two crystal wine glasses. As she poured, she said, "You really were very good out there today."

Jennifer waved a dismissive hand at the compliment. "I haven't played in years."

"Well, you'd never know it. You were right on the ball, no pun intended. And you set me right where I like it best."

"I noticed that." Jennifer nodded. "We worked well together."

"Damn right, we did. I haven't had a teammate set me that accurately in ages."

Jennifer held up her glass. "Here's to a season full of accurate sets and scorching kills."

With a smile, Alex touched her glass to Jennifer's, the crystal pinging pleasantly. Jennifer held her gaze for several seconds before releasing her to sip.

"So, what kind of dressing do you like on your salad?"

* * *

"Who would have thought a person could be stuffed to the point of explosion just from eating salad?" Alex groaned as she plopped onto the couch.

The question about whether or not Jennifer could cook had been answered with a resounding yes and then some. The salad had been overflowing...olives—both black and green, Greek and Spanish—cheese, three kinds that Alex counted, cabbage, water chestnuts, pine nuts, shredded ham. She made a complete and utter pig of herself. It was divine.

She sat in the living room on the leather couch, perfectly content to relax and wait for Jennifer to return from refilling their wine glasses. She'd never understood the appeal of leather furniture until that moment. It always seemed unspeakably frivolous to her. *Two thousand dollars for a couch? Are you kidding me? Really, how much more comfortable can it be than any other fabric?* Then she sat down and she was sure her sigh was quite audible. She had no trouble at all nestling down into the corner and tucking her shoeless feet beneath her. The leather wrapped around her like a hug.

"I may never get up from this couch," she said.

The sun had set and dusk was settling over the lake like a soft blanket. Jennifer had lit several candles around the room. The flickering light on the buttery-soft burgundy of the leather gave the whole room a warm and inviting glow and made it seem more like early fall than late spring. As she lay her head back, Alex took a good look at the room.

The coffee table and matching end tables were a rich, dark cherry and obviously costly. A large, abstract painting adorned one wall and matched the earthy colors in the area perfectly. It didn't really feel like a house by the lake. It felt like a warm, cozy library or a cabin in the woods, someplace you wanted to hunker down with a good book. The walls were a soft and richly pleasing shade of cream, but they seemed almost textured. She cocked her head to one side, trying to decide if it was the candlelight playing tricks on her or maybe wallpaper. Unable to figure it out, she stood, crossed the room, and placed her hand flat against the wall above the over-sized leather chair, expecting to feel a pattern of some sort. It was smooth under her palm.

"It's paint," Jennifer commented with a smile, startling Alex into an embarrassed grin.

"Sorry. I just wasn't sure. It looks textured."

"Color wash," Jennifer said. "I was experimenting. It came out better than I'd expected."

Alex eyes widened. "You did this?" Jennifer nodded. "Wow. It's beautiful! It sets the mood for the entire room. I'm really impressed."

It was Jennifer's turn to look embarrassed and, much to Alex's delight, she blushed. Alex managed to smother a smile.

"Thanks. I like that sort of thing, interior design. I just did this room last week. It's the only one in the house that I've completely finished, but I have plans for almost every other room." Jennifer laughed. "Eric thinks I'm insane."

"No way." Alex shook her head. "I can't do this stuff. This takes talent. Serious talent. Maybe you could help me with some color decisions in my place some time."

"I'd like that." She handed Alex her glass and they returned to the couch, one at each end, facing one another. Kinsey immediately jumped up into Jennifer's lap and curled up into a contented ball. Alex shook her head in mock-disgust, but Jennifer just smiled. "So, tell me about you, Alex."

"I'm afraid I'm not really all that exciting." Alex grinned as she sipped her wine. She was not the kind of person to open up easily, especially to somebody she'd just met. Jackie often teased her about how difficult it could be to extract information from her. With Jennifer, though, she didn't feel that foreboding sense of vulnerability that usually kept her from revealing much of anything. The expression on the younger woman's face was simply one of sincere curiosity and the desire to get to know her new friend. It was very flattering and Alex was instantly comfortable. "What would you like to know?"

"What do you write?"

"That's an easy one. I write fiction, mostly. Stories about every day people. I've always loved mysteries and suspense and action adventure, but I've never been able to write them. I love stories about private eyes and female cops, but I don't know them. I don't have those experiences." She smiled sheepishly. "And I'm lazy, so research isn't my favorite thing in the world. I tend to write about what I know. People you could run into on the street or in the local grocery store. People who live next door." She winked over the rim of her glass.

Jennifer smiled. "You like mysteries, huh?"

"Oh, God. I love them. You ever read Sue Grafton? *A is for Alibi? B is for Burglar?*"

"Nope. Can't say that I have."

"Well, then. I have an assignment for you this summer, Mrs. Wainwright. I have the whole series. She's up to Q now. You can borrow my *A is for Alibi* and let me know what you think. If you like it, help yourself to the rest. Grafton is a fantastic writer, one of my very favorites. That's where Kinsey got his name."

"Really?" Jennifer scratched the object of the discussion between his ears.

"Yup. Kinsey Millhone is the main character in all the novels. It's a she, but the breeder only had male puppies left." Alex reached over and covered the dog's ears. "Don't tell him he's named after a girl, okay?"

"It'll be our little secret." Jennifer giggled. "Do you write any lesbian stories?"

The question took Alex by surprise. "Um, no. Not usually. Well, not for public consumption anyway."

"Why not?"

"I don't know. I just don't." She quickly tried to come up with a reason, never having honestly answered the question, even to herself. "They're not as marketable." She nearly cringed at the lameness of it.

Jennifer furrowed her brow. "But, you said you write what you know."

"Uh-huh." Alex sipped her wine, feeling cornered.

Jennifer studied her for several long seconds, a question burning on the tip of her tongue. She finally filed it away for future reference and decided a subject change was in order. *We're definitely going to address this later*, she thought with determination. "Are you from here originally?"

The relief was apparent on Alex's face as she answered. "East Rochester."

Jennifer grinned. "Fight, fight, brown and white."

Alex laughed. "Go Bombers."

"What kind of colors are brown and white for a school? I mean, who decided on that?"

"Whoever it was should be shot. Brown is *not* a flattering color for most people. How 'bout you? Where do you call your place of origin?"

"Pittsford, born and bred." She watched Alex's face and then laughed. "Go ahead. You can say it."

"Say what?" Alex feigned innocence.

"*Ew!* Pittsford. Where all the snooty rich people live."

Alex burst into laughter, nearly showering Jennifer with wine. "Hey, you said that, not me!"

"Yeah, but you were thinking it. Admit it."

"You're right. I was. I'm sorry."

"Don't be." Jennifer grinned. "It's true for the most part."

Alex sighed dramatically. "It ain't easy being rich."

"Not always, no."

"Did you go to school in Pittsford?"

"Nope. Mercy."

"Ah. Private, Catholic all girls school." Alex waggled her eyebrows.

"'Fraid so."

"What about college?" Alex gestured to her sweats. "Did you go to NYU?"

"No, Eric did." A shadow passed over Jennifer's face, but she chased it away. "I spent two semesters at Parsons School of Design, but it didn't last."

"So *that's* why you're so good at this decorating stuff." Alex nodded with realization. "Why didn't it last? Did you get homesick?" She had met a couple different people in her life that had gone away to college, only to find that it wasn't for them. Their homesickness had been nearly catastrophic and they'd ended up quickly dropping out and returning home, usually extremely embarrassed. She suddenly wondered if she was being insensitive by asking.

"Something like that."

Alex knew that that was all she was going to get on the subject. Since she had shut Jennifer down on the lesbian writing topic, she figured fair was fair. *We'll come back to this,* she thought. "How 'bout your family? Any siblings?"

"One older brother," Jennifer replied. "He works on Wall Street."

"Wow."

"Yeah, it's pretty impressive," she said, sounding anything but impressed. She sipped her wine thoughtfully before adding, "Don't get me wrong. It *is* impressive. And Kevin's a great guy..." Her voice trailed off and Alex felt like she could read Jennifer's mind.

"But he's left big shoes for you to fill."

Jennifer looked surprised, then shameful. "Yeah. My mom thinks he walks on water."

"And your dad?"

"He passed away last year."

"Oh, Jennifer. I'm sorry." Alex felt awful for touching on such a fresh nerve.

"No, it's okay. I like talking about him. We got along very well."

"Daddy's little girl, huh?"

"Absolutely. Whenever Mom got too hard on me, Daddy would come to my rescue. Now with him gone, I'm forced to fight my own battles with her. I know I'm a big girl and shouldn't have trouble with it, but she always manages to make me feel like I'm twelve."

Alex snorted at the all too familiar description. "Believe me, I know just how you feel. I have very similar issues in my family, just no big brother. I'm an only child and my father left my mother when I was nine. She's never gotten over it and—though she'd never admit it—she has trouble being around me because I look just like him."

"And I bet she's exceptionally hard on you," Jennifer ventured.

"Exceptionally. It's so difficult sometimes. I get torn, you know?" She sipped her wine, gazing into space. "She's so bitter and angry and hurt because my dad didn't give her any explanation. He just went and that was that. I understand why that would be hard, I do. But Jesus, it was more than twenty years ago. Isn't it about time to get the hell over it? Get on with your life? You know? I waver between sympathizing with her—which causes me to do anything and everything she expects of me—and wanting to scream at her to just suck it up and move on, harsh as that sounds."

"It's not harsh. It's understandable and perfectly normal for you to feel like that."

"You think?"

"It sounds like our moms are very, very similar."

Alex grinned. "Eerily so. Although I will admit to being slightly relieved to find I didn't get stuck with the only insane one."

"Ditto."

They were comfortably quiet for several minutes. Alex was so happy with the way the night had progressed, she didn't want it to end. She hadn't connected so solidly with somebody since she'd met Jackie and she was having a great time. Unfortunately, all good things come to an end. When Jennifer tried to stifle her fourth yawn, Alex took pity on her, glancing blatantly at her watch.

"Oh my God, is it almost midnight already?"

Jennifer blinked and squinted at the round Eddie Bauer clock mounted on the wall. "Wow. It is."

"We should let you get some rest." She shook her head in disbelieving affection at the furry white body that had twisted between Jennifer's knees. Kinsey was on his back, all four paws sticking up in the air as he snored softly. "I think he likes you better than me. Did you know that it shows security when a dog sleeps on his back?"

"Really?"

"Uh-huh. That's the most vulnerable position he can be in. Right now, he's saying that he feels perfectly safe here with you."

Jennifer's expression softened and she flushed slightly, flattered by the comment. "Well, he's welcome here any time. As are you. I've had a really great time."

Alex stood and gently stroked Kinsey's stomach, not wanting to shock him awake. "Me, too. Next time, we'll cook for you."

"Kinsey cooks?" Jennifer teased.

"Oh, yeah. You'd be amazed. Come on, buddy. Time to go home." The Westie twisted himself back to a normal position, then stretched his entire body. Alex watched in disbelief as he and Jennifer yawned at exactly the same time. "I hate to break it to you," she said while snapping on Kinsey's leash. "But I think your soul mate is a West Highland White Terrier."

Jennifer shrugged, scratching his head. "Well, I suppose I could do worse."

"Good point."

They said their goodnights and Alex hummed her way across the yard, feeling that giddy elation she only ever felt when she met somebody she knew was going to be a part of her life for a very long time.

Chapter
Six

If there was such a thing as a beautiful cemetery, White Haven Memorial Park definitely qualified. Kept pristine and protected by an elegant, wrought iron fence, it stretched for acres off Marsh Road on the border between the suburbs of Pittsford and Fairport. There were no headstones, only grave markers that lay flat, flush with the thick, green grass. If one didn't know it was a cemetery, one might have assumed it was simply a gorgeous park, dotted with old, majestic trees and sporadic bunches of colorful flowers, with a beautiful fountain sprouting up in the center.

The day was a bit gloomy and still cool, even for early June; it seemed appropriate for a visit to the cemetery. Jennifer eased her car along the winding, paved path, following a route she had grown to know well, over the last nine months. She coasted to a stop, put the car in park, and sat for a moment or two, just looking out over the expanse of flawlessly manicured lawn.

Michael Remington had died the previous August of a massive heart attack. Though nearly a year had passed, Jennifer still had a hard time with the fact that she'd never see him again, and it was still difficult for her to accept that he wasn't available to give her advice anymore. He was the only member of the family who seemed to understand her. She knew it sounded cliché, but it was true. They were very much alike, so they tended to stick together on most issues. He had worked hard for his success, as well as his money, and he'd never taken it for granted. Over the years, they had sadly watched together as Jennifer's mother became more and more wrapped up in her image and her wealth. She hadn't started out that way, and Jennifer believed that at one time, long ago, her parents really were in love with one another. By the time her father passed away, though, they'd been basically roommates...and Jennifer wondered if they even liked each other all that much at that point. She had no idea why they never divorced. Maybe they would have eventually. That was something she'd never know.

She got out of the car, grabbed the small, Ziploc baggie from her purse, and walked past several markers until she came to his. Her brow furrowed as she stood there, looking at the small bouquet of white daisies that graced his plot. They were obviously fresh, bringing a splash of beauty to the otherwise dreary day. She knew her mother had only been there once or twice since Michael's death, so the flowers were a small mystery. Jennifer squatted down, surprised to find the grass dry, and took a seat.

"Who brought the daisies, Daddy?" she asked softly. The breeze blew delicately. Sometimes she would swear she'd hear his voice traveling by on it.

She picked a few stray blades of grass from his marker and lovingly ran her fingers over the chiseled lettering. She scooped out a handful of birdseed from the Ziploc baggie and sprinkled it evenly all around him. She doubted anybody else in the family had any idea that he loved to birdwatch. It was her own special connection with him now. Instead of bringing flowers, which is what just about anybody would do, she brought birdseed, so that even when he didn't have human visitors, he'd have animal ones.

She settled herself comfortably and prattled on, telling him about her life. It was something she did several times a month, and it was akin to a therapy session for her. She didn't think her father would mind.

"The girls are coming by for lunch today." The flat and unenthusiastic tone of her voice told him exactly how she felt about that. And they were people she called her friends. *How sad for me.* "They want to see the new lake house. I hope they go easy on me. I'm not sure it fits their 'image.'" She made the quotations marks in the air to demonstrate the sarcasm to him. "It's probably not quite artificial enough for them. I love it, though, Daddy. You would, too. It's peaceful and beautiful and being on the water is so incredibly calming. I've been working my butt off on the interior. The previous owner was a little too into reds and golds; you know, that oriental look? Ugh. Way too loud and heavy for me. I've been painting, and trying some new stuff I've been reading about in that book you got me for my birthday last year. Remember? The living room looks fantastic! You'd love it. I color washed the walls in some warm, earthy tones. It was definitely not an easy process, but I think I did it right. It looks pretty good. It feels a lot like your den. You know, cozy and inviting, like you want to sit down and read a book or something? Dawn's going to hate it. You know how she is. She's going to say it feels like a den instead of a living room and she's going to ask where I'd put the guests for a dinner party, because they certainly won't be comfortable in a *den*." She sighed, feeling the dread come over her. She knew that she shouldn't be so concerned about what other people thought, but it seemed she was always searching for *somebody's* approval. Apparently, it was her curse in life.

"But Alex liked it. A lot."

That sentence alone brought a smile to her face, and she could actually hear her father's voice, colored with a grin of his own. *Alex? Who's Alex?* He'd always made it his job to know who Jennifer's friends were, and he had his own opinion of each of them. He would have loved Alex, Jennifer was sure of it. "She's my new neighbor. She lives next door to our lake house and she's very sweet. We've become good friends. She talked me into playing on her volleyball team this summer. In the sand! I haven't played in so long and it felt great! My legs are still sore." She could hear his hearty laugh. *A little out of shape, pumpkin?* "Yeah, a little. But Alex was sore, too. First practice of the season and all, so I didn't feel so bad. She liked the living room, Daddy. Very much. She got it, you know? She got the *exact* feel that I was going for, the exact mood. It was very cool. Made me feel like I actually learned something during the time I was at school, like I knew what I was doing."

She sat quietly for a while, watching as the gentle breeze gradually swept the clouds from the sky and slivers of blue began to show. The sun kept peeking through, as if trying to decide if it was safe to make a full-fledged appearance. "Looks like it's going to clear up, Dad. I suppose I should get back and make some appropriate hors d'oeuvres for my visitors." She sighed at the prospect of the afternoon. "Kayla and Dawn hardly do anything apart anymore. It's kind of weird. When she's around Dawn, Kayla almost absorbs her personality. Like the world needs two Dawns." She shuddered at the thought. "I wish Kayla was coming alone. That's the only time she acts like herself any more." She shrugged, taking a deep breath of the clean, crisp air.

She kissed her fingers and pressed them to her father's grave marker. "I'll come by again soon, Daddy. I miss you." She stood and brushed off the grass and dirt from her behind, crumpled the baggie and stuffed it into her pocket, and waited for the tears that misted her eyes each time she visited to clear away. She bent once more and straightened the daisies, wondering again, where they might have come from. Then she walked slowly back to her car, shaking her head in disgust at the fact that she was about to have her so-called friends over to her brand new house on the lake and she was positively dreading it. At that moment, the sun broke through fully, as if to laugh at her.

* * *

"It's very...nice, Jen."

Only Dawn Chambers could make a compliment sound so uncomplimentary. She stood in Jennifer's living room surveying the walls, the furniture, the art, turning in a slow circle, disapproval written all over her impossibly perfect face, even as her lips spoke the opposite.

"Mm hmm. Very...nice," she repeated. Jennifer had to fight to keep from rolling her eyes.

Dawn was Eric's older sister. With her tan and trim body, rich, dark hair, and huge green eyes framed by astonishingly dark lashes and brows, she was stunningly gorgeous. *It's a damn good thing she looks like that*, Jennifer thought often. *She needs all the help she can get.* Dawn was the epitome of haughty and she treated most other people as if they weren't nearly as worthy of life as she was. She was definitely Claire's daughter. If Jennifer hadn't been related to her, she never, ever would have had any sort of contact with her. Ever.

"Well, I'm very happy with the way it turned out," Jennifer offered, trying not to let Dawn's obvious condemnation get to her. *This is my house, damn it. Why do I care what you think?*

"It's a little...casual, though, don't you think? Is that what you wanted?"

Here we go, Jennifer thought, thinking how her father was probably watching and chuckling as her earlier prediction came true.

"I mean, what if you have dinner guests or, heaven forbid, a party? Won't you want to have a space that's a bit more...formal?"

Jennifer bit back the urge to stick her tongue out at her sister-in-law.

Dawn shrugged and took her Chardonnay out onto the deck. That was all she had to say about the living room of which Jennifer was so proud. She stood in the center of the room, holding her own wineglass and trying not to look completely dejected, which was how she felt. Dawn had had exactly the reaction Jennifer had expected, so she wasn't sure why it still bothered her so much. She tried hard not to let her disappointment show on her face as she stood there alone with Kayla, waiting for her oldest friend to echo Dawn's opinion.

"I don't know, Jen. I kind of like it." Kayla's blue eyes moved slowly around the room, taking in every detail. "It feels kind of...warm. Inviting."

The compliment made Jennifer so happy that she decided to ignore the fact Kayla had waited until Dawn was out of earshot before she said anything.

"Thanks, Kay. I like it, too."

Kayla and Jennifer had graduated from Mercy together and

had known one another since they were twelve. They had bonded instantly then and Kayla was Jennifer's one constant all through school. She knew more of Jennifer's secrets than anybody else, including her father. Their families were very much alike and they faced many of the same struggles. Like Jennifer, Kayla also battled with her desire to be her own person, not what her family thought she should be. Unfortunately, Jennifer was sure Kayla was losing that one. It seemed to Jennifer that, not only did Kayla tend to lean toward being more like Dawn, saying things that she knew would please her and hoping to stay on her good side, but she was doing it more and more often. She was sure that Dawn noticed it, too, and liked to toy with Kayla, watching her paint herself into a corner trying to say what she thought Dawn wanted her to say instead of what she really thought or felt. It was painful for the spectators as well as Kayla, and there were countless times when Jennifer had wanted to scream at her to open her eyes and see what was really happening. Kayla never did, though, and it made her old friend sad.

The only saving grace was that every so often, a little bit of the old Kayla would peek through, saying something sweet or voicing an original thought—like commenting on the living room—and Jennifer would know that she was still in there.

Jennifer touched her arm and smiled. "You want some more wine?"

"No, I'm good." Kayla smiled back, then followed Dawn out onto the deck while Jennifer topped off her own glass, hoping to numb herself enough to make it through the rest of the visit. When she finally joined them on the deck, they were chuckling in amusement at the sight in the backyard.

A blur of white shot by, down near the water. Jennifer was surprised that he was actually heading toward his own house rather than away from it until she saw Alex, coming from the opposite direction, also running toward her own house. Apparently, she'd been chasing him for some time. The tone of her voice confirmed that assumption.

"God damn it, Kinsey! When I get my hands on you..."

Jennifer was glad she'd left the sentence dangling. Alex was not looking the slightest bit pleased. Jennifer quickly set her wine glass down and, much to the horror of her uppity sister-in-law, scrambled down the steps and into the yard, clapping her hands loudly.

"Come here, Kinsey! Here, boy!"

To the surprise of everybody, Kinsey stopped dead in his tracks. His ears pricked up and he turned his head in Jennifer's direction.

"That's it. Come here, handsome. Come on." She squatted down and continued to call to him. He tucked his tail and sprinted full speed to her, where he put his front paws on her knee and proceeded to wash her entire face with his tongue.

"Oh, good Lord," she heard Dawn mutter in disgust.

"Good boy. You're such a good boy." Jennifer lavished him with attention while holding firmly to his collar and waited as Alex approached, out of breath, disheveled, and very pissed off.

"Looks like you bought a house in the lower class neighborhood, dear sister-in-law," Dawn muttered under her breath. Jennifer blanched at the remark, praying Alex hadn't heard.

"Thank you, thank you, thank you," Alex said, putting her hands on her knees, her lungs still heaving. "He jumped on the storm door and I hadn't latched it tightly. He was out before I even had time to think." She shook her head ruefully, the concern in her eyes clearly stating that this was not funny, that she had been seriously worried.

"I think we need to build him a little kennel with a doggie door so you don't have to keep dealing with this."

Alex blinked at her. "You know, that's not a bad idea."

"Of course it isn't."

They smiled at each other.

The sudden clearing of a throat reminded them that they were not alone. Jennifer closed her eyes briefly, a move that didn't escape Alex's notice. She picked Kinsey up, not quite ready to give him up, and turned to her guests. "Alex Foster, this is my sister-in-law, Dawn Chambers, and my friend, Kayla Prince. Alex lives next door."

Alex, smiling, reached up and shook hands with each of them over the railing. "Nice to meet you."

"And this bad boy is Kinsey," Jennifer grinned, affectionately ruffling the dog's fur.

"Don't they have a leash law around here?" Dawn asked pointedly.

Alex's smiled tightly. "Yes. He got out accidentally."

"Mm."

Kayla grinned at Kinsey and leaned over the deck's railing to scratch his head. "He's adorable."

Alex smiled gratefully at her. "Well, there's something not quite right when he obeys the neighbor lady better than his mommy."

Jennifer laughed and made a comment about his good taste. Dawn rolled her eyes.

Alex decided to take her leave, certain she couldn't get away from Dawn fast enough. The woman was making her very uncomfortable the way she kept looking at her. She gently took Kinsey from Jennifer's arms, meeting her blue eyes. "Thanks again," she said softly. "I owe you." Looking up and raising her voice a bit, she nodded. "Nice to meet you both. Enjoy your visit."

Dawn had the decency to wait until Alex was out of earshot before she commented, "Well. That was...interesting." Her voice dripped with censure and Jennifer felt the sudden urge to leap to Alex's defense.

"Alex is great. She's a writer. She's working on a novel."

"A writer? Are you sure?" Dawn crinkled her brow as if trying to place a small detail. "She looks so familiar...I'm sure I've seen her before. Foster...Foster..."

"She's very nice," Jennifer reiterated.

"Oh my God!" Dawn exclaimed. "She's the teacher!"

"What teacher?" Kayla and Jennifer asked simultaneously.

"The teacher from the kids' school. The one who was fired a couple months ago."

"She was fired?" The question slipped out of Jennifer's mouth before she could catch it.

Dawn was absurdly pleased to have dirt on Jennifer's new pal and she took great pleasure in passing it on. "Apparently, she was exchanging love notes with a student. A *female* student. A parent brought the letters in to the principal. It was a scandal."

Jennifer felt sick to her stomach. "I'm sure there was an explanation," she said, irritated at the glee in Dawn's voice.

"Who knows? She was gone so fast nobody had a chance to ask questions. Makes her seem awfully guilty, doesn't it?"

Jennifer had the urge to change the subject. Dawn was enjoying this far too much and Jennifer didn't want to hear any more of her opinions about Alex. "Shall we go back inside? I've got lunch ready for us." She ushered them through the door, pausing to glance back in the direction of her neighbor. Something inside her just wouldn't allow her to believe Dawn's story. There was more to it. She was sure of it.

* * *

"Wow," Alex commented aloud as she set Kinsey down once they were safely inside the house and she had double-checked the latch on the storm door. "What a bitch, huh, buddy? We should introduce that one to Diane. Maybe we'd get lucky and they'd kill each other." She was sure the temperature was a good ten degrees cooler on Jennifer's deck that day.

She shook her head as she sat back down at the desk to pick up where she had left off when Kinsey had decided to bolt. She couldn't understand how somebody as sweet and kind as Jennifer could stand to be around such a shallow and rude person, relative or not. Didn't she see it? Didn't she think she deserved better? Alex stared off into space for a minute, pondering the train of thought.

"Huh," she said to nobody, realization dawning on her. "What if she *doesn't* think she deserves better?" Kinsey sat by her chair, cocking his head, his pointed ears perked like he was really listening.

Alex picked up a pen and jotted notes on the description of the character she'd named Kristen. She took the idea of a young woman who lacked the confidence and self-esteem she ought to have and ran with it. She created a back story that told of Kristen's domineering mother, her absentee father, and the importance of appearance in regards to the family name and image. Poor Kristen could barely think for herself, let alone choose a direction in life. She was a good girl and did what she was told without question, and often without any consideration of how *she* really felt. She managed to get away to college, but something happened there—something near scandalous—and she was forced to come home before the end of her second semester. When her high school sweetheart, Raymond, proposed to her, she knew she was *supposed* to say yes, so she did. The fact that she was not in love with him never entered into things.

"So, this is it, huh? You're really going to do it. You're really getting married." Something in Meg's tone seemed uneasy, but Kristen tried to pretend she didn't notice as they waited for the bridal shop saleswoman. Meg knew her very well, and often Kristen felt that her best friend could see right into her soul, could see exactly what she was thinking. She pasted what she hoped was a convincing smile onto her face.

"Raymond is a wonderful man. I'm very lucky, Meg."

Meg squinted at her until Kristen shifted uncomfortably. "Do you love him?"

"Of course I love him," she responded indignantly.

"You know what I mean. Are you in love with him?"

Kristen opened her mouth to answer, but nothing came out and she closed it again. The two friends held one another's gaze for what seemed like an eternity, the answer to the question sitting between them, as obvious as an elephant in the room.

"Ms. Stoddard? We're ready for you now." The pixie-like salesgirl smiled widely and gestured for them to follow her.

Alex blinked rapidly in the waning light as if awakening from a trance. She was surprised by how dark the house had grown and was shocked when she looked up at the clock on the wall. Four hours had passed since she sat down to start writing. Kinsey was curled up in a ball at the end of the couch, snoring softly and she chuckled at the fact that he'd slept right through his usual feeding time. Apparently, the early afternoon jog had tuckered the poor little guy right out.

Eight pages registered on her laptop and she sat up straighter, proud of such an accomplishment. She was usually only able to work a couple hours at a time, totaling maybe three pages. But, things were flowing and the character of Kristen was developing nicely. She was beautiful and sad and Alex wanted to save her. She hoped her readers would feel the same way. Before she was able to pat herself on the back any more, her stomach growled loudly, reminding her that she'd skipped lunch and it was time for dinner.

She stood up slowly, stretching and working out the kinks that tended to settle in on her after several hours in the same position. Kinsey lifted his head to regard her, looking irritated that she made what little noise she did.

"Don't look at me like that, mister. You're still on my shit list."

He yawned widely, telling her exactly how much he cared about her shit list.

"You want some dinner?"

His ears perked up at that, as she knew they would. He slid slowly off the couch, stretching as he did so, and followed her into the kitchen to watch her pull some ingredients out of the cupboard and refrigerator.

She heard a light tap at the side door just as she set Kinsey's bowl down. She smiled and Kinsey barked as they recognized Jennifer and let her in.

"Hey there. Come on in."

Jennifer glanced around the kitchen. "Have I interrupted your dinner? I'm sorry. I can come back." She made a move to the door, but Alex grabbed her arm.

"No, no. Please. I was just going to make some grilled cheese. Why don't you join me?" She looked skeptical. "You wouldn't want me to eat dinner alone, would you? Besides, I promised that we'd cook for you."

That made Jennifer smile. "Well, I was going to eat alone, too, and I was certainly not looking forward to it."

"Great. Have a seat."

Alex pulled out a stool from the breakfast bar and gestured for Jennifer to sit there while she cooked. Jennifer had changed her clothes and was now looking much more comfortable in old, faded jeans and a white Gap T-shirt. "Lots of cheese or a little?"

"Are you kidding? Lots."

"Girl after my own heart." Alex got out the frying pan and started constructing dinner.

"I wanted to apologize for my friends earlier." Jennifer shifted uncomfortably.

"Oh? What do mean?"

"Well, Dawn's not always...as polite as she could be."

"Really? I hadn't noticed."

"Liar."

Alex laughed. "She certainly didn't win Miss Congeniality."

"No, I suppose not. I just wanted to tell you I'm sorry."

"Mm. It's okay. No big deal." She put two slices of buttered bread butter side down into the warm pan. "You said Dawn was your sister-in-law?" she asked as she put a tall glass of milk in front of Jennifer.

"She's Eric's sister."

"And is she always a bitch on wheels to people she's just met?"

Jennifer was quiet for a minute, before answering softly. "Not always, no." She chewed on her bottom lip and studied her hands.

Knowing she'd made her feel bad, Alex's anger dissipated and she decided to let it go, for the time being. "And how do you know the other one? Kayla, was it?"

"Yeah. We went to school together."

"High school or college?"

"Both. But she stayed in college and graduated. She works for an ad agency in the city."

She sounded both proud of Kayla and jealous, which Alex thought was interesting. "Graphic design?"

"Sales."

Alex nodded, flipping the sandwiches over and smiling at the perfect golden brownness of the bread. "Is that the first time they've seen your new place?"

"Yup."

"What did they think?"

"Exactly what I thought they'd think," Jennifer replied with a bitter grimace.

"Meaning...?" Alex slid a plate with her sandwich in front of her.

"Dawn said the living room was too casual."

Alex made a face. "What the hell is that supposed to mean? It's a house on the lake, for Christ's sake. Casual is the name of the game."

"It just means that it's not what Dawn would have done with it."

"So? Why does it matter what Dawn thinks?"

They stared at one another as Jennifer absorbed the question, chewing slowly, then swallowing.

Alex tried again. "It's a terrific room, Jennifer. You did a great job on it."

She nodded and took another bite.

Alex put her elbows on the counter and looked Jennifer right in the eye. "It's *your* house. Who gives a shit what anybody else thinks?"

"You really think it's a terrific room?" Her voice sounded small and Alex had to consciously keep herself from wrapping the smaller woman in a big, warm hug.

"Absolutely. Dawn doesn't know what the hell she's talking about."

Jennifer smiled then, and Alex felt absurdly pleased with herself. "Thanks, Alex," she said softly, taking another bite.

"Any time."

Chapter
Seven

"I feel like I haven't seen you in days." Jennifer smiled across the table at Eric.

"I know, baby. I'm sorry. Things have been insane at the office." Eric's ruggedly handsome face was drawn and dark circles were under his eyes.

"You look so tired. Are you getting enough sleep?"

"Of course I'm not. What do you think?" His voice was cooler than it needed to be and Jennifer grimaced. The waitress appeared with their drinks, ready to take their orders. Eric was unnecessarily brusque, which was obvious by the expression on her face. Jennifer tried to compensate by placing her order in an extra sweet tone, not sure if it worked.

Eric picked up his scotch, swirled it once, and then downed the whole thing in one gulp. "I don't know how much longer I can keep up this schedule," he muttered, more to himself than to Jennifer. "I feel like a fucking zombie." He held up the empty glass and wiggled it in the direction of the bar, silently and rudely requesting a refill.

Jennifer watched helplessly, wanting to help if she could. "Can you take a little time off? Maybe a few days of rest would help. Hang with me at the lake and relax for a bit? You've hardly been there at all."

He snorted. "Are you kidding me? Jen, you have no idea what's been going on at the firm. Accounts are shifting like sand, attorneys are scrambling for them, Dad's been heaping more and more shit on me. Vacation time now is out of the question."

The condescending and clipped tone of his voice made her bristle. She hated that attitude, hated when he talked to her like she was completely clueless about the working world. They'd argued about it in the past, but she decided that doing so at that point would be useless. She understood that he was stressed out, so she simply nodded, let a few moments of silence pass, and attempted to change the subject.

"I've got my first volleyball game this week. Maybe if you're around, you can come and watch? It's not until seven and it's just over at the beach."

Eric grunted noncommittally as the waitress set his drink down.

Jennifer refused to be pulled down by his funk and plowed on. "The team is really nice. I'm enjoying it a lot. It's been a long time since I played."

He looked up from contemplating the contents of his glass and met Jennifer's eyes. She could almost see the train of thought chugging across his handsome features. He looked back down at his drink, then his face softened considerably. He inhaled deeply, then exhaled very slowly.

"That's great, honey." He smiled at her as she tried not to register the surprise she felt at his change in demeanor. "You used to be pretty damn good, as I recall. I don't know that I'll be able to make it, but I'll try. What night?"

"Wednesday."

He nodded, taking a much smaller sip of his drink this time. "I'm sorry I've been such a prick, Jen. I don't mean it."

"I know you don't, Eric. I know. I'm just a little worried about you, that's all. You're pushing so hard, I'm afraid you're going to crash and burn."

"I've thought about the same thing. It won't be much longer. I just have to hang in there for a few more months."

Jennifer nodded, feeling less reassured than she had hoped. "Okay. I'll try to be patient."

"Thanks, honey." He seemed relieved. "So, tell me about your teammates."

It had been so long since they'd had the time to just sit together, have a nice dinner, and talk, that Jennifer was momentarily stunned by the idea of having a simple, uninterrupted conversation with her husband. He smiled at her and she suspected that he knew exactly how she was feeling. Before anything else, they were friends. Good friends. They cared about one another and, more importantly, they actually *liked* each other.

"Well, you know Alex. She's an incredible player, very consistent. She's a hitter and I think I've picked up the ability to set her pretty well. We're a good team. Her best friend Jackie is another big hitter, a bit more powerful."

"Have I met Jackie?"

"No, not yet, but I'm sure you will. She's at Alex's a lot."

"Is she Alex's girlfriend?"

Jennifer blinked at him. "What?"

"Jackie. Is Jackie Alex's girlfriend?"

"Um, no."

"You did know that Alex is gay, right?"

"Yes, but how did *you* know?"

"I have my sources," he replied, grinning around his fork.

Jennifer absorbed that for a second, not sure why it made her uneasy. She shook the feeling off and continued. "Jackie has a partner, Rita, and an adorable little two-year-old daughter."

"Huh. Is anybody on this team of yours straight?" He kept his tone light, smiling in hopes of masking the apprehension he felt. He saw a flash of something cross Jennifer's face, but it was gone too quickly for him to identify it.

"Yes, silly. Me, for one." She grinned wryly at him. "And Steve. He plays like you." She chuckled as she recalled him throwing himself into the sand over and over.

"All over the court?"

"All over it." They laughed, easing the slight tension that had settled over their table. "He's really sweet. And there's David. He's new, but he's constantly improving and I think he'll be really good in time."

"A natural, huh?"

"Definitely." She tapped a finger against her lips. "I'm forgetting somebody. Oh, yeah. Nikki. She doesn't say much. I'm not sure she likes me."

"Why not?"

"I don't know. Just one of those things. She looks at me funny."

"Don't be silly, Jen. What's not to like?" His eyes sparkled sincerely. "You're a very likable girl."

She smiled at that, her heart warming. *This* was the Eric she had married, not the stressed-out, snappish business executive from earlier in the dinner. Despite the success of his parents and the image his family projected to the community, Eric had always been sweet and down-to-earth. That was the major reason Jennifer had been so worried about the long hours he'd been keeping and the sudden pressure put upon him by his father. Deep down, she didn't think Eric really wanted to take over the firm, but she knew he would do what he had to in order to please his father. He and Jennifer were very much alike that way. He would do what was expected of him, but the stress he'd been under was actually altering his personality, often making him snippy, abrupt, and even insulting. She was determined to grab onto this glimpse of the man she'd married while she could, because she was sure it wouldn't last long.

* * *

She lay there, staring at the ceiling for a long time, wide awake, mind spinning. Though Eric had relaxed considerably during their dinner, a ripple of tension continued to flow through him. Trying to ease his mind, Jennifer had focused on how good it was to finally have him home for the night for the first time in weeks, rather than staying in Buffalo or Pittsford. He seemed to appreciate her enthusiasm. They'd barely gotten in the door of the lake house before he began undressing her. His hands were insistent, his mouth was demanding and she knew this was something he needed. She barely had time to register being at the bottom of the stairs before he cupped her backside, picked her up off the floor and carried her upstairs to their bedroom, his tongue buried deep in her mouth the whole way.

Sex with Eric was usually pleasant enough for Jennifer, though never earth-shattering. She considered it something she did for him, almost going so far as to use the old-fashioned—and utterly politically *in*correct—phrase "wifely duty." It was true that she'd listened to women like Dawn talk about how much they despised sleeping with their husbands and how they had much better sex when they were alone, but for every Dawn, there was another woman with the opposite reaction. She was always envious of friends who had fabulous sex lives with their husbands and she didn't understand why she wasn't one of them.

She wasn't like Dawn; she didn't *hate* sleeping with Eric. He was usually quite an attentive lover. He wasn't perfect—she had faked orgasm more than once in order to escape his dogged attempts to make her come—but he was by no means selfish in bed. She had started to think it must be her and that was a little scary.

She'd noticed a change in him recently as well. If she had to pinpoint a time, she would have to say it began when his father had started grooming him to take over the family business. The frequency of their lovemaking had waned considerably after that, which didn't really concern her. She simply attributed it to the new stress Eric was under and left it at that. However, the last few times they'd made love, Eric had taken care of Eric and only Eric. It seemed that on his part, it was all taking and no giving, which was very, very unlike him. Jennifer had oscillated between relief at the shortened amount of time it was taking to perform her "duty" and worry that Eric no longer cared whether or not she enjoyed being in bed with him.

That night, he'd entered her much sooner than she would have liked and she'd tried not to tense every muscle in her body. She'd closed her eyes and done her best to move with him. He had thrust into her, pumping furiously, his eyes shut tightly, his brow furrowed in concentration, though she was not sure on what he was concentrating. Their bodies were as close as they could possibly be, but their minds were on completely different planets. Jennifer didn't know where her husband was, but she was certain that it wasn't in bed with her.

When he had finished, he'd eased out of her, panting and sweaty. He'd rolled onto his back with a sigh and within minutes, he'd begun to snore.

Jennifer continued to stare at the ceiling, trying to decide if she should go on blaming this now-chronic problem on Eric's long hours and stressful job, or if it was time to look more closely at things, to delve deeper and try to get to the real issue. She wasn't completely unaware that she had her own issues, that she brought her own crap to the table. She knew deep down that blaming things entirely on him was unfair, but she wasn't sure she was ready to look in the mirror and really *see*.

Eric snuffled and rolled onto his side, away from his wife. She looked at his back, her eyes roving over his milky-white skin, her mind thinking how he'd been shut up in his office too long and that he could use some sunshine. She ran her fingertips lightly across his broad shoulders with a heavy sigh. Then she slipped those same fingers between her thighs, probing and stroking knowingly, searching for release.

She came quietly next to him. He slept on.

* * *

At barely six thirty in the morning Eric Wainwright maneuvered his silver Mercedes through the tollbooth and onto the New York State Thruway, heading west toward Buffalo. He hated this time of the day; he hated being stuck in his car for nearly two hours. It gave him way too much time to think, something he'd been trying to avoid lately as he didn't like the direction his thoughts were taking. That's why he opted to stay in Buffalo so often. The alone time in the car was just too daunting.

He thought back to the previous night and the morning. Dinner with Jennifer had been pleasant once he'd kicked his nasty mood. She'd been a big help in getting him out of it. She always was. She knew how to change the subject or how to bite her lip to keep from snapping back at him, which he usually deserved. She'd just kept talking about her new volleyball team and how excited she was to play. Once she'd pulled him away from the subject of work, he'd been okay. And she'd seemed so happy to have him home...her voice had been a little flirty and there was a sparkle in her eyes. He'd incorrectly taken that as the signal he always longed to see, one she seemed to give less and less since they'd been married.

They'd headed home and he'd immediately made the move, doing away with her clothes and kissing her hungrily. He grimaced as he remembered the rest of the night. It seemed to be a regular occurrence now, any time they made love—which was hardly ever at this point. She made no sound, she was barely able to contain her desire to be anywhere else but with him, beneath him. A small part of him was ashamed at his own behavior lately, his failure to do anything at all to help make her more comfortable. God forbid they actually talk about it. Instead, he simply took what he wanted, released himself inside her, rolled away and fell asleep. He was disgusted that he'd become such an uncaring lover, but so had Jennifer and that made him resentful.

If she's not willing to try, why should I?

Totally childish behavior and he knew it. He also couldn't seem to do anything about it. The more he thought about the state of his marriage, the angrier and more bitter he became. He looked at the cell phone mounted on the dash and hesitated. After only a slight internal debate, he punched in the number he was embarrassed to admit he knew by heart. Even at that early hour he was not surprised when somebody picked up.

"Sensations," a pleasant and familiar female voice answered, her tones sounding intimate and affecting even on the speakerphone.

"Good morning, Stacy. This is Eric Smith."

"Well, good morning, Mr. Smith. What can I do for you?"

"I'd like to set up a meeting for this afternoon, if possible."

"Certainly, sir. Will that be with your usual contact?"

"If she's available, that would be great."

"She is. At your regular conference area?"

"Please."

"What time works for you, sir?"

"Two?"

"Two it is. Shall I use the card on file?"

"That's fine. Thank you very much."

"Thank *you*, Mr. Smith. Enjoy your meeting."

He pressed the button to disconnect the call. He simultaneously felt guilt at his own dishonesty and thrilling excitement at his impending "meeting." The thought of the small, shapely, blonde—so physically like Jennifer, but willing to do so much more—writhing beneath him and calling his name aroused him to the point where it was almost painful. He stepped on the gas and zipped past an eighteen-wheeler, the speed only adding to his exhilaration.

* * *

The morning was beautiful and clear on the lake and Jennifer took her tea out onto the deck to breathe in the clean air and listen to the lapping of the water. The air was a bit cool, but the sound was calming and she let it wash over her, taking some of her stress and worries with it.

Eric had been up, showered, dressed, and on his way to work very early. He'd been distant and quiet all through the breakfast she'd fixed him. The Eric she'd seen the night before had vanished, just as she'd suspected he would.

She refused to dwell on the growing problems in her marriage, though in reality, she knew she should have concentrated on them more. Avoidance was the absolute wrong way to handle a dilemma, but that's what she'd always done. *This is too hard to deal with, so I just...won't.* Somehow, the fact that she *knew* that's what she did, didn't seem to help or make her attempt to change things and she was often frustrated by her own pigheadedness.

She had always found that the best way to avoid a problem was to focus on something completely different. So, that morning, she contemplated her house, the one thing in her life that she was happy with, the one thing bringing her any sort of pleasure. She went inside and decided her next project would be the master bedroom. *Hell*, she thought. *If I'm going to spend most of my time in it alone, I can at least decorate it so it suits me.*

As was her modus operandi, she pulled up a chair and sat in the doorway, simply studying the room, getting a feel for the size, the scope, the possibilities...trying to envision what she'd like it to be, how she'd like it to look from the doorway—the place anybody would be standing when they saw it for the first time. It was a large rectangle with a master bath off to the left. That room, having been recently remodeled, was in fantastic shape and—much to Jennifer's delighted surprise—didn't need any help from her. Its Jacuzzi bathtub and white, ceramic tile floors were precisely what she would have picked. The bedroom itself, however, was very bland: off-white walls, off-white molding, and off-white mini-blinds. The hardwood floor was the only saving grace, the only thing that held any character. Jennifer had already decided that she liked the idea of varying shades of purple and she'd used it as an accent color in the bathroom. She was fond of the concept of carrying that into the bedroom to tie the two rooms together, so she examined the space carefully, envisioning what she thought might work and tossing away ideas that didn't quite seem to fit.

As she sat there, she remembered seeing a room she'd fallen in love with in one of the many design and home improvement magazines she'd become addicted to. She jumped up and ran downstairs, opened the bottom cabinets of a shelf in the living room and groaned at what had to be twenty-five or thirty various magazines.

She pulled them all out, situated herself on the floor, and flipped through page after page until she yelped with relief, finally finding the one she was looking for.

She glanced at the clock, then did a double take. She was utterly shocked to realize that two and a half hours had gone by since she'd started her search. Her legs shrieked at her when she uncurled them from beneath her and stood up from the floor. She carefully marked the correct page in the magazine and cursed herself for not doing so the first time. She stretched slowly, allowing the blood to reintroduce itself to her deprived limbs. With a now clear picture in her head of the way she wanted the bedroom to look, she stepped out onto the deck to get some fresh air.

It was still clear, but the temperature had risen considerably and the sun beat warmly down on her hair. She could see three boats drifting lazily on the water, fishing rods protruding into the air. She leaned her forearms onto the railing of the deck and watched them rock gently on the easy waves, letting the peace of the lake embrace her.

The quiet was interrupted by the clang of metal coming from her right. She glanced in that direction and saw Alex, standing with her hands on her hips, surveying a pile of supplies she'd dumped on the ground at her feet next to her garage. Jennifer watched her for several minutes as she looked at the pile, then up at the blank side of the garage, then down, then back up again. She went inside, but reappeared several minutes later with a toolbox and a large hammer. Jennifer smiled as her curiosity got the better of her.

"Building an addition?" she called with a wry grin.

Alex turned, then smiled, happy to see Jennifer. "Yup. I've decided to fulfill my life-long dream of being a landlady, so I'm adding an apartment."

"Need some help?" Jennifer asked hopefully as she approached.

"Four hands are better than two, or so I've been told."

"I've heard the same thing. What kind of apartment are we making?" She looked at the pile, which consisted of six large steel stakes and a sizable roll of wire fencing, all green.

"The fenced-in kind. I took your advice and I've decided to make a sort of run for Kinsey. Like a kennel, but a bit bigger, sort of like his own miniature play area. This way, he can be outside all damn day if he wants and I won't have to worry about finding his squished little body on the roadside."

"And how does *he* feel about this kennel thing?" Jennifer teased.

"Well, you see, that's the beauty of this relationship. I'm the human and therefore, the boss. He has no say and he knows it."

The kennel was by no means going to be anything extravagant. The equipment Alex had chosen was akin the items she'd purchase if she was looking to fence in a garden or protect a large bush. With Kinsey's small size, though, and short, stubby legs, she knew it would be perfect. She just needed something to contain him, something tall enough that he couldn't jump over it, and something sturdy enough that he couldn't knock it down by jumping against it. The fencing she'd picked was just right and she felt good about it.

Both women were surprised by how well they worked together, especially Jennifer. She thought about how she and Eric rarely did projects together around the house because they never seemed to be on the same wavelength. He was never able to see her vision of things and she was frustrated by his overly perfectionist ways of operating. They usually ended up at each other's throats, so they'd decided to avoid such pairings all together. Jennifer did the decorating, Eric did the repair work, and it seemed to be the right solution.

Things were different with Alex, though. It was like they only had one mind. She handed Alex tools before she asked for them, Alex nodded in agreement before Jennifer even finished her suggestions. Because of the lack of conflict, the sense of accomplishment seemed that much stronger when they finally stood straight and surveyed the finished product.

"Not bad, Ms. Foster. Not bad at all."

"Couldn't have done it without you, Mrs. Wainwright. Nice work. And thank you."

"My pleasure."

"Shall we introduce the king to his new castle?"

"Absolutely."

Alex went in to fetch Kinsey, who eyed the fence warily. They had even constructed a primitive gate for easy access, but since the fence was only four feet high, Alex simply bent over it and set him in. He wandered around a little bit, sniffing the ground and lifting his leg on several of the stakes, reluctantly marking them as his. After three or four minutes, he sat directly in the middle of the area, facing the women, and simply stared at his owner. Alex pressed her lips together with worry and Jennifer had to stifle a laugh.

"Oh, he is not happy with me. Not happy at all."

"You think?" Jennifer teased.

"See how his ears are back and he's looking at me, but not really? Like I don't deserve a full stare? That's how I can tell. Those are sure signs."

Jennifer was grinning at Alex's obvious distress. "Sure signs of what?"

"He's pissed at me."

Jennifer pressed her finger to her lips, the laughter threatening to burst forth, and just nodded. Alex picked up the nod and they stood there like a couple of bobble-heads, nodding away.

"Oh, yeah. He's annoyed." Alex turned to Jennifer, cocking an eyebrow at the expression on her face. "Are you laughing at me?" The tone of her voice was light; she was well aware of the humor of the situation.

"You know," Jennifer responded in the most matter-of-fact voice she could manage, "I've heard of a person being pussy-whipped, but the idea of being poochy-whipped is a totally new concept for me."

Alex stood quietly for several seconds, simply blinking at her friend. When she finally did speak, she tried hard for "low and menacing." Instead, it came out more like "trying hard not to burst into hysterical laughter." "Are you saying I'm ruled by my dog?"

"Well, let me think for a minute." Jennifer tapped a finger against her lips, looking up into the sky. "Um, yeah. I'd say that's exactly what I think."

Alex dropped her head, shaking it shamefully, her voice a mock-sob. "It's true! It's true! My dog is my life. I am a pathetic human being. Please shoot me now."

They both broke into laughter. Kinsey was obviously not amused, as he continued to stare at them, only serving to make them laugh harder. Once they had collected themselves, they took a closer look at the kennel, just to make sure it didn't need any final adjustments.

"Hm. I'm not sure I like this." Alex was near the garage wall where she had driven a stake into the ground. It was about an inch and a half away, leaving a space between the stake and the wall. "I got this as close as I could, but I'm afraid if he decided to work at it, he could worm his way through here. He's pretty smart."

"I bet they make some sort of bracket thingie for that," Jennifer offered. "You know what I mean? Like a horseshoe-shaped piece of wire or something that will pull the stake closer and close up that space."

Alex nodded as the item Jennifer described became clear in her mind. "I think a trip to Chase-Pitkin is in order. Care to join me?"

Chapter
Eight

Chase-Pitkin was Rochester's local version of Home Depot. There was one in almost every suburb and they housed everything from lumber and gardening equipment to furniture and birdseed. They had definitely felt the pinch since Home Depot had arrived in the area a few years before, but much to the surprise of many people, Chase- Pitkin managed to hold its own and stay in business. Despite the fact that Home Depot was a nationwide chain and thereby had some better pricing on many items, Chase Pitkin employed hundreds of local people, and Alex tried to give them her support whenever she could.

Having Jennifer along for the ride was a pleasant surprise. When Alex woke up that morning and decided to build a kennel for Kinsey, she hadn't expected to have help or company—and certainly not such charming company. She realized that the more time she spent with Jennifer, the more time she wanted to spend with her. She was funny and clever and amusing and Alex hadn't enjoyed just simply being with somebody in a long, long time. The only person who came close was Jackie and they'd been best friends for more than ten years. Alex got a happy little tingle when she thought of being such great friends with Jennifer, too.

"Pretty empty," Jennifer commented when they entered Chase-Pitkin. "I suppose it'll pick up in a couple weeks, once school's out and summer officially hits, huh?"

Alex felt a sharp pang of loss when she thought of her teacher friends. She missed her old job more than she cared to admit. She thought about what the atmosphere would be like then, thick with excitement and anticipation. Students and teachers alike would be counting down the days. The kids would be entertaining visions of lounging like blobs, sleeping until noon, and vegging in front of the television, computer, or PlayStation. The teachers would be daydreaming of their first getaway since Easter break, nearly salivating with expectation. Jackie often asked her if she missed teaching and Alex always waved her off with a dismissive flick of her hand and a look that said, *Are you kidding me? Don't be silly!*

It was a big lie.

She sighed silently as they walked through the aisles, rationalizing in her head. *We all make our own beds and then we must lie in them. Besides, I'm writing a novel! How many of my teacher friends can say that?*

"Here we go."

Jennifer's voice snapped her back to the present and Alex blinked at her. "I'm sorry, what?"

"Something like this is what I was talking about. Think these will work?" She held up some semi-circular brackets that seemed like just the thing they needed.

"I think they'll be perfect." She grabbed a couple packages off the peg. "Do you need anything while we're in here?"

"Well..." Jennifer's eyes wandered toward the giant paint display. "I'm in the process of redoing the master bedroom, at least in my mind." She smiled disarmingly and Alex felt she had no choice but to smile back. "Would you mind terribly—?" Her voice trailed off as she gestured hopefully in the same direction.

"Not at all." Alex grinned. "Any ideas so far?"

Jennifer launched into the story about that morning and how she'd stared at the room, then gone through stacks and stacks of magazines trying to come up with the perfect room. Alex decided then and there that she loved listening to Jennifer talk about her design visions. She was so structured and certain of what she wanted, how she expected something to look. It was very similar to the way Alex herself developed a story in her head or in outline form on paper before she actually started writing it. Jennifer explained how she hadn't been able to bring herself to throw away any of the design magazines and Alex remembered seeing a few scattered about the house during her visit. She had research books and materials, and articles on writing that meant the same thing to her.

Jennifer's green eyes sparkled with enthusiasm as they walked, telling Alex of the eggplant accent pillows, the area rug she'd seen in the Pottery Barn catalog that had just the right combination of various shades of purple, and her desire to paint one wall in the room a deep, rich plum, though she was leery of making that first brushstroke.

"So what?" Alex teased her about her reluctance. "What's the worst that could happen?"

"The worst that could happen? It could look like complete and total shit."

"Again, so what? It's paint. You can paint over it."

"I know, but..."

"But what?"

"I don't want people to think I don't know what I'm doing, even if I don't."

Alex squinted, noting the genuine concern in her eyes. "Jennifer. Sweetheart. You've got a serious hang-up with the What Will People Think thing, you know that?"

"Yes, I do."

Then she took Alex's arm and pulled her to the color display, cleanly avoiding the subject.

Together, they collected what seemed to Alex to be an enormous stack of paint squares in innumerable shades of purple. She laughed at the thought of Jennifer spreading them all out on the floor or the bed, which was exactly what she intended to do with them.

She looked at a paint square and snorted. "Monster Mash? Are you kidding me? I want to know how much somebody gets paid to come up with these ridiculous names." She picked up another one. "Okay, guess what Introspection is."

Jennifer furrowed her brow. "Um...green?"

"Purple."

"Damn. Okay, how about Red Riding Hood?"

"If that's not red, there's something seriously wrong with the people at Glidden."

"It's red."

"My turn. Maestro."

"Maestro? As in orchestra conductor?"

"That's what I said."

"Blue?"

"Nope. Purple."

"Damn. Okay, here's one. Malabar."

"That's a candy bar, isn't it? Got to be brown."

"Nope. Teal. And you're thinking of a Mallomar."

"Huh. Okay, here we go. Flair."

"Orange."

"Purple."

"Damn."

Alex watched Jennifer out of the corner of her eye, smirking and waiting...waiting...

"Hey!"

And we have liftoff, Alex thought with a smile.

"Yours were all purple."

"Why, yes. Yes, they were." Alex laughed as Jennifer swatted her with the sample swatch cards she had in her hand.

"Brat," she said, joining in the laughter.

They continued in their mirth, rolling their eyes over the barely discernible difference between Subtle Heather and Summer Orchid, when a female voice interrupted them.

"Jennifer? Jennifer Remington? Is that you?"

Alex was facing Jennifer, but the woman's voice came from behind her. It was a pleasant enough sound, full of cheerful surprise, and Alex was shocked to see Jennifer's face drain of color. She'd read such a description more than once in books, but she'd never actually seen it happen until that moment. Jennifer looked as pale as a ghost. Alex actually thought Jennifer might be sick right there in the aisle.

Alex turned to the source of the voice and was met by an attractive, smiling brunette who looked vaguely familiar, though she couldn't place her. She was roughly the same height as Alex, with beautifully clear, olive skin and dazzling hazel eyes accented by very dark lashes and brows. She was dressed casually in jeans and a white T-shirt, her keys dangling from long, tapered fingers.

"Sarah." Jennifer's barely audible voice cracked. She cleared her throat. "Sarah. Hi."

"Wow. You look..." Sarah gave Jennifer a visual appraisal and Alex raised an eyebrow, surprised to feel a tiny ping of jealousy. "You look fantastic."

"Thanks." Jennifer nodded, still looking vaguely nauseous. "You, too."

"God, what are the chances of us running into each other? You live around here now?"

"We have a summer home on the lake," Jennifer replied quietly.

"That's great. It's beautiful there, huh?"

"Yeah."

The conversation faltered, with Sarah gazing apprehensively at Jennifer and Jennifer's eyes darting from somewhere around Sarah's midsection to her shoes and back again. Alex stepped in quickly.

"Hi. Alex Foster." She stuck her hand out and Sarah took it, smiling gratefully.

"Sarah Evans."

"Nice to meet you, Sarah. How do you know Jennifer?"

Sarah's eyes drifted back to Jennifer. "Oh. Um. We went to college together for a while. Seems like ages ago." She chuckled nervously. Then her expression seemed to change slightly and she turned her focus fully onto Alex for the first time.

"And how do *you* know her?" Sarah tried hard, but unsuccessfully, to make it sound like a completely innocent question.

Well, isn't this interesting? Alex thought, wondering exactly what was going on and beginning to paint her own picture of the situation. "We're neighbors."

"Oh. I see." Sarah nodded, not really seeing anything.

Alex turned back to Jennifer, wondering if she was ever going to speak again.

Jennifer finally looked up, but at Alex and not Sarah. "We should go check out. I have to get back." Looking at her hands, she addressed Sarah. "It was great to see you again. You take care of yourself, okay?" Without another word, she took the brackets from Alex's hands, turned, and headed off toward the cash registers.

Alex and Sarah stood awkwardly for several seconds, neither sure what to do. Sarah was looking as green around the gills as Jennifer as she stared off in the direction the blonde had taken and Alex saw her swallow hard.

Before a word could be said, another woman came up from behind Alex and touched Sarah on the arm. She was small and thin with reddish hair and a kind face. "Did you find the paint thinner?"

Her voice seemed to jerk Sarah back to the present and she blinked several times. She smiled at the redhead, but her eyes had a hint of sadness in them. "Um, yeah. It's right over here." She pointed to her left, then met Alex's gaze. "It was nice to meet you, Alex."

"Same here," Alex replied, watching them walk away, the redhead's hand on the small of Sarah's back. Alex hurried to catch up with Jennifer.

* * *

They were halfway home before the color started to resurface beneath Jennifer's skin. She was utterly silent and simply stared out the window. Alex wasn't the kind of person who was bothered by silence, but when it was of the uncomfortable variety, it made her fidgety, so she tried hard to break it.

"Jennifer? Are you okay?"

"Mm hmm."

"Do you want to talk about it?"

"No."

"You're sure?"

"Mm hmm."

Well, this is working nicely, Alex thought, then decided to take a different approach.

"Remington, huh? Is that your maiden name?"

Jennifer turned and looked at her for the first time since they'd left the store. "What?"

"She called you Jennifer Remington."

"Oh. Yeah. Maiden name." She went back to gazing out the window.

"You do realize that I will now be forced to make endless Remington Steele references, don't you?"

"Excuse me?" This time when she looked at Alex, there was a flicker of amusement on her face.

"You know. Remington Steele. Only one of my favorite shows growing up. God, I had such a crush on Stephanie Zimbalist." Alex let her voice drift off dreamily. The corner of Jennifer's mouth twitched slightly and Alex grinned, seeing that she was starting to come out of her funk. "I'm afraid there's no way I can now know that your last name was Remington and *not* make an 80's pop reference. It's just not possible."

"Well, if I remind you of Remington Steele, does that mean I get to call you Laura Holt?" Jennifer asked, playing along much to Alex's delight. "You'd have to be my faithful sidekick."

"*Sidekick?*" Alex gasped in horror. "Ha! How dare you insult me like that? Laura was the brains of the operation, you know that. *Steele* was actually the sidekick."

"Only in Laura's eyes. As far as everybody else was concerned, Steele was the boss." She cocked her head to the side as if contemplating something. "Hmm. Yeah, okay. I think I can live with being the boss and ordering you around. I'm okay with that."

Alex grumbled and muttered to herself, which made Jennifer laugh. The sound brought great relief for both of them and Alex let go of her worry. As she pulled into the driveway and put the car into park, she turned to Jennifer. "Hey, Ms. Steele?"

"Yes, Ms. Holt?"

"If you ever decide you need to talk about Sarah, I'm right here, okay?"

Jennifer's eyes softened, her thanks clearly written in their blue depths. "I'll remember that."

Chapter
Nine

Dinner at Jackie and Rita's house was something that Alex looked forward to each and every time. Rita was an absolute magician in the kitchen, whipping up culinary delights that were actually healthy and delicious at the same time. That was something Alex often classified as impossible, at least it never seemed to happen in her kitchen. Cooking was not something she was good at, nor was she fond of it. She preferred to be fed by friends like Rita, people who actually knew their way around a kitchen and took pity on her because she didn't.

Only when she had passed thirty had Alex begun to realize a certain fact. Nobody told her when she was young that as she got older, she'd allow important relationships to drift away because she'd let herself get too absorbed in things like work. Her friendship with Jackie meant way too much to her to let that happen, so when things had started to get chaotic in their lives, the two women made a pact to ensure that they stayed in touch, even when life got crazy. Having dinner together on a regular basis helped to fulfill that promise. So, once every week or two, Alex went to have dinner with her best friend's family.

As she drove, she thought about how spending time with Hannah was another benefit of their dinners. Although Alex was the child's godmother and could see her any time she wished, it never felt like enough. She knew that kids grew fast, that if she blinked, she could miss it. *People are always saying that and you never believe it when you're a kid yourself, but it's true*, she thought. *One minute, she's two and I'm the coolest person she knows aside from her mommies. The next, she's ten and I'm not allowed to hug her in front of her friends.* Alex promised herself that she'd spend every second with Hannah that she could while she was still cool enough to be seen with. She was positively dreading the day when Hannah would choose her friends over her.

Jackie and Rita had a modest but beautiful home in Victor, which was between Canandaigua and Rochester. It only took Alex

about fifteen minutes to get there, as opposed to the forty-five minutes it took to get to the city, so having dinner with them on a week-
night was feasible. She pulled into the driveway, noting with
approval—and a little jealousy—that Rita had been hard at work on
her landscaping already. It was barely June, but her perennials
shown in a wide variety of bright colors, making their homey living
quarters that much more inviting.

"Feed me," Alex commanded as she entered the home of her
dear friends. The kitchen smelled divine, the mouth-watering aroma
of garlic floating in the air.

"Not to worry, my sweet. Feed you I will." Rita kissed Alex's
lips while deftly removing the bottle of merlot from her hands. "Hi,
love."

"Hello, gorgeous." Alex meant it. Jackie had done incredibly
well for herself and Alex liked to remind her every chance she
could. Rita was stunning, and if Alex hadn't thought of her as a sister, she might very well have entertained a fantasy or two about her.
Her classic Hispanic looks and dark eyes were seductive and sexy.
Her natural dark curls had been past her shoulder blades at one
time, but with the birth of Hannah, she had found she didn't have
the time to fuss with it and it had been easier to cut off some of the
length. Still, it was thick and wavy, and skimmed along her shoulders in an alluring cascade of rich, cocoa brown. She had a wonderfully feminine figure and hadn't lost any of her appeal since Hannah
had come along. Even during her pregnancy, she'd been beautiful
and sexy.

"Hey, what did I tell you about ogling my wife?" Jackie asked
from the doorway.

"Sorry. I can't help it. I've tried. She's impossible to not ogle. If
you get hit by a bus tomorrow, she's mine."

Rita shook her head and rolled her eyes, smiling with just the
slightest hint of embarrassment. "Take this and go sit down. I need
another half hour or so. Go. Out." She shooed them out of the
kitchen, handing Alex back the wine bottle she had taken from her
not three minutes before.

Jackie snatched a corkscrew and two glasses off the counter
and the two friends headed for the living room where Hannah sat
on the floor absorbed in a video. Alex handed the bottle to Jackie,
then crawled up behind the toddler and wrapped her arms around
her, making the child giggle adorably.

"What are we watching?" Alex asked, sitting Indian-style next
to her.

"Boo's Koos," Hannah responded, her blue eyes riveted to the
screen. The guy on the show was wearing a striped green rugby
shirt that clashed horrifically with the bright blue background on

the screen, but he didn't seem to notice and neither did Hannah. He launched cheerfully into song, inviting Hannah to help the animated blue dog find the item he was hinting at. Hannah joined him without missing a beat, singing slightly off-key, just like her mother.

Jackie handed Alex a glass of wine. "What's new?"

"Not much, really. Jennifer helped me put up a pen for Kinsey today."

"A pen?"

"Yeah, sort of a kennel. Like a big playpen off the garage. Should keep him out of trouble."

"Does he like it?"

"Hates it."

Jackie laughed. "That dog is worse than a kid."

Alex stroked Hannah's silky blonde hair. "Yeah, but he's almost as soft."

"How 'bout the writing thing?"

"It's a book, Jackie." Alex grinned. "Say it. Say 'book.'"

Jackie rolled her eyes. "Book. Okay? How's the book thing?" She knew how important writing was to Alex and she liked to check in on her progress every so often to make sure she wasn't getting discouraged.

"It's good. It's moving along. I'm really not sure where it's going yet, but I had a session last week where I was totally immersed. I felt so *great*. I was lost for over four hours. Amazing."

"Well, Rita's chomping at the bit to see it, so get a move on, would you?"

"Soon." Alex smiled. Rita had proven to be a terrific proof-reader for her in the past. She was intelligent, loved a good story, was great with spelling and punctuation, and wasn't afraid to point out when something wasn't working or didn't flow smoothly. Alex had asked her earlier in the year if she'd proof the book for her. Rita had been incredibly gracious and flattered, and Alex felt very confident with her writing in Rita's hands. "So, what's new with you guys?"

Jackie sipped her wine and Alex was sure she saw something resembling a shadow pass across her friend's face. "Not much. Same old same old." It was just a flicker, but Alex caught it and furrowed her eyebrows.

"Want to try again?"

"What?"

"What's bothering you?"

"What do you mean?"

So, we're going to play this *game, are we?* Jackie hated when Alex played the I-can't-just-tell-you-you're-going-to-have-to-drag-it-out-of-me game, but she thought nothing of turning the tables.

"Jackie. Do you think I don't know you like a book?" At her friend's sudden expression of nervousness, Alex glanced toward the kitchen and lowered her voice. "What's the matter?"

Jackie sighed, studied the contents of her wine glass with clouded blue eyes, and pushed an errant lock of blonde hair behind her ear. Throwing a glance at her daughter to make sure she was sufficiently absorbed in her program, her gaze finally met Alex's. "Rita's ready for another baby," she said quietly.

"That's great!" Alex smiled with enthusiasm. At the complete lack of such enthusiasm on the face of her best friend, she corrected herself. "That's not great?"

Jackie sighed again, throwing one hand in the air. "I don't know, Alex. I mean, I love being a mom. I do. And I want to have more kids. But..." She lowered her voice even more, very aware of her proximity to Hannah. Alex scooted away from the toddler and closer to Jackie. "I hardly have Rita to myself any more and that's only going to get worse if we have another baby. Hannah's finally big enough where we can toss in a video and keep her occupied for a little while so that we can actually talk to one another like adults. I've missed that so much and now that we have a little bit back, she wants to throw it all away and go back to square one."

"Jackie..."

"I know. I know I'm being totally selfish here. I'm aware of that. I can't seem to help it." She dropped into the recliner in the corner. "We hardly have sex any more, Alex. God, we used to have it a couple times a week. Now, if we've got enough energy for once a month, we're lucky."

She looked miserable and her best friend smiled warmly at her. Alex was one of the only people who knew that Jackie's biggest fear was the legendary Lesbian Bed Death. The idea of it scared the hell out of her and she looked it.

"Have you talked to Rita about this?" Alex asked gently.

"The sex thing?"

Alex bit back a chuckle. "Well, yeah, that. But I meant all of it. How you feel about another baby."

"Another baby right now," Jackie corrected. "We've touched on it a little."

Alex cocked an eyebrow at her and she looked away in defeat.

"A very little."

"I think you need to touch on it again. And soon."

Jackie nodded knowingly and grimaced. "I'm bad at that, Stretch."

"I know you are. But, honey, Rita's in her late thirties. She's not going to want to wait much longer for another child. You need to talk about this. Now. If you don't, it's going to fester and turn into resentment. And you don't want resentment in this relationship. You and I both know that. Talk to her."

Jackie rested her head on the back of the chair and took a large gulp of her wine. "You're right. I'll talk to her."

"Good."

"Oh Wise One."

Alex snorted. "Yeah, that's me. You can tell by the love of my life standing here by my side."

"It'll happen, sweetie. She'll show up sooner or later."

"Well she'd better hurry the hell up. I ain't gettin' any younger, you know." She sipped her wine and they watched Blue's Clues for several minutes, both of them smiling as Hannah sang along.

Jackie got up to refill their glasses. "So, you made a playpen for Kinsey today."

"Yup."

"And Jennifer helped."

"Yup. She came over when I was just starting to put things together and offered her services, so I took her up on it. We worked very, very well together. Hey, what's that look for?"

"Offered her services, huh?" Jackie waggled her eyebrows teasingly.

"Unfortunately, not *those* services."

"Maybe Ms. Right is closer than you think, hmm? Like, right next door? You got a little crush thing going on, do you?"

Alex snorted. "Yeah, right. You're obviously forgetting that extra little thing she has. What's the word again? Let me think...Oh, yeah. A husband."

"Too bad."

"Tell me about it. Although a weird thing did happen today while we were at the store." She relayed the story of running into Sarah and how oddly Jennifer had behaved. "Sarah had one of those faces I sort of recognized, like we play volleyball or softball against her or something. I'm sure I've seen her before."

"Family?"

"Definitely. Her girlfriend came looking for her right after Jennifer ran away."

"Did she say anything afterward?"

"Jennifer? No. She just got really quiet. I poked and prodded a little, trying to get her to open up, but she wasn't talking. Whatever the situation, seeing Sarah totally freaked her out."

"Huh. That *is* odd." They were quiet for a minute before Jackie grinned. "Having her next door must beat the hell out of Old Lady Cavanaugh, huh?"

Alex laughed. "Damn right."

"And she's more fun to look at."

"Much. *Much* more fun to look at."

"She's got a great ass."

"God, yes."

They were silent for another minute, but when they met each other's gaze, they dissolved into raucous laughter as their college-age selves reared their heads in an unexpected bit of regression. Then Rita announced that dinner was ready and the two friends had to grow up all over again.

Chapter
Ten

It was cool and cloudy the evening of the first volleyball game. Jennifer arrived at the beach very early, knowing she'd need to do a lot of stretching. Though she'd practiced with the team, she still considered herself quite rusty. A severely pulled muscle was not out of the realm of possibility. Plus, she'd need as much time as possible to calm the fluttering butterflies in her stomach; she was terribly nervous.

Three courts were set up right on the beach, each with a wooden tower on which the official would perch to make the calls. The sand was smooth, all three courts having been raked and sifted. They looked neat and inviting. Jennifer remembered Alex's warnings, though, not to get too lax. Despite the raking, they were still on the beach and there were always foreign objects buried somewhere.

"Dear God," Jennifer mumbled in mock-prayer. "If it's all the same to you, I'd really rather *not* step on broken glass today."

As she sat in the sand stretching her hamstrings, she noticed several other players who seemed to be as early as she was and she wondered whom they'd be playing. There were a couple women bumping a ball back and forth between them with enough competence to look like they knew what they were doing, but not so much as to seem threatening. The two young men on the middle court were another story. One was setting for the other, who snarled with anger as he clobbered the ball into the ground.

Yikes. Let's not play him today, she thought with trepidation. *Or ever.*

Alex had reassured her that the league was strictly recreational and that they were there to have fun. That, of course, was no guarantee of the intentions of their competitors.

She tore her eyes away from the Snarling Man and concentrated on stretching her quads and her lower back. Both could be problem areas for her—they had been in the past—and the last thing she wanted was to go out with an injury during her first game. When she thought she had stretched enough, she stretched some more, just to be safe, and waited for her teammates to arrive.

Jackie was first.

"Hey there, Setter Extraordinaire," she greeted with a big smile.

"Don't jinx me," Jennifer scolded.

Jackie laughed. "No worries, babe. You're going to be great." She pushed a lock of her short, blonde hair behind an ear and pulled from her gym bag a bright yellow water bottle, stamped in red with the Kodak logo.

"Where's Rita? And Hannah?"

"Our cheering section will be here in a little while. An entire game is still a little long for Hannah, so Rita brings her late. That way they can stay until the end and Rita can see how we do. She'd rather catch the end than the beginning."

"I don't blame her. She doesn't play?"

"Not any more." Jennifer detected a hint of sadness in Jackie's voice. "She's always had some knee problems and they got worse during pregnancy. Her doctor gently suggested she give it up and try something less punishing on her joints."

"Bummer."

"That's for sure. She was a damn good player. She misses it."

They stretched together for several minutes, discussing how common knee injuries were for female athletes. Steve and Nikki showed up soon after that, having run into each other in the parking lot. Steve wore baggy, plaid shorts in blues and greens and a white t-shirt with a small, illegible logo on the left chest. Nikki was dressed in red, Lycra shorts that accentuated her long, shapely legs—Jennifer pulled her eyes away before she got caught staring. Her pale yellow tank top fit loosely. The wrap-around athletic sunglasses hid her eyes, which was a bit unnerving for Jennifer, who couldn't tell if Nikki was looking at her or not.

About three minutes later, David joined them. He looked like he'd walked straight out of a magazine. His bright orange swim trunks showed off his muscular legs and the royal blue t-shirt he wore clung to his massive shoulders like it was wet. He sat next to Jennifer in the circle and they all chattered on about their respective days.

"Well, it's about damn time," Jackie scolded in jest as Alex approached.

"Sorry. Lost track of time," Alex said breathlessly.

We have the best-looking team on the beach, Jennifer thought, suppressing an embarrassed giggle as she sat in the sand and looked up to observe her friend. Alex wore black, cotton shorts and a raspberry colored, long sleeve t-shirt emblazoned across the front with the word "Provincetown" in thin, white letters. Her dark hair was pulled back into a ponytail, several strands already escaping and brushing along her ears. Her sleeves were pulled up to the middle of her forearms, revealing muscles and the beginnings of a summer tan. Jennifer looked up at Alex's face and felt an immediate jolt at the realization that Alex was looking back at her. She quickly looked down and busied herself by picking sand out of her toes.

"Hey, neighbor. You ready?"

Jennifer nodded. "I think so. We'll see soon enough, won't we?"

Alex recognized the nervousness in her voice, squatted next to her, and placed a warm hand on her back. "Relax. You're going to be fine. This is fun, remember?"

The reassurance was sweet and Jennifer felt her anxiety slip down a notch or two.

"Fun. Right." She nodded. "I'm with you."

"Good." Alex smiled, then grabbed Jennifer's hand and hauled her to her feet. "Come on."

They joined the rest of the team, who had already moved to the court for warm-ups. They passed the ball around, loosening their arms and fingers. Then they lined up to do some hitting. Jennifer stood at the net, setting to her teammates one by one. Her sets were accurate and that went a long way in alleviating some of her tension.

After half a dozen sets, she backed off to let Nikki set a few and returned to the sidelines where she stretched her quads one last time for good measure and sized up their opponent.

She remembered Alex telling her how hard it was to find a women's league in sand volleyball. There just wasn't as much interest. Because of that, there were mostly men's leagues and co-ed leagues. She said that in most co-ed leagues, a team consisting of all women was allowed, but an all-men's team was not. Jennifer winced as she realized that the team they were about to play included the Snarling Man, and was all men except one.

All boys would be a better description, she thought with dismay. Not one of them looked older than twenty-two. The only one who was under six feet tall was the girl and Jennifer's mouth fell open when she saw her vertical leap.

Alex was suddenly next to Jennifer, reaching her left arm up and behind her head, stretching her triceps. "Ick. These guys don't look like much fun, do they?"

"I was hoping you'd say you've played them before and they look much more intimidating than they are."

"Sorry, babe. They're new this year." She watched the Snarling Man spike the ball straight down into the sand, roaring with satisfaction. "And a bit too serious, if you ask me."

"This ought to be fun," Steve commented sarcastically, joining the two women in watching their opponents. "What are they, sixteen?"

"College boys, I bet," Nikki added, approaching them with a frown. "I hate playing college boys. They're assholes."

Jackie and David finished their warm-ups and joined the other four. Jackie took on the role of coach and pulled the players into a huddle merely by the sound of her voice.

"Okay, listen up. These little bastards are going to be tough. But that's all they are. Little bastards who think they know this game. The bad news for them is that they're all about power and they know nothing about skill and consistency. That's why we're going to beat them. Don't be intimidated. We were playing this game when they were in grade school, so let's take them back to class and teach them a thing or two. Stay sharp. Keep moving. Lots of talk. Okay?"

Her pep talk seemed to spark the team, building their confidence as it was meant to. Six fists stacked in the middle of the huddle. They did a quick cheer and the game was on.

* * *

By the time Rita and Hannah arrived, the match was in the middle of the second game. The good guys had taken the first game, but it had been a struggle and they were exhausted, all six of them drenched in sweat. Rita's dark eyebrows lifted in surprised. It was unusual for the first game of the season to be so intense.

The exhaustion had already taken its toll, and they were down by eight points. "Free!" Jackie hollered, as the other team's back row player sent the ball over. Steve received it with ease and sent it gracefully up to Jennifer in the front row. She set Alex, but the dark-haired woman's approach was off and the seven-foot monster on the other side of the net stuffed her easily, bellowing with delight and high-fiving his mates.

"I hate him," Alex muttered as she turned away from the net, looking defeated.

Jennifer grabbed Alex's upper arm and pulled her close to her, talking quickly in her ear. "Listen to me. You're only a step off and he's blocking you inside. Start one step closer to the net than you have been and hit down the line instead of the center of the court. Nobody's covering there."

She watched as Alex absorbed the information, and then readied herself to receive the serve. It skimmed the net as it came over and Nikki was able to make herself play it, albeit a split second later than usual. It used to be that when a serve hit the net, it was whistled dead and a side out was called. That was how Jennifer remembered it. That rule had changed. A net ball on the serve was now legal, much to her surprise. Not only did it seem like a point-less rule change, but the people who had been playing the game for ten years or more had a terrible time adjusting to playing a serve that was a net ball. As a testament to that fact, Nikki's pass was ugly, but Jennifer managed to get to it and set Alex again. This time, her approach was perfect. The seven-foot monster was up to block again, growling menacingly, but Alex kept her cool. Com-pletely faking him out, she did as Jennifer had suggested, spiking cleanly straight down the line. Sand flew and the whistle blew. Point.

Alex whooped happily in an unmistakable imitation of her blocker. Jennifer couldn't help but smile.

"Beautiful set," Alex commented.

"Nice hit," Jennifer responded, slapping Alex's raised hand. "Now you've got to pay attention. They'll probably have you cov-ered there."

"Leaving something else open." She smiled a dazzling smile and Jennifer felt her stomach flip-flop. Five minutes before, Alex had been miserable and now she was smiling. The selfish part of Jennifer wanted to take credit for that...and did.

Jackie called a time out, more for a rest than for any strategiz-ing. The team members all grabbed their water bottles or Gatorade and drank deeply.

"God, I'm glad it's only seventy out," Steve commented, wip-ing his face with a towel. "We'd have passed out by now." He was covered with sand from head to toe, as was David. All six of them were drenched.

"Nice job, Alex," Jackie commended. She waved to Hannah, who was busy building a sandcastle. "Keep your eyes peeled. That spot's been open a lot."

"Jennifer was gracious enough to point that out." She smiled at Jennifer.

"Well, it worked. They're getting pissed off. I don't think they like the idea of losing to a team of mostly women. No offense, guys."

"None taken," Steve answered.

"Watch out for the guy in the red shirt," Nikki suggested, pointing to the Snarling Man with her eyes. "He just came into the front row. I've seen him play indoors. He's not very consistent, but if he gets a perfect set, his spike is so fast you won't even see it until after it bounces."

Jackie nodded and caught David's eye. He was their tallest and strongest player and, as luck would have it, in the front row during the upcoming rotation. "He's all yours, darlin'."

"He's not really my type..." David began with a wry grin, adding a decidedly feminine lilt to his voice.

Jackie slapped him playfully. "Hey, he's got a penis, doesn't he?"

"Good point."

They did their cheer just as the whistle blew, marking the end of the time out, and went back onto the court. They were off again in a mere seven minutes, having dumped game two by twelve points.

They were feeling dejected as game three began. The opposing team was nothing short of obnoxious. They argued every call, making the referee completely miserable. They were sloppy in their approaches and landings. More often than not, when coming down from a spike, they came down dangerously under the net, taking out Jackie once and Steve three times. They had no sportsmanship whatsoever and playing them was simply no fun at all.

But they were good.

Alex was close to the end of her rope, Jennifer could tell by the smoldering disgust on her face. She was being stuffed left and right and it left her skittish about spiking at all. She'd actually asked Jennifer to set David for a while so she could get herself together.

Mirroring their last on-court conversation, Jennifer pulled Alex close once again. "You can't go through a tree. Go around him. Next one's yours."

Alex nodded, setting her jaw and swallowing hard as she set up to receive the serve. It ripped over the net and Steve received it easily. He was by far their best at service reception and Jennifer always felt a little tingle of relief when the serve headed for him. It meant she'd get a nice, easy pass, which would greatly increase the chances of her getting a good set off to Alex or David. She put the ball up for Alex, who heeded Jennifer's advice, hitting around her blocker—the Snarling Man. It wasn't an incredibly strong hit, but Alex got it past him and he didn't like it.

It was received in the back row and sent forward to their setter. She put it up perfectly for the Snarling Man, who went up with impressive form, almost in slow motion, as Jennifer dropped back and Alex and David went up to double block.

Jennifer didn't see his arm swing at all. Actually, she didn't see the *ball* at all until it hit her squarely in the face. She didn't recall falling, but when all she saw was the sky, she decided she must have. Sound seemed to be affected as well. All she could hear was the rushing of blood in her ears. She blinked rapidly, totally confused.

The next thing she knew, the whole team was bent over her.

Alex's face was the only one she could focus on, the worry clearly etched across it. She gently brushed Jennifer's bangs off her forehead.

"Rita!" Jackie shouted. "Ice!"

Okay, Jennifer thought. *I heard that. Ears are working again. That's a good thing.*

"Jennifer?" Alex asked. "Are you all right? How do you feel?"

"Did you happen to get the license number?" Jennifer replied. Alex smiled with relief and Jennifer found herself thinking how beautiful that smile was. "I feel like an idiot. I'm sorry."

"For what? That ball would have taken down any one of us. Let's put some ice on that to keep the swelling down." An ice pack seemed to appear out of nowhere. Alex put one hand on the side of Jennifer's head and pressed the ice pack to her eye and cheekbone with the other. She tightened her grip slightly when Jennifer flinched from the cold, her thumb gently stroking Jennifer's temple.

"Hey, can we finish the game?" an unfamiliar voice called.

Jennifer watched in fascination as Alex's face hardened, her nostrils flaring slightly, her lips a thin, straight line.

"Nikki, could you hold this for a second?" She gestured to the ice pack. Nikki took her place, surprising Jennifer with her soft touch. Alex was on her feet and moving.

"Alex, don't!" Jackie's calves flashed across Jennifer's peripheral vision, along with some other feet she couldn't recognize from her vantage point, and she lifted her head to see what was going on. That was a big mistake. The world tilted on her and she squeezed her eyes shut, groaning as she lay back down.

"What's happening, Nikki?"

Nikki launched into color commentary. "That was the big guy who hit you who just asked about the game. Alex is right in his face. Jackie and David are standing close enough to pull her away if she gets out of control." There was a definite smile in her voice, which brought a grin to Jennifer's face as well.

They could only hear snippets and bits of what was being said. They caught Alex's voice snapping off things like "recreational, you shit" and "good sportsmanship." The idea of Alex leaping to her rescue made Jennifer feel warm.

"Okay, Jackie's pulling her away now," Nikki reported. Then she laughed with a surprised chuckle. "The guy actually looks like he feels bad. Like a kid who just got scolded." Her voice held a tone of amusement.

"I think I should get off the court," Jennifer said, removing the ice pack from her face. She suddenly felt foolish and embarrassed by the whole thing.

"You're sure?"

"Uh-huh. You guys have to finish up and take game three."

Nikki snorted. "You *did* get hit in the head, didn't you?"

Jackie, Steve, and David all joined them, each holding onto Alex in some way to keep her on their side of the net. Alex's face was red and her eyes were flashing. "How we doing?" she asked Jennifer, visibly calming herself and replacing Nikki by her side.

"My hero," Jennifer teased.

"She wants to move off the court so we can finish the game," Nikki said.

"So you can *win* the game," Jennifer corrected.

"Now that's what I call team spirit." Jackie laughed, taking Jennifer's arm and helping her to stand. The court picked that moment to shift sharply to the left.

"Whoa. Okay. Hang on." Jennifer stood between Jackie and Alex, clutching tightly to both of them and waiting for the dizziness to subside. It didn't take long. "Okay. That's better." The three of them walked slowly over to where Rita sat in a beach chair, her brow furrowed with concern. Hannah came running up, looking closely at Jennifer as she settled back down into the sand, her gym bag propped behind her head so she could see the game.

"You got a boo-boo?" the toddler asked with concern, dropping to her knees next to Jennifer.

"Yeah, just a little one."

She squinted her big, blue eyes as she inspected the injured party closely. "Ow. Does it hurt?"

"Yeah. A little bit."

She leaned forward, her fine, blonde hair brushing Jennifer's face, and placed such a gentle kiss on her cheekbone that it made Jennifer's heart swell and her eyes mist. "Better?"

"Much," Jennifer whispered, truly touched. "Thanks, Hannah."

"Welcome."

"You are the sweetest little thing in the world," Alex said to the little girl, her face beaming with pride. "You know that?"

Hannah merely smiled and scooted back to her sand toys.

Alex took Jennifer's hand and placed the ice pack in it, then gently pressed it to her face. "Twenty minutes, okay? Rita, keep an eye on her, will you?"

"Go kick some ass," Jennifer ordered.

"Yes, ma'am." Alex gently rustled Jennifer's bangs, then was up and jogging back onto the court.

Jennifer turned to catch Rita's eye. The brunette looked far too amused for her own good.

* * *

"This is a really nice car," Alex commented, nodding with certainty as she drove Jennifer's Volvo home from the beach. After much coaxing and more than a little insisting, the plan had been settled. Alex would drive Jennifer in her car and Jackie would follow in Alex's, while Rita followed Jackie to pick her up and take her home. On a normal volleyball night—one that didn't include an injury—the team would go out and have a few drinks to celebrate its win or scowl over, then laugh about, its loss. On that night, however, the team had agreed as a whole that even though they'd won, they couldn't in good conscience go out and party without Jennifer. She'd protested, as expected, but they decided they'd definitely go out the following week, win or lose.

There was also the slight concern of a possible concussion. Jennifer swore she was fine, just a little hazy, and refused to go to the emergency room. Alex and Jackie both tended to agree with her assessment, but Alex was reluctant to leave her alone, at least for a little while. When Jennifer mentioned that Eric was spending the evening in Buffalo, that settled it for Alex. She'd announced that she would take Jennifer home, get her comfortable, and sit with her for a while to make sure she didn't fall asleep until they were sure she was okay.

So, they pulled into her driveway with Alex commenting on the car as Jennifer slumped comfortably in the passenger seat.

"Eric wanted me to get the Cross Country. Have you seen those?"

"Is that the station wagon that looks like an SUV? They're pretty cool."

"He thinks so, too."

"And you don't."

"To me, it's still a station wagon. In my opinion, you drive a station wagon or a minivan and all sex appeal goes right out the window."

Alex chuckled as she looked over at her own driveway, Rita pulling in with the minivan. She thought about how hard Jackie had fought against getting one, for exactly the same reason Jennifer had just outlined. However, after driving it for two days, she'd fallen in love with it and was singing its praises any chance she got. Alex decided to keep Jennifer's comment to herself.

She hopped out of the car and scooted around to open Jennifer's door before she had a chance to do so herself. "M'lady," she said in her best British accent. "We have arrived. Allow me to escort you." She held out a hand.

"Alex, I'm fine," Jennifer said with quiet laughter. "Really. You don't have to stay." Despite her protests, she slid her hand into Alex's, feeling the warm tingle of her skin. Her blue eyes met Alex's in a silent thank you and Alex cringed inwardly at the deep purple that was beginning to show around her eye, thinking how tender it must be. Then she grinned at the thought of Jennifer with a shiner.

"Really," Jennifer said again, as if Alex hadn't heard her the first time.

"Humor me. Okay?"

Jackie came jogging across the yard to give Alex her keys. "How we doing?"

"Just fine," Jennifer assured her. "Though I'm finding Dr. Foster here to be quite a hard ass."

Jackie looked at Alex, feigning seriousness. "She has no idea, does she?"

"Not a clue," Alex deadpanned.

"Yeah, you two are funny." Jennifer tightened her grip on Alex's hand. "Come on, doc. Get me inside. I'm feeling a little woozy."

"I'll put Kinsey in his pen, okay? I can use my key." Jackie offered.

"That would be great, Jack. Thanks."

"Call if you need anything. I can be here in a flash."

"Thanks, Jackie," Jennifer said sincerely. "And thank Hannah for me. Tell her that her kiss made me feel a million times better."

"I will." Jackie's eyes met Alex's in silent question. After over a decade of close friendship, the two of them could read one another's faces without a second thought. Alex told her with her eyes that they'd be fine. Jackie was satisfied with that and took her leave. Alex and Jennifer waved to Rita, parked in Alex's driveway, then entered Jennifer's house.

* * *

"Comfy?"

"Immensely."

Alex set a tall glass of iced tea down on a coaster on the coffee table so Jennifer could reach it. She was stretched out on the leather couch in a clean, pink T-shirt and white boxer shorts with teddy bears on them. She smelled like baby powder. The edges of her bangs were damp from washing her face and her hair hung loosely around her shoulders. The slight sleepiness in her eyes made her look all of twelve years old and Alex thought she was simply adorable, even with the nasty bruise marring the overall picture.

Alex hovered with her own glass, surveying her seating options and wishing she could take a quick shower. Jennifer lifted her legs slightly and pointed to the end of the couch with her chin. "Have a seat."

"I'm sandy," Alex warned.

"Hi, Sandy. I'm Jennifer. Sit."

I'm going to argue with a direct order? Alex thought. *I think not.* She sat obediently, sinking deliciously into the soft leather. Jennifer settled her feet in Alex's lap and that was that. Alex had no intention of ever moving again. *You're just a sucker for a pretty girl,* she chided herself.

Her conscience decided to add its two cents. *A pretty,* married *girl,* it pointedly kicked in, causing Alex to grimace.

"Hey, I thought Eric was coming to the game." Alex took a sip of her tea, trying to look anywhere but at the creamy smooth skin on the firm calves that rested against her leg.

Jennifer sighed softly and a dark cloud passed over her face. She took a swig from her own glass. "Yeah, so did I. Apparently, he got stuck at the office. Again." She grimaced as she remembered the abrupt voicemail message he'd left. She'd been excited to have him come to her game, but he'd obviously had more important things to do than spend time with his wife. As usual.

Alex studied her closely, concerned by her sudden change in demeanor. "You okay?"

"I don't even know anymore, Alex."

"Tell me."

Jennifer sighed again, weighing the pros and cons of opening up to this woman. She was sure the knock on the head had weakened her resolve slightly, and the thought of talking to somebody totally unbiased as far as her family was concerned was almost too tempting. She'd been thinking it for so long, yet she'd never said the words. Saying the words would make it real and she didn't know if she was ready for that. She looked up and met the soft, brown gaze of her neighbor, a woman who was quickly becoming the best friend she'd ever had, and felt safe. She took a deep breath, bracing herself for the impact the sound of the words would have, and spoke.

"I think he's screwing around on me."

There. I said it. She waited for the walls to come crashing down, but it remained quiet, the gentle lapping of the water the only sound. She felt a sense of near-relief.

"Oh, wow," Alex said softly. "You're sure?"

Jennifer rubbed at her uninjured eye, nodding slowly. "I'm not stupid, Alex. He must think I am, but I'm not. I've called the Buffalo office on several occasions at night when he's supposed to be there. I get the switchboard or his voicemail, but I never get him. I've tried his cell phone, but he claims the reception goes mysteriously out of whack out there and he doesn't get my calls. He's always talking about how hard he's working, but I've heard his father mention that he's concerned about Eric's lack of attention at the firm." She took another sip of her tea, carefully not looking at Alex. "We hardly ever have sex any more and when we do, I feel like I'm by myself anyway."

Are none of my friends having sex? It was the first thought to pop into Alex's head. She wasn't sure what to say or do and she found herself a little startled at the lack of ire in Jennifer's voice. She didn't seem all that angry, just a little sad and surprisingly matter-of-fact, like this was something she'd been dealing with for quite some time. "What are you going to do?" she finally asked, her voice soft.

Jennifer stared into her glass as if looking for the answer. "I have absolutely no idea."

They sat in silence for several minutes, each lost in the moment. Alex slumped a little further into the leather, propped her bare feet up on the coffee table, and gently rested her hand on Jennifer's shin in what she hoped was a show of support. She tried to pay no attention to how good the younger woman's flesh felt beneath her fingers.

As she looked at Jennifer's face, she realized that her neighbor looked more tired than sad and she knew she should keep her talking in order to keep her awake, at least for a little while longer. The Eric subject was definitely off-limits; she wanted to cheer her friend up.

"Hey, how's the decorating coming?"

Jennifer's face brightened slightly. "Great. I think I finally have all the little details ironed out for the master bedroom. And guess what I did."

The sparkle in her eyes had returned and Alex knew immediately that this was her friend's passion. She found it endearing and flattering that Jennifer chose to share it with her. "Bought new furniture?"

"Nope. Not yet, anyway."

"Ripped down a wall?"

"No." She laughed.

"I give."

"I bit the bullet and painted that wall."

"That wall." Alex furrowed her brow and shook her head, lost. "That wall, what wall?"

"The purple wall."

"The purple wall." She shook her head again, but it struck her before she needed to have her memory nudged along. "*Oh!* The purple wall! You painted the purple wall? Like, *purple?*"

"Yup." Jennifer's face was positively beaming. Alex found it intoxicating just to look at it.

"Like, *dark* purple? Like the purples we were looking at?"

"Yup."

"Like, purple like your eye?"

"Hey! Shut up." She kicked at Alex playfully. "It's called *Deep Eggplant.*"

"And? Are you happy with it?"

"It's an unbelievably sensuous color. I love it."

"Ooo, sensuous, is it? I'd say that's rather appropriate for a bedroom, wouldn't you?" Alex waggled her eyebrows in mock flirtation.

"Yeah? Wanna see it?" Jennifer held Alex's surprised gaze, unmistakably flirting back, effectively beating Alex at her own game.

Just how hard did she get hit with that ball? Alex wondered. "Tomorrow."

"Chicken." Jennifer smirked, savoring her victory even though her eyes seemed to swim slightly out of focus.

"*Deep Eggplant,* huh?"

"Uh-huh. The sales guy was great. Did you know there's such a thing as tinted primer?"

"Tinted? I thought primer was white."

"It doesn't have to be. He tinted it with the *Deep Eggplant* so the paint would cover better. He was right. It looks really rich and smooth. And it took fewer coats and much less effort than I expected."

"Then is it safe to assume that your most recent trip to Chase-Pitkin was better than the previous one?" Alex knew it was a touchy subject, but her friend's I-just-got-whacked-in-the-head-and-I'm-talking-more-openly-than-I-usually-do behavior was too tempting to resist. She wanted to take the opportunity and see if she could find out more about the mysterious Sarah.

"God, that feels good," Jennifer muttered, almost to herself, closing her eyes.

Alex crinkled her brow, wondering what she meant, then very nearly gasped out loud when she looked down. To her horror, she was gently kneading Jennifer's calf muscles with her fingers. In response, Jennifer was pushing her rear end down into the cushions ever so slightly. Alex willed herself to stop, but her hands refused to obey. Instead, she decided to keep Jennifer talking.

"So, no scary patrons sent you scampering to the check-out this time?"

Jennifer chuckled, her eyes still closed. "Sarah. What the hell was she doing there anyway?"

"She seemed happy to see you." Jennifer snorted. "You weren't happy to see her, though, were you?"

"Considering that the last time I saw her, she was ripping my heart out, no."

"Excuse me?" *Whoa! What the hell?*

Jennifer gingerly fingered her swollen eye, winced, then sighed heavily. She hadn't meant to get into this. She'd never gotten into this with anybody, but the effect of being hit in the head left her feeling almost drunk and she couldn't seem to stop her mouth from saying things it shouldn't. And she did owe Alex an explanation of some sort for what had happened that day. She took a deep breath. "Sarah and I...there was this...we had a thing."

"A thing?" Alex blinked at her.

"Yes, a thing," she retorted, more abruptly than she had intended. "I don't know what else to call it." She held Alex's gaze, her brows dipping together in tension. "What?" she snapped at the shocked expression on Alex's face.

"Nothing. Nothing. I'm just..." Alex's voice trailed off.

"Surprised?"

"Well. In a word, yes."

Jennifer shrugged. "Yeah, well, so was I."

Alex sat quietly, absorbing the fact that Jennifer had had "a thing" with a woman. Suddenly, inexplicably, and unexpectedly, all her perceptions of Jennifer had shifted. She wanted so badly to press the issue, to find out more. It was obviously a touchy subject for her, though, and Alex didn't want her to shut down completely like last time. But Jennifer didn't seem to be offering up more, not at that moment. As much as Alex wanted to explore, she decided to respectfully back off, at least for a little while. They sat in silence.

"How's your head?" Alex finally asked.

"Still attached. I think."

Alex chuckled, watching her still-traveling hands as if they had little minds of their own. They moved down from Jennifer's strong calves, massaged over her ankles, and then settled on her feet, kneading and rubbing, pressing strongly into the arch until Jennifer groaned, squirming slightly.

"Too hard?" Alex asked.

"No. Perfect," she whispered. "You have amazing hands." The tone of her voice was low and sexy and it made Alex swallow hard, the sound of her own heartbeat pounding in her head. She had a sudden flash of Jennifer using that husky voice, rasping Alex's name in her ear as Alex ravished her body using hands, mouth, and tongue.

Alex's mind shrieked at her, warning her that things were getting way too close and that Jennifer was enjoying the physical attention far too much for Alex's own good. She shook her head slightly, then ran a fingernail up the sole of Jennifer's foot, causing her to jump with surprise and pull it away.

"Hey," she gasped, slightly annoyed.

"Just making sure you're awake," Alex replied innocently, patting Jennifer's leg in a gesture that told her she wanted to get up. She *needed* to get up. Fast.

"I'm awake," Jennifer yawned. "I don't want to be, but I am."

Alex checked the clock; it had been three hours since her injury. "Are you still woozy or disoriented?"

"I feel okay. Really. A bit of a headache, but I think I'm fine."

Alex studied her face for sincerity and found it. "Me, too. Still, I don't want you to be alone. How 'bout if I go feed Kinsey, then we come back here for a little while longer. Is that okay with you?"

Jennifer smiled sweetly from the couch. "You don't have to stay, Alex, but I'm not going to turn away your company. I like when you're here."

The endearing honesty of her statement warmed Alex's heart and she smiled at her. "I'll be right back."

"I'll be right here."

Once outside, Alex took several deep breaths of the cool night air, reprimanding herself and her wandering hands as she crossed to her house.

Jesus, Foster, you might as well have just thrown yourself at her and ripped her clothes off with your teeth. What the hell is the matter with you?

Rolling her eyes, she was distracted from her self-deprecation by the shrill, staccato barks of her Westie. She bent over the little fence and scooped him up. "Hey, buddy," she cooed affectionately, accepting his kisses. "Miss me?" She unlocked the door and set him on the kitchen floor. His furry, white tail wagged continuously as he playfully scolded her for being so late with his dinner, admonishing her with disapproving *woo's*. She would have genuinely felt bad if he weren't so damn cute with his little black lips in the shape of an "O."

"I know, I know. I'm sorry." She filled his bowl, rambling on with her explanation as if talking to an irritated parent. "I would have been here sooner, but Jennifer got hurt and we were worried that she might have a concussion, so I offered to stay with her for a bit." Kinsey eyed her suspiciously as he ate. "To keep her awake, you know. Just to make sure she was okay. Stop looking at me like that." She looked away guiltily and busied herself with the breakfast dishes she'd left in the sink, her mind wandering back to the earlier conversation.

We had a thing.

A thing. That could only mean one...thing, right? The phrase "having a thing" was a pretty standard euphemism, wasn't it? Jennifer and Sarah had been lovers. Jennifer had been with another woman.

"So what?" Alex said aloud, annoyed at the path her mind was taking, but unable to stop it. A lot of women had been with other women. What was the big deal if Jennifer had? But she smiled as she felt a familiar warmth spread through her body, followed by a slight tingle in her belly. She had always thought there was something incredibly sexy and erotic about a "straight" woman who occasionally went to bat for the other team. She chuckled, shaking her head to rid herself of the thought, and went into the bedroom to change out of her sand-infused clothes.

Someday, I'll get her to tell me all about Sarah. In great detail.

"Come on, Kins," she called and snapped on his leash. "Let's go check on your girlfriend, make sure she hasn't kicked off on us."

Alex was sure she hadn't been gone for more than twenty minutes, but when she slid the door from Jennifer's deck open, she could do nothing but smile affectionately.

Jennifer had fallen asleep, her breathing deep and even. One arm was tossed carelessly over her head and hung limply over the end of the couch. The other was draped across her stomach. One leg was bent so her lower body looked like the letter 'P.' Alex stood still and studied her for what seemed like a long time. She looked different in sleep and it took Alex several minutes to figure out why. She finally realized that Jennifer looked infinitely more relaxed. She'd never thought of her young friend as a tense woman, but she must have been if the change while she was sleeping was so dramatic. *What's got you so stressed out?* she thought, wishing she could make it better.

She bent to unhook Kinsey's leash and let him roam. "Stay out of trouble," she warned softly as he set to work with his sniffer.

She debated waking Jennifer up. She laid the backs of her fingers on Jennifer's forehead, then her cheeks. She felt perfectly normal—cool and soft—and Alex exhaled a relieved breath she hadn't realized she'd been holding. She pulled the afghan off the back of the couch and draped it gently over the sleeping form. Without thinking, she bent forward and placed a tender kiss on Jennifer's forehead, and flushed with embarrassment when she stood back up and recognized what she had done.

Watch yourself, Foster. This one's gotten in deep...

She grimaced at the voice in her head, wondering why she wasn't panicking at the prospect of falling for a straight girl, and decided it would probably hit her full-force later on and send her into a horrified tailspin of some sort. She looked longingly at her previous spot on the couch, but knew returning to that place was not an option. She narrowed her eyes into a glare as she watched Kinsey hop up onto the leather and curl himself into a ball. He settled in the crook of Jennifer's knee and possessively rested his head on her thigh. Alex was certain that if he could have teasingly stuck his tongue out at her, he would have.

"Little bastard," she muttered, finding a second afghan and settling herself across the room in the oversized chair. She curled her feet underneath her, propped her head on her hand, and watched her friend as she slept, feeling a frustrating mixture of arousal, affection, and sadness.

Chapter
Eleven

God, my head hurts.

It was the very first thought that crossed Jennifer's mind as she clawed her way up from the depths of a deep, deep sleep. The ray of sunlight that woke her felt like a lance slicing across her eyelid and she winced painfully, bringing her hand up as a shield.

For a split second, she was startled by movement near her legs. She soon realized it was only Kinsey and she smiled with affection.

"Hey, handsome," she whispered as he gingerly walked up her torso, making sure to step on all her most sensitive spots along the way, causing her to grunt comically. He set to work bathing her face with his soft, pink tongue. It was something that Jennifer would have normally found slightly unpleasant, but he was so gentle and careful around her eye that she didn't have the heart to stop him. He was like a mother caring for her pup and she was touched by his kindness.

She turned her head to the left, wondering what time it was. When she squinted to see the clock, her gaze fell upon Alex.

Alex was sound asleep in the overstuffed chair directly across from her and her heart warmed as she realized that Alex had chosen that spot so she could keep an eye on her during the night. Jennifer watched in fascination as Alex's chest rose and fell in the relaxed cadence of slumber. Her right arm cradled her head, her fingers curled into her tousled, dark hair. The afghan covered her midsection, but her bare feet and legs were exposed, tangled on the ottoman. Jennifer followed the visible length of them, starting at her painted burgundy toenails and moving slowly upwards. As her eyes caressed Alex's skin, she remembered how Alex's hands had caressed *her* skin the night before. While her gaze slid over Alex's smooth-looking, well-defined calves, her mind replayed the sensation of Alex's strong, sure fingers pressing expertly into her flesh. She vividly recalled her own inability to keep from squirming and the sudden, unexpected dampness of her underwear as Alex massaged her feet and legs.

Jennifer wet her suddenly dry lips as her eyes continued their ardent journey, then stopped abruptly at the hem of a pair of black shorts, the fabric lying across Alex's thigh as effectively as a brick wall. She turned her gaze to the ceiling and blew out a long, frustrated breath.

"Shit," she whispered, simultaneously frightened and aroused by the erotic reaction of her body, caused simply by *looking* at Alex's. "This is not good. Not. Good."

Air. I need air. She needed to clear her head, which—in addition to the dull, throbbing ache—was a whirlwind of too many thoughts.

Noticing Kinsey's leash on the floor by the door, she managed to get both herself and the dog up and out without waking Alex. She slipped her bare feet into Alex's Nikes, which were two sizes too big for her, to protect her from the morning dew, and she and Kinsey headed out into the inviting sunshine.

"So much for the phase theory," she muttered as she and Kinsey strolled through the wet grass. She felt like she'd been smacked with a two-by-four, in more ways than one. Suddenly, there was nothing else to do but admit to herself the true nature of her attraction to Alex. It wasn't admiration, as she'd originally suspected—and hoped. It wasn't the hero worship of somebody who was doing exactly what she wanted in life. It wasn't even simple friendship. It was true that Jennifer was envious of Alex's confidence and that she enjoyed being her friend, but those seemed absolutely miniscule when overshadowed by the *real* truth. She turned her face to the sky, letting the warm sun beat down on her as she absorbed it.

The real truth was that she didn't really want to be Alex's friend. She wanted much, much more than that. She wanted to touch her skin, to measure the smoothness and the temperature of it with her fingertips. She wanted to taste Alex's lips with her own. She wanted to glide her tongue into Alex's mouth and over every inch of her body and she wanted to hear Alex say her name, begging her not to stop...

Jennifer sat down heavily at the end of the dock as her own reality finally started to sink in. She blinked at the water, not really seeing it, and let out a long, slow breath of defeat. As if sensing her state, Kinsey sat quietly next to her, patiently waiting for her next move.

This hasn't happened since Sarah. Jennifer had almost convinced herself that Sarah *had* actually been a phase, a college experiment. Sure, she still looked at women, still thought they were attractive and sexy. She'd even occasionally wondered what it might be like to sleep with a woman again, but for the most part, it had just been a fleeting thing, a passing fancy, an erotic daydream. No woman had ever hit her with the fiery intensity of Sarah. Not in years.

Not until Alex.

"What the hell am I going to do, Kinsey?"

He looked expectantly at her, his ears pricking up as he listened, but he offered no solutions.

She thought about telling Eric. He had known about Sarah, at least after the fact. He'd taken it surprisingly well, finding an acceptable place between his jealousy and his arousal. It helped that she hadn't gone into great emotional detail. He had no idea she'd been totally in love with the woman; Jennifer hadn't told him that. He, like her mother, had assumed she was just experimenting and she'd never corrected him. He'd never felt as threatened as he probably should have.

Back then, she'd told him out of respect, not wanting to taint their friendship or start their marriage off with a lie. Things were different now. Now, she was thinking of telling him out of spite, to cause him pain in retaliation for what he was doing to her. Telling Alex her suspicions the night before had been the first time she'd ever given voice to her husband's infidelity, the first time she'd actually said something out loud. And *now,* she was angry. No, their marriage wasn't perfect; they both knew that. But there was a line that Jennifer always assumed neither of them would cross. As far as she was concerned, he'd crossed it.

Resentment burning hotly through her, she reverted to a childish eye-for-an-eye attitude. He'd crossed the line, why couldn't she? What if she decided what's good for the goose is good for the gander and she began to consciously *look* for somebody? Somebody *not* Eric.

What if I marched right back into that house, took Alex by the hand, led her upstairs to the bedroom, and fucked her brains out? It would only be fair, wouldn't it?

Kinsey's timing couldn't have been better. He pawed gently at her, derailing her train of thought. She shook her head, disgusted with the turn her feelings had taken. She'd never thought of herself as the kind of person who would cheat on her spouse. She'd always been absolutely against such a betrayal, but at that moment, she started to understand that maybe there were actually reasons why people did such a thing. Maybe, when something was missing from a relationship, it only made sense that one half might go looking elsewhere. She wasn't particularly thrilled with that way of thinking, but she had to concede to the logic.

She got to her feet, took another deep lung full of fresh lake air, and then led Kinsey back toward the house. Just as they reached the top step of the deck, the door slid open and they were greeted by a sleepy looking Alex. Her dark hair hung loosely around her shoulders, sleep-tousled and adorable. Jennifer smiled.

"Morning, sleepyhead," she said, trying to avert her eyes as Alex reached above her head and stretched slowly with a yawn. The sleekness of her body proved too big a draw, however, and Jennifer was grateful that Alex had closed her eyes while she flexed, assuring that she wouldn't see Jennifer's as they raked over her.

Alex rubbed her eyes, then focused on her friend. "Have you been up long?"

"Maybe a half hour."

She stepped into Jennifer's space and before Jennifer had any time to react, her warm fingertips gently probed around the injured eye. Jennifer managed to wince only once, instead finding herself reveling in the touch.

"It looks good," Alex finally announced. "A bit black and blue, but the swelling is pretty much gone."

"Is it? I was afraid to look."

"Your face looks as good as it always does, but with a hint of...indigo."

"A splash of color?"

"Exactly."

They laughed for a minute. When they stopped, their eyes met and suddenly, it was as if they were the only two people in the world. Jennifer couldn't have pulled her gaze away if she'd wanted to, which she didn't. She felt so safe in the chocolate brown of Alex's eyes. All sound from the outside world faded; there was only the rushing of blood in her ears. It wasn't until Alex's lips began moving that Jennifer realized she had refocused her gaze on Alex's full mouth. Jennifer blinked several times, swallowing hard.

"I'm sorry. What?" She sincerely hoped her voice didn't sound quite as squeaky as she thought it did.

"The phone. Your phone's ringing."

As if by magic, the shrill, electronic sound beeped through the air. "Oh. I guess I'd better get it."

"Yeah."

She handed Kinsey's leash to Alex and they followed Jennifer inside. She grabbed the phone off the coffee table, catching Alex's grin as she noticed her own shoes on Jennifer's feet.

"Hello?" She smiled sheepishly and stepped out of the sneakers.

"Hi, babe. How're you doing?"

She felt the scowl cross her face at the sound of her husband's voice. "I'd be doing better if you had come to the game last night like I thought you were going to."

As she looked up to meet Alex's gaze, she watched in surprise as the playfulness slid away from her face and it made Jennifer faintly nauseous. Alex reached for her shoes and sat to put them on. Jennifer looked at the sofa cushions.

"I know, honey. I'm sorry. I got stuck. Saunders screwed up his deposition from the other day and we had to get it in this morning. I had no choice. You know how that works." His voice was sincere, heavily laden with an apologetic flavor. "I would have much rather been there with you. You know that." Against her will, Jennifer felt her anger melt like a snowflake in the sun, though she tried hard to hang onto it.

"I know. I just really wanted you to be there. You said you would."

"I said I'd try to be there. I'm sorry, babe. Did you win? How'd you play?"

Jennifer looked up to see Alex backing out the door, Kinsey in tow. Much to her surprise, she panicked. "No, stay. Please?"

"What?" Eric asked, confused.

"I've really got to get home," Alex said, not stopping her departure.

"But I didn't get to thank you," Jennifer whined, then winced at the sound of her own voice.

"Who are you talking to?" Eric asked in bewilderment.

"It was nothing. I'm glad you're feeling better." Alex seemed in such a hurry to leave and Jennifer didn't know how to stop her, short of throwing herself around the woman's ankles. "I'll catch you later, okay?" With that, she snapped the door shut. Jennifer watched her skip down the steps of the deck and head across the yard. She felt an acute sense of loss.

"Jen? Are you there?"

She sighed into the phone. "Yeah, I'm here."

"Who were you talking to?"

"Alex."

"She's over this early?"

"She stayed the night."

"Excuse me?" His tone was playful enough, but the implication was there. Jennifer toyed with the idea of not telling him anything, of letting him think whatever the hell he wanted. Then she decided to be an adult again and sat down to relay the story of the Volleyball Spike from Hell.

* * *

Eric swallowed hard as he set the phone back in its cradle. The worry that had settled in the pit of his stomach threatened to expel the breakfast he'd ordered from room service half an hour before.

He sat heavily on the king size hotel bed and sighed, leaving the ends of his tie dangling from his neck. He leaned his forearms on his knees and hung his head.

Poetic justice? Is that what this was? The fact that he woke up alone didn't take away from the actuality that he'd spent yet another night with a woman not his wife. In turn, she'd spent the night with a lesbian. No, not in the biblical sense—not like him—but spent the night just the same.

Of course, he only knew that because of Dawn. She'd taken great pleasure in warning him about their new neighbor. He shook his head, reproaching himself for ever telling his sister about Jennifer and Sarah in the first place. She'd made it her duty to look out for him by watching his wife like a hawk and he found that she enjoyed it a little too much.

Hadn't it been a phase? Hadn't Sarah simply been an experiment?

Isn't that what some girls do in college?

He'd been clinging to that hope, to that idea, since the first day of their marriage. He had vowed not to stifle her, but he had watched her carefully, paid attention to those with whom she associated. To his surprise, there weren't many. She didn't have a lot of friends, though he never understood why. She was very likable. She was kind and intelligent and witty, but somehow he could only think of a couple women with whom she spent time. She had Kayla and she had Dawn.

And now she had Alex.

The churning in his stomach continued as he scrubbed a hand over his freshly-shaven face. For the first time in years, he allowed himself to actually think the dreaded thought he'd been avoiding for so long.

My marriage is falling apart.

He closed his eyes against the threat of tears.

* * *

"God damn it." Alex tossed Kinsey's leash to the floor, then kicked off her shoes. Violently. "Damn it. Damn it. God fucking damn it." She shook her head in disgust and looked down at her dog. "How do I do this? How do I live for over thirty years and still end up this fucking stupid? Can you clue me in? Because I'm just not getting it." At the tone of her voice, Kinsey's ears went back against his head and he blinked at her, his tail between his legs, wondering what he might have done to make her so angry. She immediately felt guilty and scooped him up in her arms, hugging him tightly and showering him with kisses. "I'm sorry, buddy. I'm not mad at you. I'm mad at me."

She'd done it again. She'd let simple, physical attraction get way out of hand and she'd allowed herself to glimpse at the extra page in the back entitled *What If...*Problem was, there wouldn't be a *What If...*Jennifer was married and Alex might be a lot of things, but a home wrecker wasn't one of them.

"I just couldn't leave well enough alone, could I? I think she's cute and sexy, but I had to go and get to know her." Her voice dripped with reproachful sarcasm. "I had to find out there are other things about her that I like."

She's married, the little voice said.

"I know!" she snapped back.

Jennifer had felt it, too. Standing there on the deck, she'd felt it, too. Alex was sure of it. The electricity. She could see it in Jennifer's face; it was so obvious. She'd looked exactly as Alex had felt. She'd been staring at Alex's mouth and it had taken every ounce of strength Alex had possessed to keep from grabbing her and kissing her senseless right then and there.

"When did this happen?" Alex asked. "How?" She poured herself a glass of orange juice and pondered the question. "Yesterday, she was just my friend. Today, I wanted to kill her husband for having what I want."

Her reaction to the realization that it had been Eric on the phone had surprised her. She'd felt suddenly nauseous and totally exposed, not to mention ever so guilty and ragingly jealous. She'd had trouble breathing and felt she had to get out of there as fast as she possibly could. She knew it was rude, but she didn't think she could stay there in Jennifer's presence for one more minute while she talked to her husband without going completely insane. That feeling had scared the crap out of her.

She's married to him, the voice chimed in again.

"I said I know. Shut up!"

She stormed over to her desk and booted up the computer, determined to channel her anger into something more creative than arguing with herself. She sat down and began to type. She didn't stop for over an hour.

"You should come on over for dinner some night, Paul. Kristen's a great cook. We can shoot the shit and talk corporate politics."

"Sure. That'd be great." Paul didn't think it was possible to say it with any less enthusiasm. He pressed his lips together tightly as he watched them walk back to their own yard and up the back steps, Ray's arm around Kristen like he owned her, like she was a thing and not a person. It made his blood boil.

He returned to the shrub he'd been trimming and hacked at it viciously. Had he ever met anybody as phony as Ray Daniels? He didn't think so. Had he ever met anybody less deserving of somebody like Kristen? No way. Ray had no idea what he had in Kristen. None. Not only was she beautiful, she was smart. She was funny. She was sweet and compassionate. She deserved somebody who would appreciate those qualities. She needed somebody who would take care of her and respect her.

He blinked the sweat from his eyes and continued to work the manual hedge clippers, pretending each piece he severed was some part of Ray Daniels' body.

Kristen deserved so much more. She was special.

"She deserves somebody like me," he muttered, then, with a sigh, dropped the clippers at his feet.

She was married to Ray.

Paul felt a sharp pain of sadness stab through his heart like lightning. Instead of slicing through and out the other side, though, it stayed, settling into the dull ache of unfulfilled desire, unrequited love, and forbidden want.

She was married to Ray. Nothing was going to change that.

He felt sick.

And angry. So angry.

It wasn't fair. It wasn't right and it wasn't fair. He was a good man. He was a good man and it always got him nowhere. He'd be so good to her. Didn't she know that? Couldn't she see that? He'd treat her like a queen. That's what she deserved. Royal treatment. Somebody like Ray had no idea what that was. He wasn't worthy of her. He was nothing but a selfish prick and he certainly didn't warrant a wife like Kristen. The whole pairing was just wrong.

"And I'm going to fix it," he muttered.

Alex nodded with satisfaction as she reread the four pages she'd whipped out. They were good. The story was solid. The characters felt real to her. She cared about them and she knew that was key. She hadn't intended for it to be a suspense novel, but it seemed to be heading in that direction and she was pleasantly surprised.

"Rita's going to love this," she said, feeling the high that only happened after a good session of writing. She set the computer to print what she'd written so far. Glancing at the clock, she picked up the phone and dialed Jackie's back door office number, the one that allowed her to sneak around her friend's secretary. If Jackie was in, she'd answer, as only Alex and Rita used that number.

"Jackie McCall," she answered cheerfully.

"Hey."

"Hiya, Stretch. How's your setter?"

Leave it to Jackie to immediately bring up the one subject Alex preferred to avoid. "She's good. Got a bit of a shiner, but she's fine."

"Damn. I ought to have that little prick thrown right out of the league for messing up *that* face, huh?" Alex's lack of response went unnoticed. "What's up?"

"I was thinking of taking a drive. Can you do lunch?"

"Let me see..." Alex could hear the beeps as Jackie tapped her stylus against her Palm Pilot, checking her schedule. "Yeah, I'm good. 11:45?"

"I'll meet you at Empire. I've got some reading material for Rita."

"She'll be thrilled. See you then."

* * *

It was a sunny day and Sheryl Crow sang about soaking it up as Alex popped the sunroof on her Acura and hopped onto the New York State Thruway for the quick, five-minute ride that would spit her onto 490.

I miss the city, she thought as she sped along, remembering the little house she used to own in the northeast part of downtown Rochester. It was small and the neighbors were close, but there was nothing quite like being five minutes from exactly everything. Theaters, restaurants, stores, gyms, they were all an easy jaunt from her old two-bedroom. She walked Kinsey all over the place. She could meet her friends for happy hour and be home in just a couple minutes. There was a certain sense of connection that came from living downtown and, much as she loved her new life on the water, she still missed that feeling.

Jackie worked at Eastman Kodak's downtown location, so Alex took 490 west all the way in, passing by St. John Fisher College, muttering in disgust at the orange cones that squeezed traffic down to one measly lane for no apparent reason, since there were no workers to be seen. A running, local joke said there were only two seasons in Rochester: winter and construction. *If you're not fighting snow, you're fighting these damn orange cones,* she thought with irritation. She seriously wondered if the highway department closed lanes down just for the hell of it, for no other reason than to annoy her. *If they only knew what a prime candidate I am for road rage, they'd think twice.*

She took the Inner Loop and got off at State Street, scooted behind the WXXI public television building, and parked in the Kodak visitor's lot. She'd need a code to get out and she silently chided herself for not reminding Jackie to grab it on her way over.

The Empire Brewing Company had a prime location. Directly across the street from both Frontier Field and the main office building of Eastman Kodak, it was almost guaranteed a constant clientele, especially during the summer. If not full for lunch, it was sure to catch the crowd on the way in or out of a baseball game.

Alex arrived before noon and her host introduced himself as Jay, asking her where she preferred to sit. He was a small, cheerfully smiling young man with wire rimmed glasses, khakis, a black Empire Brewing Company t-shirt and matching baseball cap. He led her to a table by the window, pulled his pad out of his black waist apron, and wrote down her order for a glass of their home brewed root beer.

From her seat by the window, Alex watched for Jackie, who would simply scoot across the street from her Kodak office. There was no sign of her friend, so she scanned the menu.

The restaurant had an open yet warm feel to it. The high ceilings and the wood, stainless steel, and glass décor lent to the openness. The hardwood floors, chunky wooden chairs, and earth tones supplied the warmth. Large, stainless steel vats were visible through glass walls and a chalkboard listing the choices of their micro-brewed beer available on tap hung from the ceiling. The names were always colorful and creative and Alex smiled at that month's choices: Red Mulligan, Scotch Ale, and Purgatory. Had it not been the lunch hour, she might have ventured to give one a try.

The menu was eclectic with a Cajun flare. Such specialties as Big Easy Gumbo and jumbalaya stood out as favorites, combining with beer foods like sausage, chicken wings, and chili dogs, and accompanied by the most incredible side dish of roasted garlic mashed potatoes Alex had ever had in her life.

Jay returned with a frosty mug and a bottle of root beer.

"Need a few more minutes?"

"She should be here soon," Alex said apologetically.

"No problem. I'll be back."

No sooner had she settled on the Thai Chicken Taco, than she saw Jackie hurrying down the sidewalk across the street. It was always a surprise to Alex when she saw her friend in business attire, especially during the summer. She became so used to Jackie in shorts and t-shirts that the sight of her in black dress slacks and a cream-colored silk blouse was almost a shock. In a matter of minutes, Jackie pulled out the chair across from her and brushed her blonde locks behind her ears, her gold hoop earrings glinting in the sunlight. She looked very professional.

"Hey, Stretch," she greeted with a smile. "To what do I owe this pleasant surprise?"

"I missed your smiling face?" Alex replied, sliding her a menu.

Jackie snorted. "Yeah. Okay."

Jay returned to take Jackie's drink order. As she continued to scan the menu, Alex handed her a manila envelope.

"Here. Before I forget. Give this to Rita. Tell her no hurry, but to hurry up."

Jackie laughed quietly and looked into the envelope, impressed by the stack. "Wow. You've been busy."

"Fifty pages," Alex said proudly. "The juices are flowing, my friend. The juices are flowing."

"Then it looks like we have juice flowage in both our houses." She said it smugly, then returned her eyes to her menu.

Alex furrowed her brow. "Flowage...what?" Jackie's smiling face and glowing eyes gave it away. "Jackie! You got laid!"

Jackie glared at her over the top of the menu. "A little louder, why don't you? I don't think the people on the other side of the bar heard you."

Alex laughed aloud at her friend's expression, which showed that she was more happy than annoyed. "What happened?" She narrowed her gaze. "Tell me you actually talked about the situation and didn't just let your raging hormones take over."

Jay arrived with Jackie's root beer. They placed their orders with him and Alex noticed the restaurant had filled up quite a bit in the time since Jackie had appeared.

"So?" she prodded once Jay had moved along.

"We talked. We talked about it all." Jackie paused for dramatic effect. "And *then* we let our raging hormones take over."

"Details, damn it! Give me details!"

Jackie chuckled, then took a deep breath, trying to decide where to begin. "She started talking about another baby again last night. She was so enthusiastic and so excited about it and I guess I wasn't. She noticed and called me on it, so I just decided I needed to get my concerns out in the open. I thought it was only fair, to both of us."

"Good." Alex nodded. "Good for you. How'd she take it?"

"Better than expected," Jackie answered, a hint of wonder in her voice. "I don't think she was surprised. She said she'd sort of suspected that I felt the way I did and she was worried about that. And she actually apologized to me for not asking me about my feelings sooner."

"Wow."

"Yeah. So, we talked and I brought up all my concerns and laid them all right out on the table."

"All of them?" Alex asked skeptically.

"All of them. I told her that I loved being a parent, that Hannah is the most important thing in our lives, but that I missed my time with her. I told her I missed making love with her and being close with her and that I was afraid that it would only get worse if we had another baby."

"And?"

"She said she understood and she had the same concerns."

"She did?"

"She did. Seems she's been missing our alone time as much as I have, and it's actually a little worse for her because she's with Hannah all day long. I never looked at it from that angle before. At least I get to talk to adults during the day, you know? She's stuck watching *Blue's Clues* and *PB and J Otter* and reading Dr. Seuss." They both chuckled. "We laughed and we cried and we both agreed that we do want to have another child, but only if we make an extra effort to spend time alone, just the two of us. Whether it be setting up a weekly date night or spontaneously dumping Hannah off at my mother's so we can go to Niagara Falls for the weekend, whatever. We both need to spend more time together."

Alex smiled, impressed with her friend having taken the bull by the horns.

"You know what else, Alex? During that whole discussion, I learned something that I think is pretty valuable."

"What's that?"

Her face got serious and Alex knew she was about to tell her something she should pay close attention to, possibly file away for future reference.

"I realized that I love Rita more than anything in the world and that I'm incredibly lucky to have what I do with her. And..." She studied her fingernails, searching for the right words. "Making love with her is very important to me. But...we have so much more than that...and I don't know that it's worth it to jeopardize the whole thing because I think we should be having more sex. Do you understand what I'm saying?"

She looked up at Alex and in all their years of friendship, Alex had never seen her looking so sober. "I think so," she answered honestly.

"You and I have always felt the same way about sex in a relationship and lesbian bed death and all that stuff. I'm saying that maybe...maybe we shouldn't be so worried about it. Don't get me wrong. I don't mean it's not an important issue and I don't mean that it's an okay thing with me. It's just that maybe...maybe when you have something real like Rita and I do, maybe whether you have sex twice a week, twice a month or twice a year doesn't really matter. Maybe we make it a bigger deal than it needs to be. You know?"

Alex was overcome with the strangest sensation that Jackie had truly grown up and she smiled at her friend with great affection, her eyes misting. "Have I mentioned lately how insanely jealous I am of you?"

Jackie smiled a genuinely flattered and grateful smile. "Lately? I don't think so."

"And what did Rita say when you told her your theory about making sex too big a deal? You did share it with her, right?"

"Yes, I did. She said, 'You better believe it's a big deal. When we stop making love, we're roommates and I don't want a roommate. I want a partner and a lover.'"

"Wow. I think I want her."

"Sorry. She's taken."

"So I guess you don't have to worry about it going away completely, huh?"

Jackie breathed a giant sigh of relief. "I cannot begin to tell you how much better I felt after hearing her say that. Jesus."

"I want nothing more in the world than to have what you have with Rita. You two are my role models, you know."

Jackie smiled at her best friend for a long moment. "Somebody's going to be very lucky to land you, Stretch. Very lucky."

As their conversation paused, Jay wandered over with perfect timing and gracefully set down their plates. "Enjoy."

Jackie watched him as he walked away.

"Family?" Alex asked.

"Definitely."

"So, let me ask you," she said around a bite of her taco, her eyes twinkling with mischief. "How are you going to tell your giant libido that sex with Rita isn't as much of a necessity as it thinks?"

Jackie leaned forward and lowered her voice conspiratorially. "It's called a vibrator, sweetie. You should get one."

Alex nearly spewed food across the table as she burst into laughter. "Oh, I've got one, my friend, and believe me, it's getting plenty of use. It's been over a year since Nikki and I broke up. I've got needs, you know."

Jackie chewed on a forkful of her salad. "Speaking of your ex, I think she's gotten herself into a bit of a situation."

"What do you mean, 'a situation'?"

"I'm getting the impression she's less than happy with Diane."

"Shocking."

"Now, now. Let's not get catty."

"I'm not getting catty, Jackie. The woman's a first class bitch who does nothing but boss Nikki around. And Nikki doesn't help the situation by waiting on her hand and foot."

"I know. I'm not saying you're wrong. I'm just saying that I think it might be a little more serious than we think."

Alex stopped chewing. "What's that supposed to mean?"

Jackie sighed. "I mean Nikki wants to get out, but doesn't know how. She's asked for some help. She's afraid."

"Afraid?" She studied Jackie's face. "Do you think Diane hits her?"

"I don't know that," Jackie responded quickly, holding up her hand in a placating gesture. "Let's not jump to conclusions. We don't know for sure and we could be way off base. I haven't been able to get Nikki to admit to it, but if that's the case..."

"I'll fucking kill her." Alex said it with steely determination.

"Relax. I feel the same way, but we can't go flying off the handle. I could be wrong."

"I never liked Diane. From the very start, there was something about her that just didn't sit well with me."

"I know. You made that very clear to all of us." Jackie flashed her a little half-grin.

"Subtlety is not my specialty, is it?"

"Absolutely not."

"So, what do we do?"

"Rita's going to talk with Nikki, see what she can find out. Then, we'll see what the next step is. She wants to get her crap out of Diane's apartment and she's asked if we'd help. I figure you, me, and David should be enough. I'll let you know the details after Rita talks with her."

Alex nodded. Rita was definitely the mother figure and voice of reason in their little clique. If Nikki were going to open up to anybody, it would be her. "Sounds good."

Jackie paused, looking as if she was carefully choosing her next words. "You know, Stretch, Rita and I are aware of the fact that you weren't terribly pleased with us for staying friends with Nikki and inviting her to our parties."

Alex nodded again, not sure how to respond since she was absolutely right.

"She's a good girl, Alex. We know you had your issues and that's why things didn't work, but Nikki's a cool lady. She's sweet, she's kind and she deserves better than Diane."

Alex fought down the childish surge of jealousy that welled up, determined to act like the adult she was. "I know. You're right. I guess I just regressed a bit, back to my junior high persona." She gave Jackie a wry grin. "I just wanted you to hate the same people I hate."

"You don't hate Nikki."

Alex sighed. "No, I don't."

Jackie glanced at her watch. "Shit. It's been fun, doll, but I've got to get back." She motioned across the restaurant, catching Jay's eye and signaling for the check. She waved Alex off as she reached for her wallet. "I've got this one, babe." She tapped the manila envelope. "You're the starving artist. I'm just a Kodak grunt. You get this book published and you can take me to dinner someplace nice. And expensive."

"You've got yourself a deal."

Chapter
Twelve

July arrived in a wave of heat, which was somewhat unusual for that part of New York State. Summer went very quickly in that neck of the woods. During June, one started to get used to the idea of summer. July was when one actually enjoyed it. Then August arrived and one slowly became depressed at the prospect of the end of summer. It was the cycle of nature upstate and though Jennifer had lived there all her life, she never got used to it.

She rarely left her lake house. She spent every night there, with or without Eric, mostly without. She worked nonstop on the interior, slowly making each room into exactly what she wanted. She had never felt such accomplishment. Normally, she would run things like colors and patterns by Eric for his approval, but she'd decided that—given his continued absence—he had forfeited his say. Whether he liked her designs or not made no difference to her. *This house is mine.* The realization was freeing.

Since her acceptance of the true nature of her feelings for Alex, she thought about her constantly, but tried to keep herself from spending inordinate amounts of time with her. She also wondered if these feelings might be mutual, because she got the distinct impression that Alex was avoiding her outside of volleyball. They still played very well together, but the flirtatious banter had come to an abrupt halt. Jennifer had her own suspicions as to why, but she was too chicken to explore them, even in her own head.

That Monday in mid-July was a gorgeous one, hot and sunny with a light breeze...perfect for being outside. The lake was a-buzz with people. Boats, jet skis, kids swimming, people fishing. It was invigorating just to be in the area.

Jennifer wore a white t-shirt over her bathing suit, fully intending to spend the day baking herself in the sun's rays, perfecting what was turning out to be the best tan of her life. She stepped out onto the deck, towel in hand, and closed her eyes, taking a huge breath and absorbing the very essence of the lake. She had no words to describe the peace she felt.

She opened her eyes when she heard Kinsey's muffled bark. He was inside and Alex was outside, which explained his irritation. Jennifer had noticed a few days earlier that Alex had pulled a sporty-looking blue and yellow jet ski out of her boathouse, but it had simply sat untouched until that day. Jennifer studied her. Alex had pulled the machine so it was half on the shore and half in the water, a bright yellow vest on the ground by her feet. She was bent over the vehicle, doing something Jennifer couldn't make out, but assumed Alex was preparing to take it for a spin. She smiled as her mind conjured up an image of the brunette skimming effortlessly over the water, a happy grin on her face and the wind in her hair.

Alex looked up then, catching Jennifer's eye and holding it. Jennifer waved uncertainly, wondering if Alex was aware that she had been staring at her. To Jennifer's relief, Alex waved back with a grin. She stood still for a moment, as if debating something. Then she looked at the jet ski and at the life vest on the ground. She pulled an identical vest from under the seat and held it up enticingly in Jennifer's direction, letting it swing from her finger.

"Want to go for a ride?" she called. It was a perfectly innocent question, but to Jennifer, it was laden with temptation she couldn't refuse. The excitement that surged through her at the sound of those six simple words was obscene.

"I'd love to."

She scrambled off the deck and headed across the yard as Alex bent over the jet ski again. Jennifer tried not to ogle Alex as she approached, but it wasn't easy. Her dark hair was pulled back into a careless ponytail held by a red scrunchie. Her long legs were tanned a deep bronze color, as were her arms, the brown only intensified by the pale yellow tank top that reached to her hips and covered—judging from the quick peek Jennifer stole at Alex's backside—a sleek, black bathing suit.

She looked up as Jennifer approached, her brown eyes sparkling. The summer sun had sprinkled various strands of red into her dark hair and they winked at Jennifer as Alex moved. "Hi there."

"Hey. This your summer toy?"

"It is now. Used to be Aunt Margie's. Came with the house." She swept her hand over the jet ski like a model on *The Price is Right*. "Meet Jessica."

"Jessica? It has a name?"

"She. She has a name," Alex corrected, chuckling. "Two summers ago, my friends Lynda and Anne decided she needed a name. Like a boat."

"But...Jessica? Is that an ex or something?" Jennifer teased with a smile.

Alex shook her head. "I don't know where or why they came

up with it, but it stuck. She's been Jessica ever since. Here." She handed Jennifer one of the life vests. Then Jennifer watched with a dry mouth and wide eyes as Alex, her back to Jennifer, pulled the yellow tank top over her head. Her bathing suit was indeed sleek and black as expected, a one-piece that hugged her body and caressed her curves like a lover, then dipped teasingly low in the back. Jennifer's mouth ceased being dry, and filled in anticipation at the thought of tasting such unblemished skin while sliding the palms of her hands down the strong planes of Alex's back. She stood there gaping like a fifteen-year-old boy until Alex turned back to face her. "Okay, come here. You're driving."

Jennifer blinked, the words knocking her abruptly out of her little fantasy world. Alex was in the water, pushing the jet ski away from the shore. "I'm what?"

"You're driving."

"But, I don't know how."

"It's a piece of cake. Put that life vest on and I'll teach you."

At that moment, Jennifer was made fully aware of the old phrase "tit for tat," a lesson that made her understand Alex had been well aware of her staring. In retaliation, Alex waited patiently for her to don her own life vest, never once looking away. As she pulled her t-shirt off, Jennifer could feel Alex's eyes on her almost as intensely as if they'd been her hands. She knew her dark green bikini left very little to the imagination and her hands trembled slightly as she pulled on the vest and tried to work the clips, feeling as exposed as if she'd been completely naked in front of her friend.

She waded into the water after Alex, keeping her eyes downcast, hoping her face wasn't nearly as flushed as it felt. She thanked God for the chilly temperature of the water, wincing when it reached her thighs.

"Here, let me tighten this up or you're going to lose it." Suddenly Alex was very much in her space, tugging at the straps on the vest. "I think Jackie wore this last," she said, but Jennifer barely heard her. She was too busy looking down, focusing on Alex's hands, on the long, tapered fingers; the smoothly filed nails and the intricate blue veins crisscrossing the backs. She marveled at how they could look so strong and so feminine at the same time. "Okay." Alex's voice brought her back to attention. "Very simple." She clipped a long, spiral cord to Jennifer's vest, a key dangling from the end. "This is so if you fall off, the key pops out and the jet ski just stops instead of scooting away without you. Hop on."

"You're coming with me, right?"

"You can drive it, Jennifer. It's easy. You don't need me."

"Yes, I do." Her tone was a bit more pleading than she'd intended, but she was painfully aware of the dual meaning of the words. Alex blinked at her. "Please?" she added softly.

Alex swallowed and held Jennifer's gaze. Then she nodded and laughed. "All right. But if you dump me, I'll kill you."

"No dumping. Not intentionally, anyway. I promise."

Alex helped Jennifer climb aboard and she used the handlebars to scoot forward and make room for Alex behind her. It was like sitting on a motorcycle, surprisingly comfortable. Alex spun the machine so she was directly behind it, then easily slid on from the tail end, though Jennifer detected more than one grunt during the process and raised her eyebrows in a teasing manner.

"I cannot tell you how long it took me to learn how to do that. It's really hard to get on from the water without somebody to steady it."

She slid up behind Jennifer, who found herself barely able to concentrate on any words from that point forward. Alex's mouth was so close to her ear, it sent an erotic shiver down her spine. "Okay, like I said, very simple. The key starts the engine. This lever here controls the gas and thereby, your speed."

Jennifer tried her best to remain in control during such sweet torture. She was hyper-aware of Alex's body pressed to her back and she thanked her lucky stars they were both wearing life vests; she was sure the feeling of Alex's breasts tight against her back would be her complete undoing. As it was, Alex's thighs were burning against hers. Alex reached around her, inserted the key, and helped Jennifer with the throttle. The vehicle jerked forward, jerking both women with it. Jennifer laughed nervously.

"It's okay," Alex said. "You'll get a feel for it. Try again."

She was right. In a matter of minutes, they were cruising along the lake at a nice, easy pace. Jennifer gradually became more comfortable and increasingly aware of Alex's palm resting against her bare stomach—*under* her life vest. It was hard to explain the safety and protection Jennifer felt with Alex's body pressed up against hers, so rather than wrestle with it, she decided to enjoy the feeling. The roaring of the motor made conversation difficult and for that, she was grateful. She didn't want to talk; she only wanted to feel. She hardly noticed any of the other people on the lake. Every so often, Alex would point something out to her, leaning in closer and speaking directly into her ear so she could hear. Jennifer had no idea about anything that was said and it was all she could do to keep from driving them into somebody's pier.

Though she did speed up a few times, she mostly kept them at a comfortable cruising rate. It wasn't really necessary for Alex to hold onto her, but it warmed her heart—and tingled other parts of her body—to note that Alex kept an arm wrapped securely around her midsection for the entire ride. At one point, Alex's other hand dropped onto Jennifer's thigh after pointing out a particularly spectacular house. Jennifer inhaled sharply at the contact, hoping Alex hadn't felt it. The hand remained for several minutes until Alex realized it and jerked it away as if Jennifer's skin had burned her. Jennifer suppressed a grin at the idea that maybe Alex was as affected by their closeness as she.

They had literally circled the lake three times before Jennifer noticed the gas gauge approaching "E." Trying to stave off her disappointment, she headed them home.

There was one more lesson in her class that day: stopping. As she found out, halting a jet ski in a precise location was not an easy task.

"There aren't any brakes, so just aim it where you want to end up and ease off the throttle," Alex explained. The idea was to coast there without much speed, but they were moving too quickly.

"Whoa..." was all Jennifer could manage.

They were heading directly for shore and Jennifer cringed as the inevitable scraping sound of the bottom of the craft filled her head. Alex reached around her and jerked the handlebars sharply to the left, effectively halting their progress while throwing both of them into the water.

They sputtered and laughed, the water not deep enough to cover them, but certainly deep enough for them to notice that it was quite cold.

"Wow!" Alex exclaimed, coughing and laughing at the same time. "That'll wake you up, huh?" She pushed her now-wet bangs out of her face.

"Jesus, does this water ever get warm?"

"Not terribly. Not until late August, if we've had a hot summer."

Jennifer watched as Alex fastened the jet ski to the dock. "Thanks, Alex."

"For what?"

"The ride. The tour. Everything. It was great."

"We'll have to do it again so you can work on your landing."

Jennifer smiled sheepishly. "Yeah. Sorry about that."

"Hey, don't sweat it. See this?" She pointed to a spot on the dock that was seemingly missing a large chunk of wood. "This is the result of my first landing."

Jennifer burst into laughter. "Now I don't feel so bad."

"Good."

A deep, male voice interrupted them before the conversation could continue. "There you are, Jennifer."

Daniel Wainwright, Eric's father, stood on Jennifer's dock. He looked very professional, but uncomfortably out of place in his business suit and black wingtips. Jennifer was more than a little surprised to see him, especially in the middle of the day. She hurried out of the water as he came around to meet her, and she was suddenly aware of the fact that she had no towel and wore very little clothing. She decided Alex wouldn't mind if she held onto the life vest for a while.

"Daniel," she said by way of greeting as she reached him. "What a nice surprise."

"Your doors were unlocked, but you were nowhere in sight. I was beginning to worry." His voice carried genuine concern and she was touched.

"I'm sorry. I went for an impromptu tour of the lake with my neighbor." She moved her arm in an inclusive gesture toward Alex, who had followed her out of the water after tying the jet ski to the dock. "Alex Foster, this is my father-in-law, Daniel Wainwright."

"Pleased to meet you, Mr. Wainwright," Alex said, shaking his hand politely.

"Ms. Foster." His eyes registered something akin to recognition and Jennifer wondered if they'd met before.

"And to what do I owe this unexpected visit?" Jennifer asked lightly. Unlike that of his wife, she never minded Daniel's company. He was always kind and sincere.

"I was wondering if I could talk to you about something."

She furrowed her brow at his serious tone. "Of course."

Alex took that as her cue. "I've got to get inside. It was nice to meet you, sir."

"Likewise," he replied with a guarded smile.

"Thanks for the ride, Alex. I'll see you later, okay?"

She nodded and was gone. Jennifer led Daniel into the house, then excused herself to run upstairs and quickly exchange the life vest for a t-shirt and a pair of red shorts. It was very odd to have him show up unexpectedly, not to mention his desire to "talk." Jennifer wouldn't call their relationship close, but she'd always respected him. She wasn't sure what to think.

When she returned to the living room, he was standing in front of the windows. "Can I get you a drink? I made some iced tea this morning."

"I'd love some. This is a fantastic view," he commented, then looked around. "You've done a nice job with the place, Jennifer. It looks a thousand times better than when you first bought it. I'm impressed."

She was caught off guard by the compliment, but took it in stride as she handed him a glass. Eric had barely noticed all her work and he supposedly shared the house with her. "Thank you. It's getting there." She watched him fidget slightly, something very uncharacteristic of him. "Is there something wrong, Daniel? Is something bothering you?"

He sighed heavily and sat in the overstuffed chair. "I need to talk to you about Eric."

"Okay," she responded, worry tinting her voice.

"And I need you to be honest with me."

She swallowed, feeling uneasy. "All right."

He took a long drink of his tea and carefully set it on a coaster on the end table. Then he studied his hands as if looking for the right place to begin. "Eric's been...rather tense lately at the office. Have you noticed that about him?"

Jennifer nodded, choosing her words carefully. "He's definitely been under a lot of pressure. I don't really see him that often, what with him spending so much time in Buffalo, but when he is here, I do notice that he seems pretty stressed."

"I thought so, too. That's why I lightened his load considerably." He held her gaze for several seconds as if trying to convey something to her without actually saying it. "I was afraid I'd dumped too much on him, so I pulled back a bit."

Jennifer studied her own feet for several minutes, waiting for the tears that had filled her eyes to wane. Daniel had pretty much confirmed her suspicions. *He's lightened Eric's load? He's pulled back a bit on the amount of work he's given his son? Then why was Eric never home?* She knew why. She'd known why for a long time.

"When that didn't seem to help," Daniel went on, "I started thinking." He paused and Jennifer took the time to really study his face. Daniel was a handsome man, distinguished and debonair, and aging amazingly well. His silver hair was thick and his face rugged, but not haggard. His green eyes, so like Dawn's, normally twinkled with merriment. Instead, they were dull. There were lines on his face, lines she hadn't noticed before. He looked older. And worried.

"Thinking about what?"

"Jennifer, do you think Eric really wants to run the firm? I know this is what I've been grooming him for, ever since he graduated, but now I'm not so sure it's the right thing to do. For him."

She hesitated, her loyalties to her husband warring with her desire to be honest with her father-in-law.

He held up a hand, palm toward Jennifer. "I know this is a very awkward and unfair position for you. I'd never normally ask you to betray his confidence." He looked at the floor. "I'm just not sure who else to ask."

"Have you tried talking to Eric?" she asked softly.

He smiled a knowing smile and Jennifer was sure she saw a flash of pride in his eyes. "I had a feeling that's what you'd say. Honestly, though? I don't know whether he'd tell me the truth or what he thinks I want to hear."

He had a very strong point. She tried to put herself in Eric's shoes. She really wasn't sure what she would have done, how she would have answered. The fear of disappointing her parents—her father especially—was always such a huge burden and she'd carried it from her childhood into her adult life. She knew Eric felt the same way and she was suddenly angry with both herself and her husband for never being able to overcome that stigma.

She took a deep breath. "Eric has never said in so many words that he doesn't want to run the firm. Not to me."

"I sense a 'but' in there."

She nodded. "But..." She hesitated for a long moment. "I think it would be too much for him. I don't think he'd be happy. This, of course, is simply *my* opinion." She snapped her mouth shut before she spilled any more information, glad to have it on the table, but not sure she'd done the right thing by analyzing her husband's feelings without asking him flat out how he felt. In the back of her mind, she also questioned her own motivation for doing so. The possibilities frightened her.

Daniel pressed his lips together. Jennifer got the impression that he was not at all surprised by what she'd told him. He took a long, final swig of his tea and stood. "Thank you, Jennifer. Thank you for being honest with me." He sighed in resignation. "I just want my boy to be happy. I don't think he knows that."

"Maybe you should tell him some time."

"Maybe I should." He smiled grimly at her. "Thanks for the tea."

She watched him drive away, wondering what had spurred him to come to her in the first place and suffering from the niggling feeling that she may have just opened Pandora's Box.

Chapter
Thirteen

"I think that's it." Nikki's voice shook slightly as she handed a box to Jackie, who took it down to David and his waiting SUV. She wiped her clammy hands on the legs of her shorts; terrified that Diane would come home before the lot of them were gone. True, she felt much stronger with her friends supporting her, but she knew Diane didn't understand and just the thought of having to explain yet again why she was leaving was almost too much to bear.

"You're sure?" Alex stood next to her.

"I think so."

"What about this?" Alex picked up a small cactus in a purple pot, a knowing grin crossing over her face. "Isn't this yours?"

Nikki smiled back—her first since they'd arrived there—and took the plant from Alex's hand. "You know it is. You bought it for me."

"I'm glad to see you didn't kill it in retaliation."

"It's not the plant's fault you were an idiot."

"True enough." The playful tone of Nikki's voice took the sting out of the comment, but Alex still felt a flush of guilt. They stood quietly together. "Well. This is a little weird, huh?"

Nikki chuckled. "What, my ex helping me leave my girlfriend? That's just typical lesbian behavior, isn't it?"

Alex's laughter died in her throat as she turned to the front door and saw Diane standing there.

"What the hell is this?" she asked, clearly aware of what it was.

Nikki turned white as a sheet. "Diane."

"What the hell is going on, Nick?"

Alex was relieved to see both Jackie and David appear in the hall behind Diane. They were hanging back out of respect, knowing Diane and Nikki needed to have it out, but they could be inside in a flash should things get ugly.

"I'm leaving." Nikki's voice was barely audible and she studied her feet as she spoke.

"No, you're not." Diane's eyes flashed and she blinked repeatedly. It was a bit unnerving and Alex—who had been thinking about slipping out the door—decided she'd stay nearby.

"Yes, Diane. I am."

"But..."

"It's been coming for a long time. You know that."

Diane's eyes filled with tears. "Why? I don't understand. Why?" Her voice broke.

Nikki's shoulders slumped further and she covered her face with her hands in frustration. "God, Diane. We've been over this a hundred times. Why don't you ever listen to me when I talk?"

"I'm sorry. You're right." Diane spoke quickly, reaching toward Nikki. "You're right. I'll listen. I promise. I'll be better. I can be better."

Nikki shook her head. "No. No, you won't. You don't even try."

"I will. I'll try." Diane's voice cracked with desperation. "I promise I'll try."

Nikki looked like she might be sick right there on the floor. This was the Diane she'd fallen in love with. This woman, pleading with her, was the one who seemed to have disappeared. "I can't do this any more," she said softly. "I can't."

"I get it," Diane said frantically. "I get it. Okay? I do. You made your point. You've scared me. I hear you. I can change. I'll fix it. I can change."

Nikki's voice was scarcely a whisper. "No, you can't."

Alex watched the change on Diane's face in horrified fascination. She went from pathetic pleading to steely anger in a matter of seconds, her eyes hardening, her nostrils flaring slightly. When she spoke, it was a low, menacing growl.

"You ungrateful little bitch."

Nikki's head snapped up in recognition and dread. *This* was the woman she was leaving.

"Come on, Nikki," Alex said hurriedly, reaching out for her friend's arm. "Let's go."

"And who the fuck do you think *you* are?" Diane spat at Alex. "It's not enough you broke her heart once, now you've got to wreck what she's got with me?"

"I don't think I'm the one doing the wrecking."

"Alex has nothing to do with this, Diane. You know that." Nikki was visibly shaking.

Diane's laugh was chilling and her voice was a venomous sneer. "You think I don't know you've never quite gotten over her? You were nothing but her throwaway when I met you. You were pathetic." She spat the word with disgust at Nikki, who flinched as though she'd been slapped and tried to swallow down the pain of the words. "I took you in. *I* loved you after *she* destroyed you." She poked a finger in Alex's direction. "And this is the thanks I get? This is my repayment? You leave *with her*? How long has this been going on, you fucking tramp?"

Alex had had enough. After months of putting up with Diane for the sake of everybody else, after endless occasions where she'd simply bitten her tongue or stifled a remark, she'd had enough. "Oh, for Christ's sake, Diane. Get the hell over yourself, would you? She's not leaving *with me*. She's leaving *you*. Why don't you try to get that through your thick, self-absorbed skull, huh?" She tugged at Nikki's arm. "Come on, Nick. Time to go."

Diane's eye twitched once as she glared at Alex. "Good luck trying to pry her knees apart." She reached out as she spoke and shoved Nikki viciously toward Alex. "Go, you frigid little cunt." Nikki stumbled as she tried to keep her balance and the cactus slipped from her grasp, crashing loudly to the hardwood floor and shattering into several pieces, dirt flying everywhere.

Alex felt the rush of anger wash over her like a tsunami. "Don't you touch her, you psychotic bitch! Don't you *ever* lay a hand on her again, you hear me?"

David was through the door in just enough time to place his bulk between the two as Alex hurled herself at Diane, the latter egging her on. The expletives that flew from their lips made even David raise his eyebrows in surprise as he towered over the two of them, keeping them apart with a hand on each.

Jackie rushed to Nikki's side, protectively placed an arm around her shoulders, and escorted her out the door.

"Back off, Diane," David said, fire flashing in his normally kind eyes. "I have a rule about hitting women, but I'll gladly make an exception for you." He physically directed Alex to the door. "Let's go, Alex. Come on."

"Fuck you," Diane spat, her face flushed an angry red. "Fuck all of you!"

Alex pointed at her as David pushed her through the doorway. "This is *your* fault. *You* blew it. Remember that while you're cursing us. You're nothing but a coward and you have no idea what you had. Not a clue."

* * *

The interior of David's SUV was quiet as they drove. The back was full of what few possessions Nikki had chosen to keep with her when she moved in with Diane. The rest of her stuff was in storage. The foursome sat in silence as they cruised out of the city and headed east. Jackie was in the passenger seat staring out the window. Nikki and Alex sat in the back, Alex's arm wrapped comfortingly around her ex's shoulders. Nikki's head rested against Alex. Her sobs had subsided, silent tears running down her cheeks instead. Alex's heart hurt for her.

As Alex gazed out at the scenery passing by, she thought about relationships. Seeing one fall apart before her eyes—be it her own or somebody else's—always made her stop and try to put her own feelings into perspective. She considered herself a fairly cautious person and she often wondered if she was too cautious. Nikki tended to be the opposite; she jumped right in with both feet, always had, always would, and she knew it. She had told Alex once that she didn't know how to do it any other way. She'd said that life was too damn short to be guarded about everything. She'd admitted that she'd been burned—painfully—by this philosophy more than once and she was sure she'd be burned again, but it had been worth it every single time. When she sniffled from her place on Alex's shoulder, Alex wondered if she still felt the same way.

As they drove, Alex found her thoughts turning to Jennifer, something that seemed to be happening often. She wondered if Jennifer considered herself to be the look-before-you-leap type or if she just leapt. She wondered about being careful and if there had actually been times when she'd let a good thing slip away or pass her by because she'd been too busy taking precautions. The thought made her uneasy and she tightened her grip on Nikki, who lifted her head and took a deep breath.

"Thanks, you guys," she said, breaking the silence. "Sorry about the mess. She's never home early from the gym. Just my luck, huh?"

David chuckled. "No problem, Nick. I find a helping of good, old-fashioned dyke drama every so often is good for me. Reminds me how much less stressful it is to be a gay man, to just fuck whomever I want and be on my way. None of this emotional attachment bullshit."

They all knew David and they all knew he was speaking completely tongue-in-cheek. Jackie and Alex laughed. Nikki said, "I do wonder if that's the way to do it."

"The casual sex thing?" Alex asked. Nikki nodded. "I never could do it. Always wanted to be able to, but I could never bring myself to sleep with somebody I didn't care a lot about. And once I slept with them, I was hooked."

"Same here," Nikki said.

"Same here," Jackie added.

"Same here," David chimed in and they all laughed.

"So, Mr. Fuck 'Em and Leave 'Em is actually your stage name?" Nikki teased.

"I'm afraid so," he admitted. "I'm a hopeless romantic. I should have been a dyke."

"In your dreams, baby," Alex said, grinning at his reflection in the rearview mirror.

"You're sure Rita doesn't mind if I crash with you guys until my new place is ready?" Nikki asked Jackie.

"Honey, it was Rita's idea. I sure as hell don't want you there." Jackie's eyes twinkled as she tried to cheer Nikki up by taunting her.

"A glass of wine and Rita's cooking and you'll be a new woman," Alex assured her.

"I promise it won't be more than a few days," Nikki said quickly, still concerned about being an imposition. "The landlord said early next week."

Jackie reached back and grasped Nikki's chin in her hand. "Sweetie. It's okay. You're welcome at our place as long as you need to stay. Okay?"

Nikki smiled gratefully. "Okay. Thanks."

Jackie's gaze shifted to Alex. "Before I forget, Rita wants you to come by for drinks next week some time. She wants to talk about the book so far."

Alex's heart jumped. "Great. Let me know what night works best." Her nerves went on red alert; she always got incredibly nervous before receiving feedback from Rita—mostly because she was painfully honest. She had the power to send Alex's ego soaring like an eagle in flight or she could crush it like a bug beneath her heel.

"And how is the book?" Nikki asked.

"Yeah," David piped in. "Am I in it?"

"Not yet, but it's still early," Alex replied, a slight blush tinting her cheeks. "It's moving along nicely, though. More smoothly than I expected."

"You must have been *inspired*," Jackie said, winking.

Alex glared at her. "The publisher that bought my short story last fall is interested in seeing it when it's finished."

Nikki squeezed her shoulder, smiling proudly. "Alex, that's fantastic!"

"Yeah, well, I have to get it done first."

"You will."

Nikki had always been very supportive of Alex's love of writing when they'd been together and it touched Alex that it still seemed to ring true. She wanted to say a number of things to her ex-girlfriend, things about how stupid Diane had been to let her go, about how lucky she'd make her next partner. None of it seemed appropriate, though, given her status as somebody who'd left. Instead, she simply smiled and said, "Thanks, Nikki."

Nikki grinned back at her as they drove on.

* * *

Jennifer had spent most of the day soaking up the sun's rays and trying to relax. Her mind had been a whirlwind for several days. It had been a week since her conversation with her father-in-law, as well as her invigorating and arousing tour of the lake with Alex. Thoughts of the two events, along with thoughts of Eric and of Sarah, had all jumbled into a giant potpourri in her mind and she couldn't seem to get any of them to leave her alone. She was exhausted and she wished more than once that she could just turn her brain off like any household appliance, simply to have a little peace and quiet.

She'd tried to wash away some of her anxiety—along with the combination of sweat and sunscreen on her skin—with an early evening shower. As she stepped out, she heard her own voice on the answering machine in the kitchen. She swore softly, wrapped her dripping body in a thick, purple towel and tried to get to the phone next to the bed. The machine beeped just as she picked up the extension and she swore again as the dial tone assaulted her damp ear.

She padded back to the bathroom and finished drying. Tossing on a pair of black cotton shorts and a white, long sleeve t-shirt, she shivered involuntarily, having gotten a bit too much sun. She was chilly, despite the temperature still being in the seventies, and she rubbed her arms vigorously as she headed downstairs to play the message on her answering machine.

"Hi, Jen, it's me. I've still got a stack of stuff to work on, so I think I'm going to just crash here tonight." Eric had left for Buffalo that morning after being at the lake house with her for less than half a day. "The battery in my cell phone is about to croak and as soon as I hang up, I'm going to put it in the charger. So if you have trouble getting me, that's probably why. I should be back some time tomorrow and I'll try not to make it such a late night, okay? Have a good one, babe." The machine clicked to a stop.

Jennifer stood looking at the wall for a long time. "Liar," she muttered softly. The thing that surprised her most was her complete lack of anger, the missing indignation, and she realized that she needed to examine that very thing thoroughly. She should be furious. She was ninety-nine point nine percent sure her husband was being unfaithful and she didn't really seem to be concerned. He was constantly away and consistently sleeping away from home. They spent more nights apart than they did together, yet she never got upset with him or called him on any of it.

What the hell is wrong with me? she thought, horrified. *What kind of wife am I?*

The answer came immediately, clear as a bell, and the weight of it dumped her into the overstuffed chair forcing the breath from her lungs in a heavy sigh.

"The kind that doesn't want to be married," she said.

The thought was a lot to absorb, despite its simplicity. She shouldn't have been surprised, but she was...if not by the answer itself, then by the fact that it had taken her so long to accept the idea. Obviously, Eric was having concerns of his own about their marriage, given the fact that he would rather sleep elsewhere. It was depressing and sad—not so much the state they were in, but the fact that they'd let it go so far and neither one of them had said a thing to the other.

"Welcome to the Land of No Communication." She rubbed her forehead, trying to slow the typhoon of thoughts flying in circles in her brain.

She wondered if Eric had been feeling as trapped as she had. At that moment, she knew they needed to sit down and have a talk. She knew it was the only way to alleviate the stress they'd each been under, but it wasn't a comforting thought. Rather, it made her uneasy. She stared off into space for what might have been minutes or hours; she wasn't sure.

When she finally realized she was having trouble seeing, that dusk had fallen and she hadn't noticed, she decided she needed a pick-me-up. She wanted to talk to somebody, to be around people who'd make her laugh and tell her that she was okay. She stood and peered out the back window, noting with a smile of relief and anticipation that Alex's lights were on.

Jennifer was surprised at how a person could become instantly comfortable with another—that it could happen without either one even noticing. She'd only known Alex for a couple of months, but she thought nothing of popping in on her unannounced. There were not a lot of people with whom she'd feel okay about doing that, and she'd be irritated at most people for doing it to her, but she felt that her connection to Alex was different. She knew without a doubt that Alex would be just as happy to see her as she'd be to see Alex.

She had a nice bottle of Chardonnay chilling in the fridge. She quickly cut up some sharp cheddar cheese and tossed it into a Tupperware bowl, along with some stoned wheat crackers. Then she scooped up the bowl and the bottle and headed next door.

Alex saw her coming through the sliding glass door and smiled and waved. Being the one to make her smile was something Jennifer found absurdly pleasing and she grinned back at her, holding up the wine bottle. Alex scooped Kinsey up in her arms and opened the door.

"Hi, you," she said happily.

"I come bearing gifts."

"I see that. Come in. All gift-bearers are welcome here, especially those bringing food and wine. Kinsey and I were just going to sit on the deck and relax. Care to join us?"

"I'd love to." Jennifer entered, seeing papers scattered across the desk in the living room. "I didn't interrupt your writing, did I?"

Alex waved her off. "Nah. I was done for the night, anyway. My brain's fried."

Jennifer hoped her relief wasn't too visible. "Well then, why don't you and Kinsey go out and get comfortable? I'll open the wine and bring out the munchies. Okay?"

Alex's sparkling brown eyes held Jennifer's gaze for a few seconds. Jennifer could feel her heart beat in the pit of her stomach.

"Yes, ma'am," Alex said softly.

This must be what they mean when they say two people have chemistry, Jennifer thought with a slight shake of her head. The buzzing in her ears was a bit distracting.

She poured two glasses of wine, then found a small plate without a problem and arranged the chunks of cheese on it, fanned by the crackers. Turning out the inside lights, she headed out onto the deck.

A thick, squat candle was burning in the center of the glass table. Alex was stretched out on the lounge, her long, tanned legs crossed at the ankle, Kinsey sitting next to her knee and tethered to the chair. She looked amazingly comfortable in her sleeveless, button-down shirt and cargo shorts and Jennifer tried hard not to stare at her exposed shoulders, simultaneously grateful for and cursing the lack of light. Alex had moved one of the small tables next to the lounge, along with a chair for her neighbor. Jennifer handed her a glass, set her own glass and the cheese on the table, and made herself comfortable, propping her bare feet up on the end of Alex's lounge, very close to her calves.

The night was gorgeous. The breeze was warm and blew gently off the water, the soft lapping sounds soothing and relaxing.

Alex sighed in contentment. "It's totally impossible to be stressed on a night like this."

"I would think this would be the perfect place to live if you're a busy corporate executive or something," Jennifer said thoughtfully. "If you're job is nothing but stress all day long, this would be the place to unwind, I'd imagine."

"Well, what does Eric think? His job's pretty stressful, right?"

"Yeah..." She let her voice drift off into the night air.

"I'm sorry," Alex said softly. "Sore subject, huh?"

Jennifer took a deep breath and let it out slowly. "Alex? Have you ever done something you realized later that you never should have done? And you sort of knew it at the time, too, but you were too chicken to make the right decision? So you just did what was expected of you?" She waited for a few moments before looking at Alex.

Alex's eyes were focused on her and she smiled sadly. "Oh, yeah. I know exactly what you mean."

"Do you?"

Alex looked at her for such a long time, so intently, that Jennifer could *feel* it despite the growing darkness. She seemed to hold some sort of internal debate, then sighed and leaned her head back against the chair. "My mother outed me at the school where I taught."

Jennifer was incredulous. "Your *mother*?"

"Yep."

"Wow. Ouch."

"That's an understatement. My point, though, is that I left my job without even trying to fight. Like a coward."

Her voice was self-deprecating and Jennifer was caught completely off-guard by the confession. Alex didn't seem like the kind of person to walk away from a battle. "Why didn't you fight?"

"At the time, I told myself it was because I was afraid. School faculties have the most rapid grapevines you've ever seen and everybody knew in a very short span of time, even a lot of the parents."

"Oh, Alex. That must have been awful for you. Anybody would have been afraid in that position. With no support, what could you do?"

"That's just it. I had support. My principal was the greatest guy in the world. He said he had no intention of letting me go. The people opposed to my being there were loud, but the group I had supporting me was bigger. I think I could have stayed without a problem."

"But...why'd you leave?"

"Because of my mother."

"I don't understand."

"Yes, you do. Didn't you say to me when we were first getting to know each other that your parents were almost more excited about your wedding than you and Eric were? Because they wanted you to get married so badly?"

"Yes."

"Well, my mother obviously thought I shouldn't be teaching. So I was a good little girl and did like mommy wanted."

"What happened...exactly?" Jennifer couldn't help but flash back to Dawn's explanation of why Alex left her position and she suddenly wanted more than anything to hear Alex's side of the story.

Alex sighed tiredly, as if she'd told the story a thousand times. "I had a student—a female student—whom I suspect was grappling with her sexuality. She'd sent me a couple of poems. They were by no means explicit or erotic, but they were pretty obviously love poems. I had mentioned them to my mother, but I never told her they were from a girl. I had them in my apartment on my desk because I'd been trying to figure out what course of action to take when my mother stopped in for an unexpected visit. I went into the kitchen for a minute and didn't notice that she'd taken the poems with her when she left. Apparently, she'd seen them addressed to "Ms. Foster" and signed with a girl's name and decided to take matters into her own hands without even talking to me.

"The next day, she turned them in to the school. If she'd just gone to my principal, things would have been kept quiet, but she didn't. Instead, she had an in-depth discussion about them with the three administrative assistants in the district office. It just snowballed from there and everything was blown out of proportion. Ten different versions of the situation circulated, mostly ones that colored me as having an affair with my student." She snorted in disgust. "Please. My students were fourteen and fifteen years old. How sick would I have to be?"

"So, *your* mother was the parent who turned in the poems."

"Yeah." Alex gave Jennifer a suspicious look. "You've heard the rumors, too, I assume?"

Jennifer grimaced with guilt. "Dawn made a comment that day she and Kayla visited and met you. Her kids go to your school."

"Ah." Alex nodded. "That's why she kept looking at me funny."

They sat in silence for a long while, sipping their wine and looking out onto the water.

"Alex, could you still get your job back? If you wanted to, I mean."

Alex blinked in surprise. "I don't know; I never really thought about it. Maybe."

"Mm." They were silent again. Then Jennifer got up to retrieve the bottle of wine from inside. Kinsey got up, too, and Alex untied him and handed him off to Jennifer without a word. She took him inside with her just as if she'd done so a million times, as if he was her dog, too, and they all lived together. The Westie immediately curled up on the couch and Jennifer lovingly scratched his head before returning to the deck with the wine. She refilled both glasses. "I think you and I need to make a pact."

"What kind of pact?"

"From this point on, we do what *we* thing we should do. Not what our mothers think. Not what our friends think. What *we* think."

"In what types of situations?"

"In all types. Every type."

"Every type?"

"Mm hmm."

"That's a lot."

"Yup."

Alex stared out onto the water, looking pensive. When she looked back at Jennifer, there was a sparkle in her eyes reflecting the moonlight and the almost indiscernible flickering of the candle. When she smiled, Jennifer's heart melted right into her knees. Alex held up her glass. "To exercising our own free will."

They clinked glasses and sipped.

The breeze kicked up a bit and Jennifer shivered involuntarily. It didn't escape Alex's notice. "Cold?"

A sheepish smile crossed Jennifer's face. "I caught a few too many rays today."

"Come here." Alex said it without thinking. She set her glass down, sat up, and opened her arms and legs to make room on the lounge.

Warning flags popped up all over the place, but Jennifer refused to acknowledge their existence. It took all of three seconds for her body to veto her brain and make the move to the chair. Her head screamed at her in alarm, but her body moved of its own accord, settling comfortably in front of Alex. When Alex gently pulled her back against her, Jennifer couldn't hold in the sigh of contentment.

They sat quietly for a long time, just listening to the wind blow and the waves lap and the occasional boat hum slowly by, the red and green lights the only other proof of its presence. Jennifer couldn't recall ever having felt quite so comfortable in her entire life. At the same time, though, she felt totally and utterly alive, as if every nerve ending in her body was standing at attention and her nervous system could short circuit at any moment. It was delicious and unpredictable and she never wanted the night to end. Ever.

Alex's bare legs were warm and much longer than Jennifer's. Their knees were bent, Alex's legs surrounding Jennifer's lower body, keeping her safely on the lounge. When she wrapped her arms around Jennifer, the smaller woman felt like she was in a giant cocoon, protected and cared for.

"Better?" Alex asked, her lips so dangerously close to Jennifer's ear that she felt an immediate surge in her belly.

"Much." Jennifer's voice was so low it cracked. Alex's chin

rested on her right shoulder and Jennifer turned to look into her eyes. That small movement proved to be her absolute undoing. Alex's face was flushed, her eyes dark, her lips moist. Jennifer could feel the heat coming off Alex's body and it seemed that she had no course of action but one.

She reached back with her right arm and hooked it around the back of Alex's neck, pulling her face the last inch to her own. Without stopping to think twice—without stopping to think *at all*—she crushed her mouth to Alex's, dual moans escaped from each of them at the moment of contact.

There was no tentative uncertainty. There was no taking of time to gently brush and softly nibble one another's lips. There was only hunger and want and not just from Jennifer. Alex felt it, too, and was just as swept away as Jennifer. Warning bells clanged loudly, but neither woman paid any attention to them. They had simply gotten too physically close to one another and all the willpower they'd been using to resist temptation had basically fallen in on them.

Jennifer went by pure instinct. For the first time in her life, she did what felt right at the time. Alex's lips were the softest she'd ever felt and she wasted no time pushing her demanding tongue between them. Alex pushed back and they battled back and forth as Jennifer twisted in Alex's arms, trying to gain herself a better angle for which to explore her friend's incredible body with her hands.

There was a sharp crack and the back of the chair jerked down harshly to a flat position, leaving Jennifer lying directly on top of Alex. Their eyes met in amusement over their new position and Jennifer raised one wicked eyebrow before descending upon Alex's mouth again, ravaging with pure delight.

She felt like a teenage boy. Her hands fumbled with the buttons on Alex's shirt as she tasted the skin of her friend's cheek, her ear, and her neck. She wanted so badly to touch, to feel with her fingertips that skin that had been taunting her for weeks.

Alex's hands were in Jennifer's hair, her breathing ragged. She pulled Jennifer's face back up and plunged her tongue possessively into her mouth, moaning as she did so. Jennifer pushed the shirt open and cupped one lace-covered breast in her palm, enthralled by the feel, the weight of it. She ran her thumb over the nipple, causing Alex to arch into her hand.

"Oh, God," she groaned, suddenly wrenching her mouth from Jennifer's. "Wait." Panting, she shifted beneath Jennifer. She slid her off to the side and sat up. "Jennifer, wait. Please." She swallowed, catching her breath. "Wait."

Jennifer blinked at her, still immersed in a haze of sex. "What?" she asked breathlessly, struggling to sit up. "What's the matter?"

"What are you doing?" Alex gasped, trying to clear her head. "What are you doing to me?"

"What?"

"I can't...I can't do this."

"Alex..." Jennifer reached for her again, kissing her neck, murmuring against her skin. "Please. I know you want this as much as I do. It's okay." She slipped her hand back under Alex's shirt, softly stroking the same breast. Alex closed her eyes briefly, reveling in the aura of this woman who seemed to inexplicably know just how to touch her. Her legs felt like they were made of jelly and the ache in her groin was insistent. She was vaguely aware of Jennifer's hand slipping around behind her and fumbling with the clasp on her bra; it was enough to snap her back to reality.

"No." She grabbed Jennifer's hands and held them both in her own. Looking her in the eye with difficulty, she said, "We can't do this."

"Why not?" Jennifer felt like she'd lost all ability to think clearly.

Alex closed her eyes, letting out a long, slow breath. The anger seeped slowly in and she covered her eyes with her hands. "Damn you, Jennifer," she said through clenched teeth. "Damn you."

Jennifer reached to pull away Alex's hands. "Alex...talk to me." She pried gently at the fingers, her voice soothing and sweet. "Come on. Come on, sweetie. Please."

"Stop it," Alex said, lowering her hands. Her voice was almost firm and the crack in it almost unnoticeable. "Stop coaxing me like that. I can't...I can't...It can't be like this." Her eyes filled with tears. "I don't want it to be like this."

Jennifer's heart filled with dread at the sight and she wanted nothing more than to make it better. "Alex," she said again in the same loving tone. She brushed a strand of hair out of Alex's face, surprised when her hand was pushed roughly away.

"Stop it! Stop touching me and stop saying my name like that. Please. God, why can't you understand? Why can't you understand what it does to me? Don't you have any idea what it does to me?"

Jennifer blinked as Alex stood up and put distance between them. She leaned on the deck's railing with her hands, staring out onto the water. Silent tears rolled down her face. Jennifer had no idea what to say, so she waited until Alex finally spoke.

"You're married, Jennifer." Alex's voice was barely discernible in the night air.

"I know."

"I'm not your experiment."

"I know that, too."

"Do you think this makes you any better than Eric?"

Jennifer flinched, surprised by the accusation in the question. "Excuse me?"

Alex turned to face her. "Do you think your sleeping with me is any different than him having an affair on you?"

"*What?*" Jennifer felt her face flush with irritation. "Pardon me, Little Miss I'll Warm You Up, Come Here And Sit Between My Legs. What was that, a test?" Alex looked away, guilt written all over her face, visible even in the dark as Jennifer continued. "In case you hadn't noticed, your tongue was in my mouth just as often as mine was in yours. I'm not the only guilty party here."

"*You're the married one!*" Alex shouted. "Jesus, Jennifer, make up your mind. Go buy some courage. You're not in love with your husband; anybody can see that. If you're not happy, then leave. Leave him. Do *something*. Have the guts to be who you are for a change."

Jennifer's fury grew so dark that it clouded over the hidden message Alex was sending. Her eyes crackled with rage. "Let me see if I've got this right. *You're* judging *me*? You? The lesbian author who only writes about straight people? The out and proud gay woman who let her own mother run her out of a job without the tiniest of whimpers? *You're* telling *me* I need to find the courage to be who I am?"

Both women were breathless and the angry tension on the deck was so thick it could be cut with a knife. Alex swore she could hear Jennifer's heart pounding as hard as her own. Kinsey had left his place on the couch and was standing at the door, sending disapproving looks at the pair through the screen.

Jennifer was the first to break eye contact; she did so when she felt the anger recede and the tears begin to well. She looked down at her feet for a minute. Then, swiping angrily at her wet cheek, she turned, walked down the steps of the deck, and left.

Alex watched her go, unable to move, still feeling the remnants of her own resentment, though they were quickly eclipsed by guilt and the desire to wipe Jennifer's tears away. She scrubbed her hand over her face with frustration.

"Shit."

Chapter
Fourteen

"Awek!"

A little blonde-headed body torpedoed itself into Alex's mid-section and she scooped it up. She kissed Hannah's face and smelled her hair, closing her eyes and reveling in the sweet, inno-cent scent of Johnson's Baby Shampoo. Sometimes, just holding on to Hannah was all she needed to do to make the world seem not so bad after all.

"Hey, Stretch. How's life?" Jackie asked, handing her friend a glass of Merlot.

"It's there," Alex replied, taking a too-large mouthful of the wine and setting Hannah down on her feet. "Sometimes it's just there and that's all."

Jackie looked at her a little oddly, like she wanted to explore the comment. Instead, she nodded. "Ain't that the truth."

Rita's kitchen was bright and sunny, filled with yellows and floral designs. Alex always thought of it as "Rita's kitchen" because Jackie absolutely despised cooking and rarely spent any time in there unless she was getting herself a beer from the refrigerator.

Alex watched with a mixture of awe and envy as her best friend wrapped her arms around Rita from behind, as the dark woman stirred the contents of a pot on the stove. They stood like that, swaying together slowly, making a striking contrast. Jackie was tall and light, Rita was small and dark. Alex couldn't help but think how she and Jennifer would create a similar dichotomy. The love her friends had for each other was so obvious, she could actually feel it in the air. It made her at once happy for them and sad for her-self.

"Can I set the table?" she asked suddenly, finding it hard to breathe.

"Sure."

She knew where everything was and helped herself to the place settings and carried them into the dining room and away from the sickening aura of love that threatened to suffocate her where she stood.

Later, she sat back in her chair and patted her stuffed belly. "Dinner was delicious, as always, though I was only expecting drinks." She let out a big sigh. "Honestly, I don't know how you two don't weigh three hundred pounds."

Jackie stood and collected the plates. "We find creative ways to work it off." She grinned, kissed Rita's blushing cheek, and headed into the kitchen.

Boy, things have obviously changed in the sex area around here, Alex thought, surprised to find herself feeling bitter and envious.

"I all done," Hannah said from her booster seat next to Alex.

"Good stuff?" Alex asked.

"Yup." The child's plate was nearly empty and Alex wondered, not for the first time, how Rita got so lucky as to give birth to a child who ate almost everything.

"Good girl." Getting the nod of approval from Rita, Alex wiped the toddler clean, unfastened her bib and safety strap, and set her on the floor. "Go make sure your mama is doing a good job on those dishes," she ordered, playfully swatting her behind.

"So," Rita began, sipping her wine. "Let's talk about your book."

Alex's heart jumped. "Okay." It must have been her fragile writer's ego that always made her so nervous when she was about to get feedback from Rita. She was always terrified that one of these times, Rita would turn into some cackling, witch-like creature dressed in black who would loom high above her, laughing and pointing and accusing Alex of having absolutely no writing talent whatsoever. The image sent a shuddering chill along her spine every time and she took another sip of wine, hoping to warm her blood.

"First of all, it's moving along very nicely," she began with a smile. "I like the characters very much, especially Paul. I feel like I know him."

Alex nodded. "Good. That's how I want you to feel."

"And Kristen. She seems *very* familiar."

"Does she?"

Rita sipped from her wineglass and studied its contents. "Mm hmm. Is she based on somebody we know?"

The question was posed in a perfectly innocent tone of voice, but Alex knew Rita and she also knew the question was a loaded one. Alex shrugged. "Could be. Sometimes, I'm not even aware of it."

Rita nodded, looking her square in the eye. Alex, of course, looked away, not good with direct eye contact when she was lying through her teeth. Rita seemed to be searching for the right words.

"We're worried about you, Alex."

Alex's eyes snapped back to Rita's. *We?* "What do you mean?"

"You're the one who always told me that a writer writes from his or her own experiences, whether it's intentional or not."

Alex searched the inside of her cheek with her tongue, very leery of the direction her friend was headed. She opted for another sip of wine rather than a verbal response.

"I saw some glaring similarities between your book and your life. They concerned me, so I showed Jackie what I meant."

Alex couldn't decide how she felt about her sharing this sort of thing with her best friend, though Rita certainly reserved the right to do so. Her heart pounded, but she tried to remain calm and innocent. She was terrified that Rita could see right through her. "What are you talking about?"

"Come on, Alex." Rita's voice was soft and gentle. "Your story's about a thirty-five-year-old guy who has fallen in love with—not to mention, become dangerously obsessed with—his married next door neighbor...the next door neighbor who's small and blonde and has just moved in. What do you think I'm talking about?"

Jackie entered the room slowly and it was clear she'd been listening. Alex figured the two of them had probably rehearsed the whole conversation. "What's the deal with you and Jennifer?"

"Me and Jennifer? What are you talking about? There's nothing going on." She tried to sound innocent, but wasn't sure if she was pulling it off.

"I'm just worried about you, Stretch. I don't want to see you get messed up in this. She's straight and she's married."

Alex thought about slyly commenting that Jackie was one for two, but she managed to keep that thought to herself. She plastered on her best reassuring face. "There's nothing going on. Jennifer and I are friends. That's all." She could feel Jackie's eyes on her and she felt like her friend could see right into her brain, knowing exactly what she was thinking.

"Do you have feelings for her?"

"What?" Alex felt her patience waning.

"I know you, Alex. I know how easily you fall. You've spent a lot of time with her. She's a married woman—a married, straight woman—with a rich and successful husband. I just don't want you to get stuck in a situation that will prove to be nothing but bad news and heartache, that's all." She smiled to ease the tension of the circumstances. "It's my job as your best friend to look out for you."

Alex smiled back, determined to reassure her friends and not to let them in on the fact that they were much closer to the truth than even they suspected. "You know me, Jackie. I've probably got a little crush thing going on her. I mean, have you seen her? Can you blame me?" She hoped her smile was playful enough. "I took the crush and used it as inspiration for my book. It'll pass. It always does."

Both Jackie and Rita searched her face; it took every ounce of willpower Alex possessed to keep from shifting under the scrutiny. She sipped her wine.

"You're not planning on killing Eric, are you?" Jackie asked softly.

The question took her completely off guard and she coughed up the swallow of wine in her mouth. Regaining her composure, she looked incredulously at her friend. "*What?*"

"I'm just making sure," Jackie said, realizing what a silly question it had been.

"I told you not to ask her that." Rita glowered at her partner.

"Jack..." Alex took a moment, wiping her chin and trying not to burst into laughter. "You guys. Please. I appreciate your concern. I do. But, no, I am not planning on killing Eric. Is that really what you thought?"

"Of course not," Rita said, standing. "The bottom line here is that we're just looking out for you. We love you and we don't want to see you hurt. Okay?"

"Okay." Alex finished her wine. The conversation had ended on an up note, but she had the sneaking suspicion that she hadn't covered the truth as well as she'd hoped. As always, she was sure her best friends could see right through her as though she were made of glass. If that was the case, they'd surely see the name written all over her heart.

* * *

Whenever Jennifer was confused, there was only one person she could go to. Only one person who could help to put things into perspective, help her to look at her situation from another angle— usually an angle she'd never realized existed.

If I'd gone to this person a few years earlier, she thought sadly as she drove, *I might have avoided the situation I'm in now.* If she'd gone to him when Eric had hesitantly proposed and her initial reaction was to say no, maybe her life from that point forward would have been more fulfilling and less disappointing. Maybe she wouldn't be stuck where she was and maybe she'd have no trouble sorting out the jumble of emotions that filled her heart and her mind, and represented everything she felt for and about Alex.

The fact that she had to go to a cemetery to see that person only made her sigh with sadness as she maneuvered the Volvo into the familiar parking lot. The day was beautiful, breezy and sunny, so instead of following the paved and winding road around to her father's grave, she opted to simply park in the lot and walk, thinking the fresh air and exercise might help to clear her head. Stuffing her keys in the pocket of her shorts, she began the trek.

White Haven was quiet with few visitors, being the middle of a weekday. Not a person was in sight and Jennifer found the solitude incredibly peaceful.

She found her father's marker easily and took a seat in the soft grass.

"Hi, Daddy. Your daisies are on their last legs. Or should I say their last stems?" She picked up the drooping flowers from the hole in the ground and set them aside, wishing she had something with which to replace them.

She sighed heavily, leaned back on her hands and looked up at the puffy clouds floating by. "No birdseed today, Dad. This was sort of an impromptu visit. I need to talk."

What is it, honey? She could hear his voice as the soft breeze carried it by. *What's bothering you?*

"I've got this problem. Actually, it's not a new problem. It's an old problem. It's something that's been hanging around for quite a few years now and I should have dealt with it a long time ago. I'm afraid I let Mom's genes take over momentarily and I decided that if I ignored it, it would just go away. Always works for her, right?" She chuckled bitterly. "Well, it worked for me, too, for a little while. But now it's back."

She slowly picked at a few blades of grass, playing with them, until she realized her own stalling technique and rolled her eyes at herself. *I'm killing time so I don't have to explain things to a dead guy. Brilliant.*

"You're probably not going to like it," she went on, "but I don't think you'll be surprised." She took a deep breath and dove in head-first.

"Remember Sarah from college? Pretty girl, dark hair, hazel eyes? You used to sing *Sarah Smile* to her whenever you saw her and make her blush. Mom hated her." She paused, remembering her mother's immediate disdain for Sarah and realizing that she must have pegged Sarah's sexuality before Jennifer even had. "Well, she didn't hate her for no reason. Sarah became my girlfriend. I mean lover. Like, we had an affair." She tried to picture her father's expression as she stumbled over her words.

"I know I should have told you; I should have come to you, but I was so scared and I just tried to deal with it on my own first. And then Sarah left me." She nearly winced aloud as she recalled the pain of her first broken heart. "See, I was her first female lover, just like she was mine, and she dealt with the possibility of an alternative lifestyle much better than I did. She embraced it. She wanted to explore it. I didn't. I was nothing short of terrified and I wanted to hide—literally—in a closet. I held her back; I know that now. I was stifling her. I can't blame her for leaving, but I was a mess.

"I started to sink into a depression. I didn't want to go out. I barely went to class. It was bad, Daddy. Poor Kayla was so worried about me, she didn't know what else to do, so she called Mom." It had taken Jennifer a long, long time to forgive her oldest friend for that move, but she had finally understood that Kayla only had Jennifer's best interests at heart.

"Mom completely freaked out. She said I was just going through a phase, that it was a college thing and now it was over and that I'd better get myself together or I would lose Eric for good. She kept talking about what people would think if they found out, how embarrassing it would be for her. I know she kept it all from you. She said you'd be so disappointed in me and I believed her like an idiot." She shook her head in disgust with herself and looked up at the sky again as she remembered the endless browbeating she'd taken from her mother because of her prejudice.

"Anyway, long story short, I pushed all that into a little, dark corner, locked the door, and figured I'd never have to deal with it again." She snorted. "I should have known better."

His expression was clear in her mind this time, his green eyes intently fixed on her, making her feel like the only person in the world. *What happened?* he'd ask with concern.

"Alex came along, that's what happened. God, Daddy, she just...she just *gets* me, you know? She's warm and she's kind. She's talented, she's beautiful. When I'm with her, I feel like I can be who I am. There are no roles I'm expected to play, no images she wants me to uphold. I can just be myself. It's so..." She searched for the right word. "Freeing. It's freeing, Dad. I wish you could have had that with Mom or somebody, because it's the most amazing feeling in the world."

And what about Eric? He would say it without accusation, but the point would be made.

She had no answer to that. She sighed heavily, then sat in silence, soaking up the fresh air and the warmth of the sun. The birds chirped nearby and the leaves on the trees rustled gently, but the peaceful sounds did nothing to relax her mind.

"I don't know what to do, Daddy." Her voice was small, barely audible. She obviously didn't expect an answer from her dead father, but she found herself straining to hear his voice anyway.

After a long while, she took a deep breath, then stood to go, thanking her father for listening and promising she'd be back again soon. She was almost to her car when she felt in her pocket for her keys and realized they were missing.

"Damn it," she muttered under her breath as she retraced her steps back. As she approached her father's plot, she noticed a slim, dark woman crouching down near it.

She was putting fresh daisies in the holder.

Jennifer's heart hammered, as she was sure she'd never laid eyes on the woman before. She approached slowly, not wanting to intrude on the woman's privacy even though the curiosity of who she might be was killing her. The woman wiped an errant tear from her face and her shoulders convulsed in what could only have been a quiet sob. Jennifer stopped, embarrassed that she was spying on the poor woman. She dropped her gaze to the ground.

Her keys were in the grass by her feet.

She stooped to pick them up as the woman pressed her fingers to her lips, then to the grave marker. The fact that she'd been in love with her father was so glaringly apparent, it almost knocked Jennifer over with its weight.

She stood riveted to the spot as the woman stood and headed in Jennifer's direction. She met Jennifer's gaze for a short second, then lowered her red-rimmed eyes apologetically, wiping at her dampened cheeks. Jennifer smiled and, much to her surprise, spoke to the woman.

"I'm sorry. You obviously cared very much about him."

The woman stopped and nodded, not the least bit startled that a perfect stranger had said something to her. She studied Jennifer carefully as if wondering if she was supposed to recognize her. "Very much. He was a wonderful man."

Even close up, she was unfamiliar to Jennifer. She was a plain woman with no spectacular features except the noticeable kindness in her hazel eyes. "Was he your husband?" She couldn't believe she'd actually gotten the question out, but for some reason, she felt the need to find out more about this woman's relationship with her father.

The woman chuckled sadly. "Oh no. Only in my dreams." She looked wistfully back at the gravesite. "I could never get him to just follow his heart."

Jennifer blinked at her. The lack of response didn't seem to faze the woman any more than Jennifer's initial comment had. She sighed with sadness and went on her way, leaving Jennifer standing in the cemetery, absorbing the fact that her father had had a lover she'd known nothing about.

* * *

That night's volleyball game was a disaster. It was an early game, six o'clock, and the first time Alex and Jennifer had been in close proximity with one another since the fiasco on Alex's deck a few nights earlier.

Aside from a nod at one another and a quiet hello, no words were exchanged between the two. Jackie noticed this right away and narrowed her eyes with suspicion, but said nothing.

Alex didn't play well when she was distracted or frustrated and that night, she couldn't seem to bump or spike the ball cleanly to save her life. Her returns went shooting off at sharp angles. The timing on her blocks was way off. Her spikes went either directly into the net or so far out of bounds, the opposite team had to sprint after the ball to prevent it from bouncing into the water. Her lousy level of play only served to frustrate her further and she snapped at her teammates when they tried to encourage her. Because of that, they began playing in silence, the kiss of death in any team sport.

Jennifer played just as poorly. Her fingers were stiff and her sets had no height, assuming she was lucky enough to actually get beneath the ball. Her legs didn't seem to want to cooperate and her movements on the court felt sluggish and slow. Each time a set didn't get to Alex, the taller woman would huff with annoyance, which only ticked Jennifer off and made her play worse.

Their opponents were not that great. A win shouldn't have been difficult, but by the middle of the second game, all six players were drenched in sweat and completely stressed out from the animosity permeating the court. Jackie was getting frustrated for her team. As she watched her best friend and the newest member of the team, she quickly put two and two together and knew immediately that whatever was going on between the pair, it was more than the simple crush Alex had claimed. Jennifer had never played this badly with them; something was obviously bothering her. Alex had her moods, but she was usually able to pull herself out of them with the help of her teammates. Now, she seemed to be instigating the poor volleyball performance, rather than trying to help fix it. The more Jackie thought about it—and the fact that Alex had lied to her—the more agitated she became.

Steve smacked a beautiful serve. The other team received it cleanly, then put it up for a spike. As Alex went up to block, Jennifer crouched behind her to cover. As it had been throughout the match, Alex's timing was a little off. The ball hit her hands, then dribbled down her arms. Jennifer dove near Alex's feet to save the point, but as she did so, Alex stepped backwards, also flailing for the ball. She fell back over Jennifer and the two of them lay sprawled in the sand, panting and annoyed, legs tangled like wet spaghetti.

"You can stay in your own part of the court, you know," Alex muttered.

"Yeah, well, your blocks obviously need all the help they can get," Jennifer shot back.

Jackie squatted down and was very much in their space. Her eyes flashed with anger and when she spoke, her voice was no more than an incensed hiss. "I don't know what the hell is going on with you two, but I suggest you get a grip on yourselves right now, because you're pissing off every last one of us. Get your shit together and play like you're members of this team, God damn it."

Alex and Jennifer exchanged embarrassed glances and stood, brushing the sand from themselves, looking properly chastened.

The game continued.

* * *

The weeds didn't stand a chance, not given the state Jennifer was in. She'd come directly home from the beach, covered with sand and sweat and buzzing with nervous energy from her frustrations with Alex on the court. It was still light out and she needed to do something or she was sure she'd simply explode where she stood.

She had discovered gardening to be very therapeutic and was amused by what one could learn when doing something one's self, rather than hiring an outside party to do it instead. Her family had always hired gardeners when she was growing up. Getting her hands dirty was certainly not something that had interested Jennifer's mother. Jennifer, on the other hand, had spent this summer realizing that digging her fingers into the earth, smelling the richness of the soil, and helping along the beauty of nature was one of the most calming activities in which she'd ever taken part.

So she sat in her flower bed that evening, pulling weeds and loosening the soil around the thriving blossoms, trying hard to quiet her brain. Between the woman at the cemetery, her dilemma over Alex, and the disastrous volleyball game, her head was buzzing loudly and all she wished for was an on/off switch for her mind.

She had so many questions—questions that could only be answered by the woman with the daisies.

How long had she been my father's lover?

Was he in love with her?

Did my mother know?

God, did they have any children?

She yanked viciously at an unsuspecting dandelion, unsure how to feel. On the one hand, she was furious with her father for cheating on her mother. She'd always thought of him as an honorable and noble man and this put a *big* chink in his armor. On the other hand, she knew her parents didn't have a warm and fuzzy relationship. She knew her mother could be cold, distant, and unemotional, so there was a part of Jennifer that actually applauded her father for finding somebody to love him the way he deserved.

She looked up and took a deep breath to steady her nerves. That was when she noticed Alex sitting on her deck. She'd obviously decided not to go out with the team either. They made eye contact for barely a split second, both of them shifting their gazes away at the same time.

Another weed fell victim to Jennifer's wrath.

Before she had time to delve into the quadrant of her brain labeled "Alex," Jennifer was interrupted by her husband's voice.

"Jen!" He was in the house and he did not sound happy.

"Great," Jennifer mumbled. She had too much churning in her head already. She had no desire to add Eric to the mix. She continued to weed.

"Jen!" he shouted again as he stepped out onto the deck and spotted his wife. His steps were purposeful as he marched toward her. She looked up at his approach and the scowl on his face made the hairs on her arms stand on end. She got to her feet, feeling like she had a better shot at handling his obvious anger if she was standing.

"Hey," she greeted.

"Don't 'hey' me," he snapped, causing her to flinch. "Did you talk to my father?" His eyes flashed with fury and his face was flushed.

Oh, shit, Jennifer thought. *Here we go.*

"Um..." she stalled, trying to figure out how she was going to gracefully get through this one.

"Did you talk to my father recently?" He annunciated each word slowly and carefully through clenched teeth. Jennifer had never been afraid of her husband before, but his anger was so intense that it caused a little spark of fear to ignite in the pit of her stomach.

She swallowed hard. "Yes."

"And did you tell him that I didn't really want to take over the firm?"

She grimaced. "Yes?"

"Jesus Christ, Jennifer!" He threw up his hands in exasperated anger. "What the hell were you thinking? What are you trying to do to me?"

"Eric, I—"

"Are you trying to destroy me? My future?" He was yelling at the top of his lungs, his anger feeding his volume.

"No, of course not." The spark of fear had become a full-blown fire at that point and she tried to subtly take a step back from him. The wild-eyed expression on his face matched the booming level of his voice and she was torn between being embarrassed by what the neighborhood was hearing and being frightened of him.

"He thinks you're right. He agrees with you, God damn you, and he's exploring other alternatives." He glared at her. She felt the bottom drop out of her stomach. "You had no right, Jen. No right."

"I was trying to be honest with him, Eric. He was worried about you. He thought you were too stressed out. He was afraid he'd dumped too much on you." Her voice was pleading, but Eric wouldn't look at her, tried to turn her words off. "You haven't been happy since this whole thing started, since he started training you to take over. I just want you to be happy."

"You want *me* to be happy? Are you sure this doesn't have anything to do with you? That there are no ulterior motives here?" His voice dripped with accusation.

"What?"

"I'm not stupid, Jen. I see things. I know things."

Jennifer's stomach roiled; the sense of dread she felt was almost too much to bear. "What are you talking about?"

His back was to Alex's house, but he jerked his thumb in that direction. "Do you think I'm unaware of your little girlfriend over there? I know your history. Don't forget that."

Jennifer's eyes hardened. "Do you really want to do this? Do you really want to get into the subject of infidelity, Eric? Because I'm not stupid either."

His face registered surprise, then guilt, but they only seemed to fuel his anger and he quickly steered the conversation back to its original topic. "You have ruined me. You have ruined my career."

"No, Eric. That's not true—" She needed to get him on track, to explain why she'd told Daniel the truth.

"You've ruined me!" he shouted.

"No, let's talk about this—"

"I am the laughing stock of that firm now. Everybody thinks I can't cut it, that I cracked under the pressure." He looked at her and the rage in his eyes burned a hole right into her heart. "You did this to me! Why couldn't you have kept your mouth shut? This is *your* fault!" He turned to leave, but Jennifer grabbed his arm.

"Eric, please. Don't go. Let's talk about this. Please..."

With a growl, he viciously yanked his arm from her grip and raised it as if to backhand her across the face. She gasped in fright, automatically turning away, squeezing her eyes shut, and bracing herself for the blow. When it didn't come, she opened one eye to see why.

Eric was still standing there, but he was looking at his own hand in horror, his eyes wide with disbelief and self-loathing. "Oh, God," he murmured. "Oh my God." His eyes filled with tears and he blinked several times, lowering his arm. "I'm sorry," he whispered, so softly Jennifer could barely hear him. "I'm sorry, Jen." Then he turned and sprinted away like a ten-year-old boy. Jennifer heard a car door slam and an engine turn over. Then he was gone.

She had no idea how long she stood in her yard, blinking at the grass, trembling, unable to absorb what had just happened. All she knew was that it was about to become a very important day in her life. When she finally looked up, her eyes met those of Alex, who stood on her deck facing Jennifer, her hands on the railing, looking completely alarmed and unsure what to do.

Jennifer felt the first sob work its way up from her stomach and she clamped a hand over her mouth. She turned and ran into the house.

* * *

The voices were all so far away. They were muffled and distant, as though she was hearing them from under water. She'd lost track of how long she'd been lying in bed, drifting in and out of fitful sleep. She didn't seem to have the energy to move, to even lift her head. Instead, she just lay there, straining to make out the words coming from the answering machine in the kitchen without getting up or even shifting the position of her head on the pillow.

Beep. "Jennifer, it's Daniel. Listen, I was wondering if you'd seen Eric tonight. I'm afraid he left here a bit upset. I've tried his cell phone, but I keep getting voice mail. I'm worried about him."

Beep. "Jennifer Elizabeth, would it kill you to call your mother once in a while? An invitation to your place on the lake would be a nice gesture, you know."

Beep. "Hey, Jennifer. Um, it's Alex. Listen, I know we've had our share of problems, but I wanted to put those aside and check on you. I sort of...overheard your argument with Eric. It was pretty intense and I wanted to make sure you're okay..."

That one had been interesting, but still Jennifer had lain there staring at the wall. Night had fallen. Dawn had broken. She rolled over to stare at the opposite wall. The phone rang again at ten o'clock.

Beep. "Jennifer, it's Alex again. Are you there? Pick up. Please?"

At ten fifteen, the doorbell rang. She knew it would be Alex and she was almost disappointed in herself for having locked all the doors. For reasons she couldn't seem to grasp at the time, Alex's arms seemed to be the only place that held any safety for her. She pulled the pillow over her head to block out the insistent ringing.

At noon, she managed to get up and walk the five steps to the bathroom to relieve herself. After that, she fell back into bed, her energy level so low she was surprised she was breathing. She sighed, looking at the ceiling, and unable to hold it all at bay any longer, she finally gave in. She let her brain open the door to all the confusing feelings that she'd tried to lock away or ignore. Eric, Sarah, Alex, the daisy woman. She looked at them all one by one, examining each, letting her mind understand her heart and vice-versa. It took more than twenty-four hours.

The phone continued to ring.

Chapter
Fifteen

Three days.

It had been three days since Alex had witnessed the ugliness in the backyard of the Wainwright home. It has also been three days since she'd seen hide or hair of Jennifer. At first she had worried terribly. The fight had been a nasty one, not to mention an incredibly loud one, and Eric had come so close to hitting Jennifer that Alex herself had gasped in horror at the sight. She'd been so torn, standing there on her deck. When she'd met Jennifer's eyes, they were wide with a combination of fright and humiliation and her skin had been drained of color. Alex had had no idea what to say or do. Before she could make a decision, Jennifer had turned and fled into the house. And three days had gone by.

She'd left a dozen messages on Jennifer's answering machine and she'd gone to the house three times to pound on the door. It was just when she was about to call the police because her worry that Jennifer might have done something to harm herself was consuming her whole, that relief came. She saw the kitchen light snap on and noticed the light fabric curtains had been drawn over the enormous windows in the back room. She knew Eric hadn't been back—she'd been keeping an eye out for him—so she heaved a sigh of relief at the shadow moving behind the sheer panels. She'd watched carefully until it had become clear that the shadow was making something to eat. Only then had Alex ventured to bed, feeling like fifty pounds of stress had been lifted from her shoulders.

Sleep was elusive. She was exhausted from her vigil and constant worry, apparently too exhausted to actually drift off. She tossed and turned restlessly. It was stiflingly hot, as it was known to get in that part of New York State in the dead of summer. No breeze at all came off the lake. The air felt thick and heavy, making sleep next to impossible. Though she was satisfied that Jennifer was all right, Alex's mind continued to spin around the situation. She finally got to the point where she was about to scream with the insanity of it all. Kinsey groaned his annoyance as she threw off the sheet and swung her feet over the side of the bed.

"Oh, shut up," she snapped as she reached for her terrycloth robe. The simple white cotton panties and matching tank top she wore to bed felt like much more fabric than they actually were in such heat and she debated the robe. Glancing at the clock and noting the late hour, she tossed the robe back up on its hook. "Screw it," she muttered. "If the neighborhood gets a show, so be it."

Kinsey yawned and resumed his almost constant panting. The house had central air conditioning, but Alex was always reluctant to use it. She hated the way it dried her sinuses and made the atmosphere feel stale, and she hated closing the windows in the summertime. The breeze coming off the water was always peaceful and relaxing. The lack of it and Kinsey's lethargic panting, however, made her seriously contemplate flicking the switch.

"Come on, buddy," she said, lovingly scratching his head. "I need some milk and we'll get you some cool water, okay?"

He blinked at her several times, then slid languidly off the bed to follow her.

"And don't get any ideas," she warned. "It's one thirty in the morning. You're not going out."

The moon was incredibly bright and she didn't need to turn on any lights as she strolled through the living room to the kitchen, her mind still on Jennifer. She couldn't recall the last time a woman had affected her so intensely...and against her will. She didn't *want* to feel anything but friendship for her neighbor. She was constantly berating herself for falling so quickly and so completely for somebody so unattainable.

Jackie was always telling her that everything happens for a reason and on many occasions, Alex had been inclined to agree. In this case, however, she just couldn't grasp what the point might be—not just the bringing of Jennifer into her life, but making Alex fall for her. She supposed if the point had been to break her or to make her feel miserable, then it was working. Otherwise, she just didn't get it. She'd never wanted something so badly, and she simply couldn't have it. It was excruciating.

She refilled Kinsey's water bowl and dropped a couple of ice cubes in it. He sniffed at them, then proceeded to push at them with his front paw. He was making a small mess, but he was so cute, Alex didn't care. She poured herself a glass of milk and leaned against the counter, smiling down at him.

The tapping at the sliding glass door was so gentle, even Kinsey wasn't quite sure he'd heard it. He let out a little half-woof as he and Alex both turned surprised heads in the same direction. His tail wagged immediately. A wave of relief washed over Alex as she met Jennifer's blue eyes through the glass. She nearly flew to the door to let her in.

"I know it's late," Jennifer blurted out as she stepped through the doorway. "I'm sorry. I saw the fridge light go on and I just...I had to see you."

She was wearing a pair of light blue, cotton boxer shorts with *Victoria's Secret* embroidered subtly on the waistband. A loose-fitting, pink tank top covered the upper half of her, her deep tan apparent even in the light of the moon. Her blonde hair was pulled back into a very loose ponytail, the baby-fine hairs at the nape of her neck damp and curly from the humidity. Her small feet were bare.

Alex fully expected to see physical signs of emotional upheaval, given the circumstances the last time they'd seen each other—red, swollen eyes, blotchy cheeks, *something*. Instead, Jennifer looked calm, strong, confident, and incredibly sexy. Alex blinked in surprised, more than a little curious and more than a little turned on.

"No, don't apologize," she admonished gently. "I don't care how late it is. I'm glad you're here. I was worried about you."

"I know. I'm sorry. I did get your messages, I just couldn't face you. I couldn't face anybody. I had a lot of thinking to do."

"I can imagine." She studied Jennifer's face in the moonlight. "Are you all right?"

Jennifer contemplated that question thoroughly before answering. "Yeah." She nodded with confidence. "For the first time in my life, I think I am." She held Alex's gaze. "It's amazing how things that were once so blurry can just pull into focus when the time is right. Suddenly, everything becomes perfectly clear." Her eyes drifted from Alex's and slid down her neck to rest momentarily on her breasts. She rolled her bottom lip in, running her tongue slowly across it, and Alex felt a jolt shoot through her body. Only then did she become aware of what she was wearing—or more accurately, what she *wasn't* wearing. All the moisture from Alex's mouth suddenly flew south and ended up in her panties.

Jennifer's gaze was unwavering as she looked Alex in the eye once again and Alex realized that she'd never seen the woman look quite so alluring, standing in the kitchen, bathed in the ethereal blue of the moon. Her resolve to stay away from Jennifer was diminishing at an alarmingly high rate of speed.

It seemed at the moment that Jennifer's boldness was directly proportional to Alex's nervousness. As Jennifer stepped toward her, Alex took a step back until, much to her dismay, she was leaning against the counter, trapped. Jennifer's eyes never left Alex's and she was so together, so *not* flustered. Suddenly, Alex wanted nothing more than to just hang on and see where this went, where Jennifer would take them. She forced herself to relax, and tamped down the panic threatening to surface. Instead of excusing herself and scurrying off to find a robe, she leaned back casually and grasped the edge of the counter with each hand, fully aware of the tank top pulling taut across her breasts.

"Pulled into focus, huh?" she said softly. "What kinds of things are we talking about?" She took great pleasure in watching Jennifer swallow hard as her blue eyes slid down again, this time not stopping at Alex's breasts until her gaze had traveled the entire length of Alex's body and back up again. Alex was sweating and trembling at the same time, gripping the counter so tightly that her knuckles were white.

"Life things. Decisions. Expectations. Happiness." Jennifer's voice was husky as she took a step toward Alex, then another. "Wants. Needs." She pinned Alex with her eyes. "Desires."

It was Alex's turn to swallow hard.

Jennifer was so close, Alex could smell her baby powder. "Jennifer..." What was supposed to sound like a warning came out like a whispered plea instead. Alex felt as though she was dangling from the edge of common sense by her fingertips, swinging dangerously in Jennifer's breeze.

"I've made some choices, Alex." Jennifer's voice was as soft as Alex's was. She closed the remaining space between them, looked up, and put her left hand on Alex's waist. Alex was sure that if she let go of the counter, she'd be swept away into oblivion, so she held on as tightly as she could. She felt the fingertips of Jennifer's other hand on her wrist and then sliding teasingly up her arm.

"Choices?" Alex was barely able to choke out the word; her body was in serious betrayal mode.

Jennifer nodded. "My marriage is over; it has been for quite some time." Alex looked down at the hand on her waist, surprised to see no sign of her wedding band but a tan line. "It's time for me to stop doing what's expected of me. It's time to stop doing what I'm supposed to do." Her fingers grazed Alex's shoulder, sending goose bumps across her body despite the heat of the night. "It's about time I understood that it's okay to want what I want."

Alex wet her Sahara-dry lips with her tongue and was scarcely able to find her own voice. "And what is it that you want, Jennifer? Hmm? What do you want?"

"You."

Without another word, she hooked her hand around the back of Alex's neck and yanked her head down roughly, kissing her with such certainty, command and utter confidence that Alex's knees went weak and she nearly lost her balance. Jennifer had her pinned against the counter; her tongue was deep in Alex's mouth, her right hand clutching a fistful of dark hair, and her left hand snaking deftly up the tank top to take possession of Alex's right breast. There was absolutely no question in Alex's mind who was in control of the situation.

Good Lord, a sweet little femme with a butch streak! she thought. *Who knew?* It was all Alex could do to hold on for dear life.

She felt like she was lost inside a fantasy—the kind she used to have in college when she was just starting to understand her sexuality. They were all very similar: middle of the night, moonlight pouring in the windows, a beautiful woman having her way with Alex, who was absolute putty in her hands. Somewhere deep in her head, a little voice was trying to get Alex's attention. She could only make out a few words here and there...stop...regret...experiment...but at that point, Jennifer's hands were nimbly sliding Alex's panties down her bare thighs and the voice was completely drowned out by the sound of her own heart hammering in her chest.

After dropping Alex's underwear around her ankles, Jennifer straightened and kissed Alex again. "God, your lips are so soft." She slipped her fingers between Alex's legs and both women groaned at the wetness she discovered there. "I've been dreaming about this for so long," she whispered against Alex's mouth. "Wondering. Imagining. It only got worse after I'd kissed you on the deck. I wanted so much more." And then she dropped to her knees, causing Alex to jump slightly at the sudden movement. Looking up at her, Jennifer's eyes were almost apologetic. "I have to know. I have to know how you taste." With something akin to desperation, she pushed Alex's thighs apart enough to run the flat of her tongue along the swollen flesh.

"Oh, my God." The words were forced from Alex's throat and had she not been hanging on to the counter top for all she was worth, she was sure she would have slid to the floor, a puddle of useless goo.

It became suddenly, astonishingly obvious to Alex that Jennifer had indeed done this very thing before. Her mouth was like magic, probing and teasing as she used her thumbs to separate the drenched folds, allowing her tongue better access. She ran her hands up the backs of Alex's thighs to her rear end, cupping it and pulling her tighter against her mouth. All the while, she made various noises of pleasure; it was apparent she was thoroughly enjoying herself. Alex managed to let go of the counter with one hand and laid it lovingly on the top of Jennifer's head, trying to keep her own groans of satisfaction under control, lest she wake the entire neighborhood.

She could feel her climax building. At the same time, her legs weakened uncontrollably. "Jennifer," she gasped. "I don't...I don't think I can stand up any more."

Jennifer simply planted the palm of her hand against Alex's sweat-slicked belly under her top, holding her there. "Yes, you can." It was a command, gentle but firm.

Alex swallowed, knowing she'd be staying on her feet for this one.

With her tongue, Jennifer increased both the pressure and the pace of her movements and Alex had no more time to prepare for her impending orgasm. Despite the fact that she knew it was coming, it took her by surprise, hitting her full force before she was ready. Her head fell back, her eyes squeezed shut. She clenched her teeth, growling through them. She clutched at Jennifer's head with one hand; her other hand—and Jennifer's on her stomach—were the only things keeping her standing.

She managed to keep her composure as she slid to the floor with her eyes closed, ending up in a sitting position with Jennifer on her knees between Alex's. When Alex finally opened her eyes, Jennifer smiled somewhat sheepishly. For the first time that night, Alex caught a little glimpse of the shy and naïve Jennifer she was used to peeking through the shroud of confidence and strength. She smiled back at her, reaching out her arms and pulling her to her.

"Hi," Alex said as she tightly hugged Jennifer.

"Hey there."

"That was..." Alex exhaled as her voice drifted off. "I have no words."

"Told you."

"Told me what?"

"That you could stay standing."

Alex felt herself blush in the darkness. "You were right."

"And don't you forget it." She burrowed into Alex's chest.

"No, ma'am. I won't."

They sat that way for what seemed like ages. Alex had so many questions for her new lover, so many worries. She was simultaneously ecstatic and terrified. She knew she should give voice to her thoughts, but the closeness of Jennifer's body, the sparse amount of clothing, the smell of her sweat and of Alex's own arousal on Jennifer's face...the combination was too much. She tilted Jennifer's face up with her fingertips, and covered Jennifer's mouth with her own. She didn't want to deal with the details of their lives or with how she really felt about this woman. She only wanted to lose herself in her. And she did.

* * *

Had it been a dream?

Jennifer was afraid to open her eyes. She was afraid that if she did, she'd see purple sheets and familiar surroundings and she'd be lying in her own bed alone, the wonderfully relaxed feeling in her body simply the aftermath of a very vivid dream.

She was on her stomach and she was naked, two facts easily ascertained. It was humid already and there was only a sheet covering her, her right leg curled around and on top of it. She inhaled deeply, immediately aware that the sheets did not smell like her laundry detergent and that there was definitely another distinctive scent in the room. She smiled, her eyes still closed, and took another deep breath.

Sex.

Could anything else smell so intoxicating?

She stretched slowly, wincing at the soreness of several muscles, her arms sliding under the pillows, then around the rest of the mattress. She realized she was alone at the same time she heard dishes clattering in the kitchen. The sound was oddly comforting.

She rolled onto her back and finally opened her eyes. She blinked at the unfamiliar ceiling and remembered the previous night, her skin flushing with heat as she recalled the sounds, smells, and touches of Alex. She couldn't pinpoint the moment, sitting alone in her house for the third day in a row, when she realized that this was what she wanted. Alex was what she'd wanted all along and the acceptance of that fact was so sudden, so unmistakably *clear*. She hadn't cared that it was after one o'clock in the morning. She'd thrown on some clothes and marched across the yard to claim what she'd felt was rightfully hers. It was the first truly selfish thing she could ever remember doing and it felt fantastic.

The sun peeked through the slats of the mini blinds and Jennifer realized she'd never been in Alex's bedroom before. She hadn't seen much of it the previous night, so she took the opportunity to look around.

It was very tastefully decorated in khakis and dark blues, but an array of floral accents kept the earthy colors from seeming masculine. The sheet covering Jennifer's body was navy blue; the khaki bedspread was bunched at the foot of the bed near the slatted footboard. The hardwood floor was strewn with half a dozen floral-patterned toss pillows in various combinations of beiges and blues. The head- and footboard, the two dressers, and the freestanding, full-length mirror all matched in a rich, light oak finish. There was a baseball cap hanging from each side of the mirror. One was from the Hard Rock Café in Toronto and the other was embroidered with the X-Files logo. Jennifer smiled at the thought of Alex as a fan of the quirky show.

To the left, mounted on the wall, was a large piece with three shelves. All three were cluttered with knick-knacks. Surrounding the shelves were six frames, three on each side. Jennifer got up and crossed the floor to get a better view, noting with pleasure the ache in her thigh muscles.

The knick-knacks varied in size, color, and worth, but they all had the same theme. They were all about teaching or English and were quite obviously gifts from Alex's past students. There was a miniature Smurf writing on a chalkboard. There was a tiny ceramic stack of books. There was a beautiful pen in a transparent box. There was a little, cast-iron typewriter. Each shelf was full of such treasures. Jennifer shifted her gaze to the frames. Each one held a certificate of some sort. Some were from students; some were from the staff of the school where Alex taught. All were flattering and impressive. Jennifer was not surprised by Alex's teaching ability, or by the fact that her students obviously adored her. That she had kept all the gifts was a testament to how much she loved them. Jennifer was suddenly filled with pride.

Smiling, she decided she was famished and wanted to see Alex's face again. The mingled smells of coffee and bacon wafted into the room, making Jennifer salivate. As she moved, she caught a glimpse of her own naked reflection in the mirror and gasped at what she saw. She hardly recognized herself. The woman staring back at her looked totally different than the one she was used to. This one was grinning like an idiot. Her skin was flushed pink and her blonde hair was tousled. Her eyes sparkled with some secret knowledge and there were several angry red marks along her body— one on her shoulder, one on her hip, and one on the inside of her right thigh. She stifled a giggle and pointed at the glass.

"You got fucked, didn't you?" she asked quietly, her voice teasing. "Apparently quite well."

Instead of an answer, her brain gave her a quick flashback— naked, sweating bodies; tongues and fingers and lips and teeth; sounds she hadn't heard or made in ages. She swallowed at the onslaught of the memories, simultaneously excited and embarrassed by her own uncharacteristic boldness. Again, she remembered doing the taking for the very first time in her life. The shock and unmistakable expression of arousal on Alex's face had been well worth the price of admission.

She looked around for her clothes. She had the vague recollection of her shorts being somewhere in the living room and she had no idea of the whereabouts of her tank top. Noticing Alex's white robe on a hook, she grabbed it and tied it around her body. It was too big and it really was too hot for it, but Jennifer figured she would simply borrow some other clothes later. At that moment, she just wanted to see Alex. She needed to lay eyes on her, to know that the previous night had been real. She made a quick stop at the bathroom, then headed for the kitchen. She got as far as the dining area.

Alex was working busily, humming softly to herself as she cooked. Her hair was pulled back into a ponytail and she was wearing red shorts and a white t-shirt with a dishtowel flung over her shoulder. Jennifer could only see her from the back, but it was enough to stop her in her tracks. It was an indescribable pleasure to watch her new lover while she was unaware of the scrutiny. She took the bacon out of the pan and turned off the stove, then took a carton of eggs out of the fridge and popped some bread into the toaster. Jennifer leaned against the table, folded her arms across her chest, and enjoyed the view for as long as she could, completely taken with the glow of Alex's skin and the curves of her body. Once again, she was pleasantly assaulted by periodic flashbacks from the previous night and wondered how long her body could keep up the state of perpetual wetness with which it seemed to be afflicted.

She wasn't ready for the sizzling tremor that shot through her body when Alex finally turned and their eyes met. Alex wiped her hands on the towel and tossed it blindly onto the counter. Then she slowly crossed the space between them, her eyes never leaving Jennifer's. She stopped mere inches from her. Looking down, she smiled sweetly, and brushed her fingers through Jennifer's blonde and tousled hair.

Before Jennifer could utter a word, Alex's mouth came down hard on hers and they kissed deeply, as if they'd never left the bed from the night before. The height difference between them was significant, and Jennifer found herself surrounded by Alex. Rather than feeling closed in or smothered, she felt safe and loved. She slid her hands up Alex's chest and around her neck, pulling her head down more forcefully. Alex pushed into her, directing her backwards until the edge of the dining room table hit her rear end. In the next instant, she was flat on her back on the dining room table, her robe totally open, her body completely exposed to Alex. Her legs found their way around Alex's waist, Alex's fingers were buried deep inside her, and she moaned Alex's name in ragged breaths.

She came fiercely, as she had done every time the night before, gasping for air, her chest heaving and her muscles tensed into rocks. She had to literally untangle her fingers from Alex's hair, which made them both grin with amusement.

Alex nuzzled her face against Jennifer's neck, kissing the skin softly, then pushed up on her hands so she leaned over her lover, propped on her palms against the table. Jennifer's legs dangled uselessly on either side of her thighs.

"Good morning." Jennifer smiled.

"It is, isn't it?"

"That is an absolutely incomparable way to start the day."

"It is, isn't it?" Alex repeated. She looked like she might say more, but instead, she stood, held out her hand, and helped Jennifer to her feet. "Hungry?"

Jennifer closed the robe, tied the sash, and tried to get a fix on what Alex was thinking. "Famished."

"Follow me." Alex headed back to the kitchen and picked up where she'd left off. "How do you like your eggs?" she asked, without looking back at Jennifer. Then she turned, panicking, "You *do* like eggs, don't you?"

"Over easy, please. Can I help with anything?"

Alex stepped to her and kissed the top of her head. "Nope. Just sit there and look sexy."

Jennifer blushed. "Yes, ma'am." She watched Alex in silence for a few minutes. "What time did you get up?"

"Kinsey got me up at his usual six thirty, so I put him out. When I came back into the room, you looked..." She turned to Jennifer with a sheepish grin. "I wanted you to be sure to get some sleep, but I can't tell you how badly I wanted to wake you up."

Jennifer flushed a deeper red as she smiled.

"I decided I'd better get right out of the room. Less temptation." She pulled the coffee pot out of its housing and reached for a mug. "So I read the paper and had some coffee." She set the cup in front of Jennifer. "Let my raging hormones cool down a bit, you know? Though I have to say that the sash on that robe is giving me very naughty ideas." She winked at the raising of Jennifer's eyebrows and kissed her mouth quickly, then returned to her work.

Jennifer swallowed as the erotic jolt that had zapped her lower body eased to a dull ache. It was becoming obvious to Jennifer that Alex wasn't ready to talk about anything deeper than their sexual connection at that point. Maybe she was right; that connection was red hot after all. Jennifer did want to talk about things; she knew they *needed* to talk about things, but it had been so long since she felt this desired by somebody—somebody whom *she* desired—all she wanted to do at that moment was sit and bask in the glow of it. She could understand Alex's avoidance. They could talk later. They'd *have* to talk later.

She sipped her coffee.

* * *

Alex and Jennifer spent the entire day in various stages of undress. Like two children with brand new toys, they couldn't keep their hands off each other for longer than an hour or two. Alex delighted in Jennifer's stamina. In past relationships, Alex had always been the one with the higher sex drive; her partners inevitably ended up pushing her away at some point, murmuring, "no more" as exhaustion took over. Not so with Jennifer. She matched Alex touch for touch, stroke for stroke, orgasm for orgasm, and was ready for more.

When darkness had fallen and they'd opted to return to the bedroom rather than the couch, the kitchen counters, or the bathroom floor, things shifted. The raw, intense passion was replaced with tenderness. They made love slowly, deliberately, sharing eye contact and emotion, though avoiding the words that would make things all too real. They mapped one another's bodies, learning what touches made the other gasp and filing the information away for use in the future.

Jennifer was getting used to this new side of her, the boldness, the aggression. The only time she lost her lead was when Alex physically took it from her, using their size difference as leverage. She reversed their positions, flipping Jennifer beneath her and pinning her arms above her head, Jennifer struggling feebly to play along.

"Careful," Alex warned against her mouth. "You don't want me to have to get that sash out and tie you to this bed."

Jennifer gasped at the words, the intensity climbing up another notch as Alex's tongue plunged possessively into her mouth. They kissed hungrily, the tenderness morphing back into the animal passion from earlier. Alex used her mouth to travel the length of Jennifer's body and settle between the legs that opened to her unbidden. Jennifer was already very close and crested almost immediately, her orgasm striking without warning and burying her. When she finally reached for Alex's head to push her gently away, Alex caught both her wrists and held them captive, preventing Jennifer from escaping the probing tongue and lips still exploring her oversensitive flesh, forcing her to ride out the sensation of "too much," ride it through to the other side. Her groans of protest quickly changed to gasps of erotically pleasurable shock as a second climax enveloped her with its power.

Alex stopped stroking and waited for her lover to come down, still gripping the smaller wrists in her hands, reveling in the moans, gasps, and whimpers as she felt Jennifer slowly relax.

"God," Jennifer murmured in wonder. "I've never done that before...in a row like that. Nobody's ever...Jesus."

"Good," Alex replied, happy to have such a memorable sensation belong only to her. She slowly crawled up Jennifer's body, showering it with light kisses along the way. She scooped Jennifer up and arranged their bodies in a comfortable position. "You're like a rag doll," she chuckled as Jennifer's limbs flopped uselessly.

"I can't move. I feel like Jell-o."

"I'll take that as a compliment."

They lay cuddled together for a long while, listening to the gentle lapping of the water against the shore as the sound drifted into the bedroom on the soft breeze that tickled the blinds. Jennifer's head was tucked under Alex's chin, resting on her chest.

"I love the sound of your heartbeat," she said softly.

Alex kissed the top of her head and squeezed her tighter. Kinsey hopped up onto the bed and settled down with a sigh, his head resting on Alex's ankle. She lay there, replaying the summer to that point, amazed by the way things had ended up. Her mind stopped on the argument she'd witnessed between Jennifer and Eric; the image of Eric raising his hand to strike his wife was still burned into her brain.

"Jennifer?" Alex whispered, wondering if her lover had fallen asleep, expecting she had.

"Hmm?" She startled Alex by responding.

"What happened that night? In the backyard with Eric?"

Jennifer was silent for such a long time that Alex started to wonder if she'd been out of line by asking the question, that maybe Jennifer wasn't going to answer at all.

Finally, Jennifer took a deep breath and spoke quietly. "I'm not totally sure, not really, but I have my own ideas. I think he'd probably just had enough."

"Of you?"

"Of everything. Eric and I are a lot alike. He's been so stressed out trying to do what's expected of him—take over the family business, be happily married to his high school sweetheart, have just the right cars and just the right house in just the right neighborhood. He's been trying so hard to uphold that image—the image of the Good Son. I honestly thought I was doing him a favor. My intentions were good, I swear they were."

"What do you mean?" Alex asked, noting the tone of guilt that had crept into her voice.

"Remember when Eric's father came to see me? The day we took the jet ski out?" She felt Alex nod. "He seemed very concerned about his son's stress level. He said he was worried about him. Frankly, I was ecstatic that somebody had finally noticed. When he asked me if I thought Eric really wanted to take over the firm, I thought honesty would be the best policy." She sighed. "I told him no."

"Oooooh," Alex drawled out, wincing with understanding.

"Yeah. Probably not my swiftest maneuver."

"And Eric found out."

"Yep." Jennifer propped herself up on an elbow so she could

look Alex in the face. "Look, Alex, I know how you must feel about him."

Alex looked at her, but said nothing.

"He wouldn't have hit me. He's not like that."

Alex bristled at the idea of Jennifer defending her husband; she didn't like the sensation. She didn't know if she agreed with Jennifer's assessment of his actions, but she felt it was not the time nor place to argue them. Instead, she simply nodded. "Okay."

"He's a good man. We've both just made some bad choices in our lives."

Alex stiffened further and hoped Jennifer didn't notice. She didn't want to talk about Eric, but she knew it was a subject that wasn't going to just disappear. "Okay," she repeated. Jennifer returned her head to its previous spot on Alex's shoulder.

Jennifer hadn't been back to her own house since she'd shown up on Alex's doorstep more than twenty-four hours before. She'd made no attempt to locate her husband and she had no idea if he'd been trying to get in touch with her. Much as Alex would have liked for them to hole up in her house and forget about the rest of the world, she knew that would never happen...that it couldn't happen.

They were quiet for several minutes before Alex spoke again, gently. "You're going to have to go back and face him sooner or later, baby." She hoped she didn't sound as terrified at the prospect as she felt. Thinking about Jennifer with Eric made her feel nauseous.

"I know," Jennifer answered, her voice small.

Chapter
Sixteen

After more than three days together doing nothing but talking, making love, and having food delivered, Alex and Jennifer finally managed to wrench themselves away from each other. It wasn't easy, but their bodies were sore and their answering machines had been working overtime; people were getting worried. Alex sent Jennifer on her way across the yard mid-morning on Wednesday and they managed to make it through to the evening with only six phone calls to one another.

That night was their last volleyball game of the season. Alex could hardly believe it was the end of August already. *Summer goes by so fast around here*, she thought as she warmed up, bumping the ball with Jennifer. She looked through the net at their opponents, noting the weak links. They had no shot whatsoever at first place, but the battle for third was on. The humidity from the weekend had subsided and a refreshing breeze was blowing off the water. It was a beautiful night.

Speaking of beautiful... They lined up to take turns spiking as Jennifer set for each of them. She wore black, lycra shorts and a white tank top she'd borrowed from Alex. "I want to keep you close to me," she'd said as she'd stolen it from Alex's clothesbasket. Alex smiled as her eyes followed the lines of her lover's body, sleek and tan, muscles flexing as she moved. She could still smell the scent of Jennifer's skin, feel the smoothness beneath her fingers. She could still hear Jennifer gasping her name as she came, begging her not to stop...

"Hey." Jackie snapped her fingers in Alex's face. She shook her head and was quickly zapped back to reality. "You're up." Jackie's voice was blunt.

"Sure. Sorry." Jennifer smiled knowingly at her, causing her to blush. "Quit smirking and set me."

The team played well as a whole, but Alex and Jennifer were so completely in sync, it was almost unreal. They couldn't miss. Jennifer set Alex dead solid perfect every single time and Alex's hits were right on the money. She had kills left and right, leaving the other team lying in the sand in various awkward positions. Jennifer grinned through the entire game and Alex was practically giddy. They high-fived often.

It wasn't until halfway through the third and final game that Alex became aware of the subtle glares and scowls coming from both Jackie and Nikki. At one point, Jennifer threw her a questioning glance, telling her that she noticed, too. Alex shrugged at her in confusion. They were playing well and the game was as good as won, so she was unsure of what the problem could be.

When their opponents called a time out, everybody broke to find their Gatorade or water and gulped thirstily. Alex followed Jackie to her pile of belongings near where Rita sat in the sand watching Hannah.

"Hey," Alex said. "You okay?"

"Fine." Jackie didn't look at her, just took her bottle from Rita's hand and drank. Alex knew Jackie like a book and the tone of her "fine" said she was anything but.

"Talk to me, Jack."

"I said I'm fine."

"And you're lying. You've been shooting me looks all night. Something you want to tell me?"

Jackie finally met her eyes and the hostility there took Alex by surprise. "Is there something *you* want to tell *me?*"

Alex blinked at her and swallowed, knowing full well that she'd been busted.

"I know you, Alex. You may think you're being subtle, but you're not. Not to me." Her voice was harsh and nothing more than a heated whisper. "I see the way you look at her. You're a friggin' puddle. You told us you were just friends."

"We were." Alex said quietly, her eyes on the sand.

"You were. And now you're suddenly more than that."

"Yes."

"Just exactly where do you think this is going?"

Alex swallowed. "I don't know," she answered truthfully.

"Really. Well, allow me to help you out with that. The general order of things goes something like this: she's going to wait until you fall in love with her—which has already happened, judging by the look on your face. She's going to let you think she's in love with you, too, at least for a while. Then she's going to grow tired of the experiment and decide it was much easier and less controversial living in Boystown and she's going to head back there. You, my friend, will end up on the other side of the tracks, a sniveling wreck holed up in Heartbreak Hotel and your friends will have to clean up the mess even though they *warned you profusely* that you were making a huge mistake with her." Her eyes bored into Alex, flashing with frustration. "Jesus, Alex, you *know* this. You've seen it happen a million times around you. What makes you think this will be any different?"

Alex swallowed hard. She *had* seen it, over and over. The danger of falling for a straight girl was not imaginary; there were very real consequences. She had seen friends have their hearts ripped out by women just like Jennifer. Her stomach churned as the fears she'd been working so hard to ignore reared up full force. She simply looked at Jackie, having no response whatsoever.

Jackie tossed her bottle to the sand and nodded. "I hope you know what the hell you're doing." She turned and headed back to the court without waiting for her friend.

Alex looked down at Rita, who had observed the discussion quietly. Somehow, she managed to appear both sympathetic and stern at the same time, just like a mother. Alex sighed and joined her team, smiling a weak reassurance at Jennifer's questioning glance.

The team won third place.

* * *

The celebratory drinks didn't last long. Though third place was a nice finish, considering there were a dozen teams, the tension was fairly obvious. Jackie was quiet. Alex was worried. Jennifer was confused. The party broke up quickly.

The game had been an early one, finished in less than an hour. When Alex and Jennifer returned to Alex's house, the sun had not yet set and both women were famished. Alex set her hunger aside long enough to wrap her arms around Jennifer from behind and hold her tightly, burying her nose in the blonde hair, closing her eyes and losing herself in the scent.

"Was Jackie okay tonight?" Jennifer asked.

Alex swallowed. "Yeah. She's been having a tough time at work." The lie slid out so easily, it surprised her.

"She was kind of cold to me."

"She gets that way when she's stressed. Don't take it personally."

Jennifer thought about turning around and looking Alex in the face, but decided against it. "Okay. I think I'm going to jump in the shower."

Alex kissed the side of her neck. "The shower, huh?" She tongued an ear, causing a shiver to shoot through Jennifer.

"Uh-huh." She turned in Alex's arms and their mouths met. After several minutes, Jennifer pulled herself away. "Okay. I'm going. To the shower."

Alex followed her all the way to the bathroom. When they got to the doorway, Jennifer turned and planted her hand in the center of Alex's chest and gave her a gentle shove, knowing full well what would happen if they showered together. "No," she said with a smirk. "I don't want to be in here for days on end. Go order a pizza. You can have the shower when I'm done." And with that, she closed the door and locked it.

"You're locking me out?" Alex cried, feigning hurt.

"I don't trust you," Jennifer said through the door, the smile plain in her voice.

"Smart girl," Alex muttered as she left and went to order dinner.

Jackie's words came back to her as she hung up the phone a few minutes later. She took a Heineken from the refrigerator and leaned against the counter, trying not to think about what her friend had said, but unable to shut off the worry. It really would be so much easier for Jennifer to stay in her current life, her life with Eric, wouldn't it? Why on earth would she want to sacrifice all that she had?

Am I worth it? Really, am I?

She suddenly felt the weight of the world pressing down on her. Who the hell did she think she was? Jennifer had money and status and a normal life. Who was Alex to make her question all that? She closed her eyes and exhaled slowly, willing her mind to shift from the subject, lest it drive her completely mad.

The water had stopped, so she busied herself fetching plates and napkins from the cupboards. When the doorbell rang, she glanced at the clock on the microwave, surprised by the speedy delivery.

"I've got it," Jennifer called before Alex could make a move.

"The money's right there on the table," Alex called as she headed out with her armload of items.

Alex had heard the phrase "time stood still" on many occasions, but she'd never actually experienced it until that moment. Jennifer stood in the doorway, her hair wet and combed back from her face. She was dressed in a pair of Alex's boxers and her Rohrbach's Brewing Company t-shirt. Both were very obviously too big for her.

On the other side of the screen door stood Dawn and Kayla.

It seemed the four of them simply stood there looking at each other for an eternity. Finally, Kayla spoke up in a flurry of words as Dawn's eyes focused on her sister-in-law.

"Jen, where have you been? We've been worried sick. You haven't been answering your phone at either house. I tried to call

Eric at work, but somebody told me he was no longer employed there and he's not answering his cell phone. We came here because we thought maybe your neighbor could tell us if she'd seen you."

It was only a second before Dawn opened her mouth that Alex noticed she'd been fixated on Jennifer's shoulder for an unusually long period of time. The t-shirt was slightly askew on her, the neckline hanging to one side, revealing a bright red mark on her skin, one that Alex had put there with her own teeth just before the volleyball game.

Dawn sneered. "I see we were right. Your neighbor obviously *has* seen you. All of you." Jennifer realized to what Dawn was referring, flushed, and pulled the t-shirt up over her shoulder. "College all over again, Jen?"

Jennifer's face showed horror and embarrassment; it was obvious that she didn't know Dawn was aware of the situation with Sarah.

"That's right. I'm all up to speed on your extracurricular activities—the whole family is. Eric is my little brother, after all. It's my duty to look out for him." It was glaringly apparent that Dawn was taking great delight in skewering Jennifer. She could barely contain her glee. "I was sure to warn him about her." She jutted her chin in Alex's direction. "I told him he couldn't be too careful, especially after that fiasco of yours in New York. I see I was right to be concerned." She threw a disdainful glance in Alex's direction and the expression instantly reminded Alex which of her former students were Dawn's.

Jennifer hadn't uttered a single word. Alex wondered if she was in shock. She was very visibly shaken by Dawn's diatribe. And visibly shaking; Alex could see her hands trembling. Simultaneously, she felt her own do the same thing. She quickly set the armload of dishes and utensils on the table, clattering loudly. Approaching the door, she tried to focus all her concentration on keeping her voice steady. The last thing she wanted was for Dawn to know how terrified she was...terrified of the repercussions of this meeting, terrified of what was going through Jennifer's head at that very moment, terrified that she was about to run screaming into the night, never to return.

"I was not fired from my teaching position. I resigned." Thankfully, her voice didn't waver. She stole a glance at Jennifer, who was looking at the floor. When she looked back at the twosome on her doorstep, she set her gaze on Kayla. "You came here to find Jennifer. You found her. Now please go." She gently guided Jennifer backwards so she could shut the door, closing out the triumphant expression on Dawn's cold, beautiful face. Alex leaned her forehead against the wood, trying to keep from collapsing under the onslaught of worry that threatened to bury her like an avalanche.

The door vibrated against Alex's forehead as somebody knocked. She lifted her head, wondering if Dawn had come back for another round, wondering where Jennifer had gone, wondering how this whole thing had become such a mess so quickly. She opened the door warily and was greeted by a pimply-faced kid wearing a dirty baseball hat and holding a pizza box. The smell of food nauseated her.

She wandered into the kitchen with dinner, finding Jennifer standing with Kinsey cradled in her arms, staring out onto the water. After setting the pizza on the counter, she approached Jennifer quietly, and wrapped her arms around her from behind. Kissing the top of her head, she felt the slight tremor run through Jennifer's body. Alex tried to swallow her worry.

"You okay?"

"I don't know," Jennifer whispered. "I did face Dawn. I've never done that before. I didn't say a goddamn thing, but I faced her."

"Which is the equivalent of facing Satan, if you ask me," Alex muttered, attempting to inject a bit of humor into the situation, but failing miserably.

"But, she knows now. The cat is out of the bag—and you can be sure it is because everybody and their brother will know soon enough. Dawn isn't one to keep such a scoop to herself." Her voice shook slightly, whether with anger, fear, or terror, Alex couldn't be sure. Jennifer sighed quietly. "God, my mother is going to freak."

"They all do, babe."

They stood silently for several long minutes before Jennifer spoke again, her body snapping to attention with sudden realization.

"I have to talk to Eric." She moved out of Alex's embrace, set Kinsey down on the floor, and looked around the room.

Alex's heart skipped a beat as she followed her lover's frantic movements with her eyes. "Now?"

"I have to find him. He can't hear this from Dawn; it's not fair to him and you can bet she's going to want to be the one to tell him her good news." She located her sandals and slipped them on. "He needs to hear it from me."

Alex swallowed and nodded, unable to find words, sure that if she opened her mouth, she'd burst into sobs and beg Jennifer not to leave.

"He needs to hear it from me, Alex," she repeated as she opened the sliding glass door.

"Okay."

Alex watched her scurry across the yard and into her own

house, knowing that this was something Jennifer had to do, but trying to tamp down the sickening feeling that she was watching her
dream walk away from her.

Chapter
Seventeen

Jennifer and Eric had spoken only once, by phone, since their fateful argument in the backyard. Jennifer thanked the gods above that she'd been able to get in touch with him as quickly as she had—she wasn't sure she could stay in such a state of heightened panic for any longer without exploding. They made arrangements to meet in a neutral place the next day and to talk. She wasn't really sure what to expect, but she longed for some familiar territory and right then, Eric seemed to be it.

She'd abandoned Alex abruptly—too abruptly, she knew. She winced when she thought of how she'd left her new lover standing in the kitchen the night before, blinking in confusion, but she hadn't felt that there was any other option. She'd thought about Eric hearing things from Dawn, about the betrayal he'd surely feel, about the embarrassment if his family found out before he did, and she couldn't bear it. He deserved more respect from her and she knew it. She owed him that...at least that. She'd become frantic trying to locate him. Once they'd made contact and set up a meeting, Jennifer had forced herself to stay in her own house, to sleep in her own bed, to *be* alone. It hadn't been easy to know that Alex was just a short walk away. Her warm eyes, warm voice, warm body called to Jennifer, pleaded with her, but she'd managed to stay put for the entire night. As a precaution, she'd taken the phone off the hook and locked all the doors.

"I've probably completely freaked her out," Jennifer muttered to herself as she steered the Volvo into a parking space. She felt intense guilt about the way she'd deserted Alex without so much as a peck on the cheek, as well as intense guilt over the impending discussion with Eric. She rubbed at her temples with her fingertips, trying to stave off the headache that was approaching with all the speed and power of a freight train. "What the hell am I doing?" she asked nobody in particular.

She and Eric had agreed to meet at Kershaw Park so they could wander along the lake and not be tied to a table, as they'd be if they

met in a restaurant. Jennifer arrived first and, not seeing Eric anywhere, strolled down to the water. She took a deep breath and tried
to relax, but every thought, fear, and emotion seemed to hit her at
once. Questions flew at her from all directions. *What if I hurt Eric
beyond repair? What if he can't handle this? Is this really what I
want? What if it isn't? What if I haven't given my marriage enough
of a chance? Am I doing the right thing? How does Alex feel about
me? Does she love me? Could she? What if I'm not what she wants
at all? What if I leave Eric and then Alex leaves me? Where will I be
then?*

"What the hell am I doing?" she said again. She grabbed her
head with both hands and ordered her brain to calm its whirlwind
of thoughts, told herself to breathe steadily, commanded her hammering heart to slow down. After a few minutes, the questions
eased and she felt slightly better. She opened her eyes and looked
out onto the water. It was a beautiful day, sunny with blue skies and
a light breeze that rearranged her hair as it saw fit. She inhaled
deeply and tasted the lake air.

"Hey."

She jumped as Eric's voice startled her and she turned to meet
his eyes as she got to her feet. "Hi."

He was dressed comfortably in jeans and an old Eddie Bauer t-
shirt that had faded from dark red to a washed brick. He hadn't
shaved and his dark hair was windblown. Despite the dark circles
that had formed under his eyes, he seemed surprisingly at ease and
she felt the sudden desire to tell him so.

"You look good, Eric."

He smiled. "I was just about to tell you the same thing."

"Thanks."

They stood awkwardly for several minutes, then began a slow
stroll along the path.

"Rumor has it you've left the firm," Jennifer finally ventured.

"Rumor is correct. I resigned last week."

"Wow." Jennifer nodded, impressed. "That's big. How did your
father take it?"

"Surprisingly well, believe it or not."

"I believe it."

"Jen..." Eric stopped, faced her, and gently placed a hand on
her arm. He was normally very smooth and knew just what to say in
any given situation; instead he uncharacteristically fumbled for the
right words. "I need to apologize. For that day last week in the back
yard."

Jennifer wanted to stop him, to save him the discomfort and
tell him she understood, but rather she nodded for him to continue.

"I'm so sorry," he went on. "I never would have hit you...I suppose that's an easy enough thing for me to say and it certainly doesn't make it okay. I just...it was all falling in on me, you know? My workload at the office was so huge and I was so stressed out about that and about us. When my father asked me point blank whether or not I really wanted the firm, I just wigged out. I ended up taking it out on you and I'm really, really sorry for scaring you like that."

His sincerity brought tears to her eyes. She inhaled deeply, letting the relief seep into her bones. "It's okay," she said softly. "Apology accepted. I knew it wasn't you. I feel bad for spilling the beans to your father, but I think leaving the firm was the right thing for you to do."

"Yeah?"

"Yeah. You weren't happy practicing law."

"No, I wasn't."

They stood side by side, looking out onto the calm waters of Canandaigua Lake. After a long silence, Eric swallowed and looked at his feet. His voice was barely audible. "I want a divorce, Jen."

She'd known it was coming, even thought she might have to say the words herself. But hearing it come from her husband was like a punch in the stomach. All the air left her lungs and she struggled to breathe, her eyes welling. It was one of the strangest feelings she'd ever experienced, the combination of relief and sheer terror. On the one hand, she knew that they couldn't maintain their sham of a marriage. On the other, she was looking at letting go of the person with whom she'd spent over a decade of her life and she felt the panic leaching in on her once again.

The tears spilled over and ran freely down her cheeks. "Are you sure?" she asked in the small voice of a child.

Eric swallowed again, grief closing his heart in its fist. He took Jennifer's hand and led her to a nearby bench where they both sat. He gently brushed her bangs out of her eyes. "I think we both know this is the right thing to do. I tried to pretend and so did you."

"But..."

"You don't want to be with me, Jen. I've know that since Sarah."

Jennifer swallowed the lump in her throat.

"I just thought..." He looked away and snorted. "I thought I could change it. You know the old cliché. 'She just hasn't met the right guy yet.' That may be the case, but the right guy isn't me. You know that as well as I do."

"Eric, I..." She searched her mind, as well as her heart, for the words to make everything all better, but she came up empty. Deep down, she knew he was right. Despite the panic and the desperation to hold onto the only life with which she was familiar, she knew he was right. The realization was both a relief and heartbreaking. A sob worked its way up from her gut, bursting out around the hand she'd clamped over her mouth. A flood of tears over which she had absolutely no control followed it.

Eric closed his eyes, anguish filling his heart, and pulled Jennifer to his chest, holding her as she cried. His own eyes filled with tears, not for the first time since this mess had all begun. Jennifer was his touchstone, his anchor in a world of tidal waves and whirlpools. Letting go of her was the hardest thing he'd ever done in his life and he was terrified of being without her. Although he was confident that they were making the right move, the pain wasn't any less excruciating.

He held her for a long time, until her sobs subsided into small hiccups, then into silence. She stayed with her head on his chest, knowing it was the last time she'd be there and reluctant to let the feeling go. He kept his arm tight around her shoulders, also not wanting to let go. She spoke quietly, not moving.

"I'd like to keep the lake house, if that's all right with you."

He took a deep breath and nodded. "Sure. I don't see why not. I'll talk to Jake about it and get it put exclusively in your name; your trust fund should take care of things." He paused, then added gently, "I'll have him list the place in Pittsford. Is that okay?"

"Makes sense."

She sat up, wiping at her eyes and nose with her hands and inhaling deeply to collect herself. They sat quietly for a long while.

"This is kind of weird, huh?" Eric commented.

"That's a good word for it." She rocked her head back, stretching her stress-tightened neck muscles, then looked out onto the water. "I can't believe this is happening."

"I know. Me, neither."

They were silent again.

"I should probably get going," Eric said finally.

"Yeah, me too."

"Will you be okay, Jen?"

The sincerity of the concern in his voice brought tears to her eyes again. She nodded. "I think so."

He cleared his throat as he stood, his eyes darting away from her. "If...if she's...what you want, then make it work, okay?" His gaze landed on hers and riveted her to the spot. "Make it work." He pulled her into a fierce hug before she had a chance to say a thing in response. Then, taking her head in his large hands, he placed a gentle kiss on her forehead. "You take care of yourself, Jennifer. I'll be in touch." With that, he walked quickly away before his emotions got the better of him. Jennifer watched him all the way to the parking lot, her feet still rooted to the ground. With a quick wave, he got into his Mercedes and pulled hastily out onto the street.

Jennifer stared at the vehicle, knowing that the biggest part of her life was driving away for good. She sat back down on the bench and spent the next hour just staring out blankly at the water, silent tears rolling steadily down her cheeks.

* * *

Alex arrived at Chili's before Nikki and grabbed a small booth by the window. She had been surprised by the phone call—an invitation to lunch from her ex. Nikki had a doctor's appointment that morning and had decided to take the whole day off, give herself some down time. She'd told Alex she wanted to thank her for her help in making the break from Diane the month before and wished to buy her lunch. Alex was flattered—and more than a bit taken off-guard—so she accepted the invite.

She also looked at the lunch as a welcome distraction. Thinking about Jennifer and Eric was enough to make her stomach revolt in terror. She was doing the best she could to give Jennifer time and space, but it was incredibly difficult. She was still reeling from Jennifer's quick departure the night before and she couldn't fight the sick feeling that she'd get a call from Jennifer any time now, telling her that she and Eric were going to give it another try. *Thanks for such a fun time, Alex. It was great. You were so entertaining.* She swallowed down the bile that rose in her throat; she could almost hear Jennifer's voice in her head, along with a bevy of I-told-you-so's from her friends.

She forced herself to focus on her surroundings and the wonderful aromas hanging in the air—cheeses, spices, the scent of freshly grilled vegetables. Sizzling assaulted her ears as a waitress scurried by carrying a steaming tray of fajita makings.

Chili's was in a great location for Alex to meet with her friends who lived further into the city. The restaurant was in Victor, down the road about half a mile from Eastview Mall and right off the New York State Thruway. It was a good halfway point and the margaritas were fantastic.

She ordered herself a Margarita Presidente and an order of tortilla chips and salsa to occupy her while she waited for her lunch date. The waitress brought her drink in its own little blue, plastic container, showing Alex how to pour it without spilling it all over herself. Alex smiled in delight, knowing that it would actually turn out to be nearly four margaritas. She took her first salty-tangy sip, sighed with relief, and looked around.

The crowd was a good size, mostly women with toddlers and kids out of school for the summer, probably stopping in for lunch after a morning at the mall. The floor was a terra-cotta tile and the open design and earthy colors were reminiscent of the southwest. Alex pulled the Tex-Mex menu from its holder on the table and perused the selections, trying hard not to let her mind wander back to Jennifer and what she might be thinking at that very moment. She sighed at the feelings of helplessness and frustration as she crunched down on a chip, letting the spicy salsa steal her attention. Looking out the window, she saw Nikki's Toyota pull into the lot.

Nikki looked great and Alex found herself surprised to admit it. It wasn't that Nikki had looked bad before, but there was something different about her since she'd left Diane and Alex couldn't quite put her finger on it. She tried to, watching her ex through the window as she walked to the front door. Nikki seemed to walk a little prouder. Her head was held up a bit higher than Alex remembered. Spotting her date from the foyer, Nikki smiled and waved. It struck Alex at that moment how little she'd seen Nikki smile in the previous months. She seemed so much happier now.

Nikki slid into the booth across from Alex, set down her purse, and grabbed a chip from the bowl. She looked tan and healthy, her brown eyes sparkling. Her curls were bouncy, the light blonde highlights brought out by the summer sun making them shimmer slightly. Her khaki cargo shorts and white camp shirt hugged her body nicely and Alex couldn't help but grin at her as she stared.

"What?" Nikki asked, suddenly self-conscious. "Am I late?" She looked at her watch.

"No." Alex kept grinning. "No. It's just...I'm sorry. I didn't mean to make you uncomfortable. You just...look good. That's all. You look great, Nick."

Nikki blushed, tucked a lock of hair behind her ear, and focused on the menu. "Thanks."

The waitress stopped by their table and it didn't take much coaxing on Alex's part to get Nikki to have a margarita with her.

"To celebrate your day off," she said.

"You're such a bad influence," Nikki chided.

"Are you ready to order or would you like a few more minutes?" the waitress asked.

They'd been there enough times to know what they wanted, so they went ahead and ordered.

"I'm being a good girl," Nikki said, ordering the grilled chicken salad.

"Not me," Alex countered. "I prefer to feel my arteries harden right as I'm sitting here. I'll have the nachos, please. Hold the jalapenos." Her mouth watered at the thought of all that cheese smothering the plate. She picked up her glass as the waitress hurried away with their orders. "So," she said as she sipped. "How's it going?

New place working out?"

"Yup. I love it. I'm doing great."

"Any trouble from Diane?"

"Not really. I got a lot of phone calls for a while, so I just screen most of the time."

Alex grimaced.

"It's okay now," Nikki assured, a slight hint of defensiveness creeping into her voice. "She wasn't a psychopath or anything. I mean, give me a little credit. She was just hurt, that's all."

Alex nodded, sipping again.

"You never liked her." It was a statement, not a question, but the smirk on Nikki's face softened it.

"I didn't like the way she treated you," Alex answered honestly.

Nikki studied her drink thoughtfully, as if searching for her next words in it. "Alex, do you know what I liked about Diane?"

Alex snorted. "Haven't a clue."

"I'm serious."

"Me, too."

Nikki held her gaze. "Diane wanted to spend time with me. She *wanted* to be around me. Maybe not for the right reasons, but I never felt like I was too needy or too smothering with her."

Alex swallowed, her stomach doing a little flip-flop of guilt. "Like you did with me."

"Yeah."

Alex examined the table. "I'm sorry, Nick."

"I don't want you to be sorry," Nikki replied vehemently. "I'm not here to force an apology from you. I just wanted to thank you. I've learned a lot from the time we were together." She sipped and smiled at Alex's look of uncertainty. "Therapy is a wonderful thing. You know that? Understanding what makes you tick is such an empowering feeling."

"Is it?" Alex had her doubts, thinking that there were times she had no desire to know what was really going on inside her own mind. They were quiet as the waitress brought their plates. Once she was gone, Nikki resumed the conversation.

"I'm learning so much about myself, Alex. You'd be amazed by how much of our personality can be attributed back to our parents."

Alex gave a sarcastic chuckle. "Oh, terrific."

Nikki laughed, having met Alex's mother on more than one occasion. Then she grew serious. "I guess the most important discovery I've made so far is the absolute necessity to speak my mind. Not doing so is something I've discovered I learned from *my* mother. She's the martyr type. She loves to complain to other people when something's bothering her, but she doesn't complain to the right person. She never has the courage to face whoever is upsetting her and calmly say, 'Hey, you're upsetting me and this is why.'"

Alex nodded as she ate her nachos. She was impressed by the determination with which Nikki spoke. She was really making some discoveries about herself and she knew it and was embracing it. Alex felt strangely envious.

"I fell into that same pattern," Nikki went on. "I was always perfectly happy to keep my mouth shut when it mattered and then seethe about it later, usually to the people who couldn't make a damn bit of difference anyway. I didn't speak up with you," she said softly, looking Alex in the eye. "I knew why you were leaving, but it was easier to pretend it was my fault than to confront you on your insecurities and fears, so that's what I did."

"You knew?" Alex was amazed.

Nikki chuckled at her ex's surprised face. "You're really not that big a mystery, Alex. I hate to be the one to break it to you. You didn't contribute to or take much from our relationship because it made you feel too vulnerable to do so. Of course, I tried to make up for that by contributing way too much. That just made me look like some sort of pathetic cling-on. The more I gave, the less you took. I have this vision of me handing you things and you pushing them back at me. And then you left me before I'd have the chance to leave you, thereby saving yourself the inevitable pain. I suspect I wasn't the first one."

Alex felt herself blush at being so easily read when *she* hadn't even been aware of what she was doing at the time. "I didn't know it then," she said in a small voice. "It wasn't intentional."

"Oh, Alex, I know that. I'm not trying to blame you here. Please don't think that." Nikki set down her fork, put her hand over Alex's, and ducked her head to catch Alex's downcast gaze. "Please don't. That all came out a little heavy-handed, maybe because there's a part of me that's still bitter about it, and I apologize. I'm not accusing. I'm just sharing. Okay?"

Alex nodded and sipped her margarita, still stung by the accuracy of Nikki's remarks. "What about Diane?"

Nikki picked up her fork and stabbed a piece of chicken. "I did speak up with Diane. I told her how I was feeling and she didn't get it. She didn't understand why I was unhappy. I tried to explain how I was feeling like a housewife in the fifties, but she didn't see it. She couldn't grasp it. She was so completely different than you were." She chuckled, partially with humor and partially with resentment. "Seems I went from somebody who didn't want to take anything from me to somebody who took everything."

"Now you just need to find somebody in between."

"Exactly. And I will." She smiled confidently.

"Yes, you will." Alex shook her head at how much she'd under-

estimated her ex, thinking how lucky she would make her next partner. "I'm impressed with this new Nikki."

"Oh, she's not new. She's just been...uncovered. She was buried for a little while."

"Well, your therapist deserves his money."

"Peter's the greatest. Now I'm trying to share all my discoveries with my friends so they can all avoid ending up in his office
themselves." She laughed charmingly, her eyes dancing. Then she
became a bit more somber, her stare boring into Alex. "Open your
mouth, Alex. This thing you've got with Jennifer isn't going to be
easy as it is; if you can't be honest with her about how you're feeling or what you're thinking, you're already doomed. I think you
know that."

"She thinks you don't like her." Alex tried to steer the subject
away from Nikki's grave tone.

"I know." Nikki smiled wickedly. "I was very leery of her and I
wanted her to know that. We were all leery. Some of us still are."

"'Some of *us?*'" Alex gaped at her. "'Us' who?"

"I'll say it again. You're not that big a mystery, my dear. Your
friends can read you like a book."

"Jesus." Alex drained her glass, then refilled it from the blue
container.

"Make it work, Alex. If you love her and this is what you want,
make it work." She studied her ex for a long time. "Do you love
her?" she asked softly.

Alex swallowed the lump that had formed in her throat and
was annoyed by the tears welling in her brown eyes. She nodded.

"Have you told her that?"

Alex shook her head no and gazed out the window.

"Why not?"

Swallowing again and swiping at her face with her hand, Alex
choked out, "I'm afraid."

"Of what?"

"I'm afraid that she's talking to her husband right now and that
she's not going to leave him. I'm afraid she's going to decide that it
was easier to be straight. I'm afraid I was just an experiment, a fun
time. I'm afraid she doesn't love me back. I'm afraid of being with
her and I'm afraid of losing her."

Nikki smiled gently. "That's a lot of fear."

Alex snorted. "Yeah."

"Don't you think you need to talk to her about this stuff?"

Alex took a deep breath, calming her racing heart. "Probably.
You know me, Nick. I'm not good at opening up."

"You need to decide if this is what you want, if *she* is what you
want. If she is, you need to open up about it. That's the only way.

Talk to her." Her voice was imploring.

Alex nodded, feeling a strange sense of relief. She held Nikki's loving gaze for a long time. "Since when did you become so wise, hmm?"

"She's a lucky woman, Alex."

"Thanks, Nikki."

* * *

Jennifer was feeling heavy.

She felt heavy, drained, and just plain worn down. She felt like she was wading through molasses as she made her way through the house and out the back door. It was close to dusk; the air had cooled considerably and she grabbed a sweatshirt on her way past the coat rack. She dragged herself to the Adirondack-style loveseat she'd placed near her flowers and sat down with a weary sigh.

The color of the evening reflected her mood. The sky was a slate blue/gray, the stars just beginning to twinkle into view. The water was calm, mirroring the somberness of the sky, and it was quiet. Jennifer sighed again and leaned her head back, closing her eyes against the world.

She felt an impending depression weighing down on her. She knew deep inside that she and Eric were doing the right thing, but she also knew that few other people would see it that way. The thought of all the inevitable crap soon to come her way—between Dawn, the rest of Eric's family, her own mother, and her friends, there'd be plenty to go around—made her feel tired and part of her wondered if it wouldn't just be easier to stay in her old life.

Pretend to be straight.

She swallowed hard, cursing the fact that it all had to be so difficult. *Why does it have to be such a big, frigging deal?* she thought angrily. *If I'm happy, why should anybody care which gender I prefer to sleep with? Why does it matter?* But it would matter. It would matter a lot, especially to her mother.

She thought about her life up to that point. She had always been such a good girl. She'd done everything she was supposed to do; she'd obeyed all the rules put upon her by those who thought they had the right to do so. When she had slipped out of line with Sarah, she had tried her hardest to correct things and get herself back on the track she was expected to follow. Always on that right track, because she was a good girl.

God, being a good girl is wearing me out.

Much to her surprise—and for the first time—she felt a little pellet of anger form in the pit of her stomach and she allowed it to grow. She realized that the people who had made her rules had, for the most part, done so for them and not for her. She remembered her mother's anger over Sarah and finally allowed herself to accept the fact that she wasn't worried about Jennifer, she was worried about *herself*, about her own image. She was terrified of what people would think of *her*, not her daughter. At that moment, Jennifer realized the full impact of the selfishness with which her mother had acted. The pain was nauseating.

Dawn had done the same thing. And Kayla. And Eric at the time. Even Sarah, to a certain extent, for there was a part of Jennifer that would always feel that Sarah didn't try hard enough to hold onto her. She was so busy rejoicing in her newfound sexuality that she didn't have the time to try to help Jennifer out of the closet. *She let me stay there and she watched as my mother slammed the door and nailed boards over it.*

She took a deep breath and tried to force herself to relax, knowing the bitterness would get her nowhere. Soon, the anger ebbed, making way for the emotion to return. Jennifer couldn't decide which was worse, being pissed off or crying her eyes out. She told herself that the past was the past and there wasn't a damn thing she could do to change it now. *All I can change is the future. All I can change is the future. All I can change is the future.*

She was still chanting that mantra in her head when she heard footsteps scuffing through the dew-covered grass and looked up to see Alex leading Kinsey on a leash. It was almost dark, and Jennifer couldn't make out the expression on her lover's face. Her heart began to hammer. She was perilously close to the edge; if this was going to be an emotional discussion, she didn't know if she'd survive.

"Hi," Alex said softly, as if not wanting to disturb the peacefulness of the twilight. She perched on the rock wall next to the chair. Kinsey's tail wagged rapidly and he put his wet front paws up on Jennifer's knee. Waves of affection washed over her and she bent forward, allowing him to lavish kisses on her face.

"Hi," she replied, her attention still on the dog.

They sat quietly.

"How did things go?" Alex asked finally, her voice tinged with apprehension.

That worried quality alone was enough to start Jennifer's tears all over again. She let them fall silently for as long as she could before a sob managed to work its way up and out. Alex blinked at her and swallowed, her heart breaking at the sight and at the implication. She wasn't sure if her physical presence would be welcomed, but she decided to chance it. She scooted over and sat next to Jennifer, putting an arm gently around her. "Oh, sweetie. It's okay. Everything will be okay."

Jennifer was so relieved at the contact. She could hold nothing in any longer. All the emotion came pouring out in great, wracking sobs. She cried in Alex's arms, Alex rocking her gently, murmuring words of comfort, kissing the blonde head, trying to reassure her, all the while feeling the acute sense of loss settling in on her.

It was a long time before Jennifer's sobs subsided. Still, Alex held her, stroking her head. When Jennifer finally spoke, her voice cracked, her throat raw from crying.

"Do you think we can do this?"

"You and Eric? If you love each other, sure."

Jennifer lifted her head and blinked at Alex. "Me and Eric?"

Alex blinked back at her. "Isn't that what you meant?"

"You think Eric and I are back together?"

"I...kind of assumed, yeah."

"Why? Why would you assume that?"

"I don't know. I just...you were so upset. I thought maybe you...didn't know how to tell me."

Annoyance replaced the emotion in Jennifer's gut. She sat up straight and looked Alex square in the eye. "Alex, do you love me?"

There it was. Point blank. The big question. Alex swallowed hard, feeling like she was frozen in time.

"Do you?" Jennifer asked again.

Alex heard Nikki's voice in her head. *If this is what you want, make it work.*

"Yes." Her voice was barely a whisper. "More than you know."

"God, you're so insecure," Jennifer said, her voice filled with a combination of frustration and pity. "Why? Is it because your friends disapprove of me? You are a wonderful, amazing, sexy woman, Alex. Why did you automatically assume I'd choose to go back to Eric?"

Suddenly Alex knew it was time—time to make a decision. She decided then and there that this was the moment. For the first time in her life, she forced herself to be completely, utterly honest. She was terrified of the consequences, but she knew she had to let Jennifer in on everything she was thinking, feeling, and petrified of. She took a deep breath. "Jennifer, I...I know how hard this is for you. I know how scary it is to embrace an alternative lifestyle. I know what it feels like to disappoint your mother and get weird looks from people that you thought were your friends. I don't want that for you.

"You're right. I'm *terribly* insecure. It's a problem I've had all my life and much as I'd like to blame it on my mother, I'm learning that it's as much my fault as it is hers." She studied her hands for several minutes. "I was sure Nikki would end up leaving me, that she'd figure out I was a big fraud and she'd leave. So, I left her first.

She never really understood, but she does now. I did the same thing to my first girlfriend. And my second. None of them ever picked up on my pattern; how could they?" She looked up at Jennifer, who was watching and listening intently. "But then you came along and you saw right through me. Just like that. Do you know you're the only person who ever gave me shit about leaving my job? The only one. I think Jackie and Rita just know me too well and it didn't surprise them that I gave up without a fight. But you didn't get it and you called me on it. You were right. You couldn't understand why I'm gay, but only write about straight people and you called me on that, too. And you were right again."

Jennifer felt a lump forming in her throat at the soft gratitude in Alex's voice. Alex reached for her hand and played with her fingers as she continued to pour out her heart.

"Yes, my friends are worried about me. They aren't thrilled about our pairing. For all intents and purposes, you're a straight girl in their eyes. Straight girls only hurt the gay girls that fall for them. It's standard operating procedure." She winked and Jennifer grinned. "They're just looking out for me and I get that. I appreciate it." Her voice softened considerably. "But it doesn't change the way I feel, Jennifer. All their warnings and speeches don't make a damn bit of difference to my heart. I'm terrified that they're right. It scares the hell out of me that you've gone from Eric to me in a flash and I really want to tell you that you need to be on your own for a while, that you should take some time away from me to sort things out in your head. I really want to tell you that. But I can't. I love you so much and I'm so afraid of losing you. I know how selfish that is, but I can't help it."

Tandem tears were coursing down the cheeks of both women. Jennifer wanted to speak, but her throat had closed up on her. She was sure she couldn't possibly have more crying to do, but she was mistaken. She wrapped her arms around Alex's neck and held her tightly.

"I love you, Alex," she whispered. "We need to work on your insecurities. I want to help."

Alex tightened her hold, relief washing through her entire body. "I've already decided on a big step."

"Yeah?" Jennifer pulled back to look at her. "What's that?"

"I'm going to call my old principal tomorrow, see if there's anything—even part time—available." She sighed. "I miss teaching, Jennifer."

Jennifer hugged her again, her excitement contagious. "Alex, that's great! I'm so proud of you." She was quiet, holding tightly to her lover. Then she spoke softly. "I know this won't be easy. As a matter of fact, I'm certain that it will be very hard much of the time.

There will be lots of bumps and I can guarantee that I won't handle all of them well. It's going to be a rough ride for a while, but there's nobody I'd rather take it with than you."

Alex pulled back to look Jennifer in the eye. "You're sure?"

Jennifer nodded.

"What about Eric?" Alex nibbled her bottom lip.

"Eric and I talked. We understand each other. I'll go see a lawyer tomorrow. It was much more amicable than I'd expected." She focused on Alex's mouth, a pang hitting her low in her belly. "And stop doing that with your lip or I won't be held responsible for my actions."

Alex grinned. "*I* certainly won't hold you responsible."

Jennifer leaned forward and kissed Alex softly. "Then follow me inside..."

Chapter
Eighteen

The snowflakes were falling softly to the ground. There hadn't been a good covering yet, just a dusting or two, but it was only early December. *We never get off that easy around here,* Alex thought. *We're in for it; we just don't know when.*

Despite the fact that there was very little snow, it was downright *frigid* as Alex sat in her car with the engine running, the heat blasting on her feet as she waited for Jennifer to do her thing. She blew on her icy hands, which had her fingers crossed inside her mittens. She knew Jennifer was nervous, but Alex had a good feeling.

After talking about it for weeks, Jennifer had actually worked up the nerve to have more than a superficial conversation with the Daisy Woman. That's how the two lovers referred to the mysterious woman in the cemetery until they finally learned that her name was Carol. Jennifer had told Alex the story of how she'd run into Carol that first time at the cemetery and watched as she'd put fresh daisies on Jennifer's dad's grave. She told Alex of her theory, that her father had had an affair with the woman and how she was just itching to find out more. She wisely waited until she'd worked through her own anger and demons about her father's infidelity. She'd used her relationship with Eric and her attraction to Alex as a comparison, finally understanding how what her father did could happen, and finally able to let her anger with him go.

Alex remembered the day Jennifer actually spoke to Carol for longer than sixty seconds, actually had a mini conversation. She was giddy. She'd come home so high and excited, it made Alex smile just to watch her animated retelling of the conversation. She'd come clean to Carol right away, which was a relief to Alex. She'd been afraid that Jennifer wouldn't tell the woman exactly who she was and that would only be hurtful down the line. They'd only spoken a little bit; it was obviously quite awkward for both of them, but Jennifer said she'd felt a real connection, like Carol was somebody with whom she could be friends. *Good* friends.

It took a while for them to trust one another. They still only talked at the cemetery, but Jennifer was about to take a big step. As Alex waited in the car on that Saturday morning in December in the cemetery parking lot, Jennifer was going to invite Carol to Christmas dinner with them.

"She doesn't have anybody," Jennifer had said sadly to Alex, earlier in the week. "She's going to be alone on Christmas. That's just wrong."

"You don't have to convince me, baby. I think it's a great idea."

"You're sure? You don't feel like it will be an intrusion on our day together?"

"Christmas is for sharing. You're right. Nobody should be alone. Invite her. It'll be great."

They were each feeling the sting of rejection by their own families, made more painful by the approach of the holidays. Jennifer's mother had completely cut her off. Alex wasn't speaking to hers. Neither mother could handle the relationship of their daughters and both made it about them. Alex slumped down in her seat and thought back on the last three and a half months.

Leona Foster was flabbergasted that her daughter would have the nerve to return to the same school where everybody knew she was a *lesbian*—Alex could almost hear her voice as she sneered the word in a harsh whisper. She'd called to admonish Alex, make her understand how humiliating it would be, and though Alex could feel the pellets of guilt developing in the pit of her stomach as they always did, she managed to hang up the phone and then take it off the hook. She had taken to screening her calls ever since—nearly two months. She was sure Leona, tired of being ignored, would just eventually show up at the front door to make sure her opinion was heard, but that hadn't happened yet. She lived a good forty-five minutes from the lake and she didn't like to drive, so with winter settling in, the chances of her popping in grew slim, much to Alex's relief. Still, she felt like she was constantly bracing herself for the showdown. It would be ugly, that was a certainty, but Jennifer by her side gave Alex strength and she was *almost* sure she'd survive it.

Jennifer's mother was much bolder than Alex's. Alex sat in the car, shaking her head, still amazed by the audacity of the woman. Upon hearing things from Dawn, Kathleen Wainwright had driven straight to the lake house, busted right in, and spent over an hour screaming at her daughter, telling her how worthless she was, what a terrible choice she'd made, what an awful thing she'd done to Eric, never once mentioning that Eric had also been unfaithful. *Apparently, that wasn't the same thing,* Alex thought bitterly as she recalled the harsh words. She'd stayed at her own house for as long as she could, trying to respect their space, knowing that this was something that had to be aired. But it was a warm, fall afternoon and Jennifer's windows were open. After hearing nothing but vicious insults being hurled at the woman she loved, Alex couldn't take it any more. She'd stomped across the yard, entered through the sliding glass door, much to the surprise of both women, and simply stood behind Jennifer, trying not to show alarm at the redness of her face. Jennifer seemed to take strength in Alex's presence. She stood a little taller, stuck out her chin, and took a deep breath. She stepped back so she was side by side with her partner, and took Alex's hand, tightly entwining their fingers together.

"I'd like you to leave now, Mom." Her voice had only shaken slightly.

"Excuse me?" Kathleen was simultaneously sickened by the sight of their hand-holding and astonished that her daughter was actually throwing her out.

"Get out."

She blinked at the pair, stunned, then got in a good parting shot as she turned the knob on the front door. "Your father would be so disappointed in you, Jennifer." Alex felt her lover stiffen, heard her swallow as they watched Kathleen depart.

Alex had spent the next two hours holding Jennifer in her arms while she sobbed like a child.

The only bright spot from Jennifer's former life was Kayla. She'd stopped by a few days after Kathleen and though things were initially tense between the two of them, the former roommates lightened up quickly and were soon giggling like school girls. Alex chuckled as she reminisced. She had left them alone, but got the scoop from Jennifer in bed later that night. It seemed that Kayla, too, suffered from the Do The Thing Expected Of You disease. It was expected that she'd drop Jennifer like a hot potato, just like the rest of her friends and family. *Bless her heart, though, she had trouble doing that*, Alex recalled with a grin. She had told Jennifer that their friendship was too old and meant too much and that, though it was hard, she was trying to pull away from the stifling grasp of her family and to think for herself for a change. Jennifer was elated when telling Alex the story and Alex knew they'd be seeing more of Kayla in the future.

Early fall had turned quietly to mid-fall, much to the surprise of the couple. Alex had started teaching on a part time basis, but just as her principal had warned her it might, the position went quickly full time. Alex had forgotten just how much she loved teaching. It gave her such energy and confidence that she actually wrote faster and more often than she had when she wasn't working. It was very, very difficult for her, but Jennifer finally convinced Alex to change her main character, Paul, to Paula and to write what she knew. It turned out Jennifer had known what she was talking about. The story was so much better and Alex felt better writing it and she made sure that Paula got the girl—*without* killing the husband.

Alex's friends were becoming more comfortable with the relationship. They were all wary, and Alex understood that it was for her own protection. As time went on, though, her friends started to understand that maybe it wasn't just a fling; maybe Alex wasn't simply an experiment for Jennifer. David threw a Halloween party—a costume party.

"Of course," Alex had said to Jennifer when they'd received the invitation. "Because every gay man I know has to have a *theme* when he hosts a gathering."

"Why?" Jennifer had asked innocently.

"I have no idea. I just roll my eyes and go along."

With their coloring and height difference, it was a no-brainer for the two women to go as Xena and Gabrielle. They'd been a big hit. Plus, Alex had found Jennifer so incredibly sexy in her costume that when they returned home, it was as though the warrior and her sidekick had *finally* consummated the relationship so many fans of the TV show believed existed, right on Alex's living room floor.

November had rolled around in a flurry of blowing red leaves. The lake seemed deserted. Alex and Jennifer had spent Thanksgiving with Jackie and Rita, who were finally understanding what the relationship meant to Alex. Once they saw how happy she was, they embraced Jennifer, pulling her lovingly into their fold. Aside from a pumpkin pie, some new coloring books for Hannah, and a couple bottles of wine, Alex and Jennifer had brought two other, important items to their house. Alex brought the first draft of her book, handing it over to Rita proudly for a thorough run-through, smiling as her proofreader's face lit up, impressed. Jennifer brought paint swatches so the three of them could pick a color scheme for the new baby's room. The couple had decided that after the holidays, they were going to try for baby number two and they'd been so impressed with the way Jennifer had decorated her place, they'd asked her to help with theirs. Though she balked at it, they insisted on paying her as they'd pay any other interior designer. They also gave her two phone numbers of friends who needed some decorating advice. Alex recalled how Jennifer had looked at her with such glee in her eyes that it warmed her heart. She'd shot a grateful look to her best friend, Jackie, who simply winked at her and popped the cork on the Chardonnay.

Spending Turkey Day with their friends had been wonderful and it had helped take the sting out of the rejection of their families, but Jackie and Rita went away to spend Christmas with Rita's family downstate and Alex and Jennifer were left to fend for themselves. That wasn't necessarily a bad thing; they loved spending time together, just the two of them. The hard part was, despite their messed up home lives, they'd always been with their families for Christmas and the fact that it wouldn't be that way this time was a difficult fact for them to absorb. Alex realized that it was why asking Carol to join them was such an easy thing to do. If their families didn't want them, then they'd make their own.

Neither one of them said much of anything about the half dozen presents that sprinkled Jennifer's guest bed, all with tags to their mothers.

Alex blew on her mittened hands, gazing out the window at the swirling, sporadic snowflakes falling from the stone-colored sky. It was strange to her to feel so content in a relationship; she'd never experienced the feeling before. There had always been some sort of cloud hanging over her and whomever she was with. She realized then that it was a cloud of her own making and that somehow, she'd managed to grow up and reach some understanding. She now recognized what it meant to simply accept the love of her partner, to know in her heart that it was something she deserved, not some fluke, and that it wouldn't be ripped away as soon as the gods discovered that she didn't really merit it. She had a quick flashback of the previous night, of her and Jennifer making love in her bed. She remembered how perfectly they'd fit together, how well they knew each other's bodies, the sounds, the smells, the tastes. She swallowed down a sudden rush of adrenaline, smirking at the now-familiar quiver in her belly and marveling over the fact that after nearly four months together, their sex life had grown stronger rather than waning as in her previous relationships. Jennifer knew Alex's looks and Alex knew hers. Often, they didn't even have to say anything. They would catch one another's eye and thirty seconds later, they'd be naked. They were completely in tune, totally in sync with each other.

It's like we were meant to be.

Alex rolled that around a little bit, liking the way it sounded despite its corniness. She liked the way it felt.

She was still smirking out the window when she caught a glimpse of Jennifer's green coat as she came into view on the path from the parking lot into the cemetery. A tall, sophisticated, friendly-looking woman walked next to her and judging by the way Jennifer's hands were moving, she was talking animatedly with her.

The infamous Carol, I presume, Alex thought.

When Jennifer looked toward the car and met Alex's eyes, the brilliant smile on her face told Alex that all was good. Santa Claus had come early.

Alex couldn't remember the last time she'd so looked forward to Christmas.

THE END

Another Georgia Beers book available from
Yellow Rose Books

Turning The Page

Melanie Larson is an attractive, extremely successful business executive who shocks herself by resigning from her job when her company merges with another and relocates. While trying to decide what to do with her life next and at the urging of her uncle, Melanie heads to Rochester, New York, to stay temporarily with her cousin Samantha. She hopes to use her business savvy in an attempt to help Sam sort out the financial woes of her small bookstore. During her stay, Melanie meets and becomes close to the family that owns the property on which Samantha lives, the charming Benjamin Rhodes, a distinguished, successful businessman, as well as his beautiful and intriguing daughter Taylor. Surprised by what and how she feels for each of them,
Melanie is soon forced to face the facts and re-examine what's really important to her in life, career and love.

ISBN: 1-930928-51-3

Georgia Beers lives in Rochester, New York, with Bonnie, her partner of nine years, and their two dogs. Visit her web site at www.georgiabeers.com.

Printed in the United States
64671LVS00004B/13-18